Praise for *Meow If It's M...*

"Nick and Nora are a winning team. The ... ...es to stay one paw ahead of his new owne... ...s in ...Cruz, California."

—Rebecca M. Hale, *New York Times* ...elling
author of *How to Paint a Cat*

"*Meow If It's Murder* is an absolute delight and Nick and Nora make a purr-fect mystery-solving team! I couldn't put it down!"

—Michelle Rowen, national bestselling
author of *From Fear to Eternity*

"Nick and Nora are the *purrfect* sleuthy duo!"

—Victoria Laurie, *New York Times* bestselling
author of the Psychic Eye Mysteries

"If it's murder, meow for the fabulous new crime-fighting team on the cozy crime scene, Nick and Nora. T. C. LoTempio concocts a triple-decker sandwich of murder, danger, and delight as feisty former big-city crime reporter Nora partners with small-town Nick, a loner with a mysterious past . . . and a tail. Nick so brims with street smarts and feline charisma, you'd almost think he was human, and Nick and Nora pursue suspects aplenty in an action-laced start to an exciting new series."

—Carole Nelson Douglas, *New York Times* notable
author of the Midnight Louie series

"A clever debut featuring a wild and furry sleuthing duo . . . a big 'paws-up' for *Meow If It's Murder*! . . . a fast-paced cozy mystery spiced with a dash of romance and topped with a big slice of 'cat-itude.'"

—Ali Brandon, author of *Literally Murder*

MEOW
IF IT'S
MURDER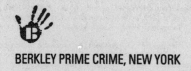

T. C. LoTEMPIO

BERKLEY PRIME CRIME, NEW YORK

THE BERKLEY PUBLISHING GROUP
Published by the Penguin Group
Penguin Group (USA) LLC
375 Hudson Street, New York, New York 10014

USA • Canada • UK • Ireland • Australia • New Zealand • India • South Africa • China

penguin.com

A Penguin Random House Company

MEOW IF IT'S MURDER

A Berkley Prime Crime Book / published by arrangement with the author

Berkley Prime Crime Books are published by The Berkley Publishing Group.
BERKLEY® PRIME CRIME and the PRIME CRIME logo are trademarks of Penguin
Group (USA) LLC.

For information, address: The Berkley Publishing Group,
a division of Penguin Group (USA) LLC,
375 Hudson Street, New York, New York 10014.

ISBN: 978-0-425-27020-2

PUBLISHING HISTORY
Berkley Prime Crime mass-market edition / December 2014

PRINTED IN THE UNITED STATES OF AMERICA

10 9 8 7 6 5 4 3 2

Cover illustration by Mary Ann Lasher.
Cover design by George Long.
Interior text design by Kristin del Rosario.

For Charlotte and Dominick LoTempio
aka Mom and Dad—
the first one's for you!

ACKNOWLEDGMENTS

They say writing is a solitary journey, but what goes into the preparation in getting a novel ready for publication is anything but. That said, I owe a ton of thanks to my fabulous agent, Josh Getzler, and his marvelous assistants, both present and past, Danielle and Maddie, and my amazing editor, Faith Black, for believing in this series and for taking a chance on me, Nora, and Nick. Kudos also to the entire editorial team at Berkley Prime Crime: especially George Long, cover designer, and Mary Ann Lasher, cover artist—this cover rocks!

I have a host of loyal friends (not enough room to list you all, but you know who you are!) to thank for understanding that writing is indeed a solitary business—if I've ignored you guys during the process, please know it wasn't intentional. There are a few, however, who deserve special mention for support above and beyond: Barbara Quellen and her husband, Danny Corleone, who generously lent his name to a character; Heather Massey, who's always willing to proofread and share helpful ideas; Vi Kizis, my muse—enough said; Kurt Hanson, a fellow "indie"; Debbie Scassera, owner of Footnotes Bookstore in Clifton; and Garrett Lothe, who jump-started my lagging writing career when he hired me on the staff of *Susabella Passengers*. I've got to give a shout out, too, to *all* the authors who have appeared on Rocco's blog over the years. I wish there was enough room to list each and every one of you! I do have to give special mention to the authors who agreed to read an ARC of this novel (and with no arm-twisting, either!): Mary-Janice Davidson, Carole Nelson Douglas, Michelle Rowen, Victoria Laurie, Miranda James, Rebecca M. Hale, Ali Brandon, Rose Pressey—thank you!

Speaking of Rocco's blog, I would definitely be remiss if I neglected to thank my tubby tuxedo—the inspiration for Nick—and the good folks at the Clifton Animal Shelter, from which I adopted him some years ago. Thanks also to Liz Taranda at CAS for her patience and assistance with the taking of the photo, and also a special mention to Fred!

A special note of thanks also goes to two extraordinary people: my former supervisor at my day job, John Erdos, who looked me in the eye and said, "Forget the vampires . . . why don't you write a book about your cat?" (always have a backup plan!), and the amazing author and creator of Midnight Louie, Carole Nelson Douglas, who advised me to "do the rewrites and don't look back." Wise advice from both of you, and I thank you from the bottom of my heart.

Last but not least, a special shout-out for a dear friend no longer with me: MaryLou Ricciardi. You were always my biggest supporter, and you would have been so proud. RIP, dear friend.

PROLOGUE

L ola never knew what hit her.

She was exhausted; Kevin's "business slash pleasure" cruises always took a toll on her, and she was more than a bit annoyed he'd chosen this particular weekend for one—after all, tomorrow was their fifteenth wedding anniversary. She knew he'd been under a lot of strain lately, though, what with the new laser device KMG was developing for the Army—not only was he under pressure to deliver the product on time, but there had been rumblings of a corporate spy in KMG's midst. She wondered vaguely if that was the real reason behind this impromptu cruise. Why else would he have dragged his three key people along on a weekend that should have been meant solely for the two of them? And people she didn't particularly like, to boot?

Not to mention the fact she'd much rather be celebrating on dry land. A shudder rippled through her. She'd always been fearful of lakes, rivers, the ocean in particular. The only water she felt comfortable in was a tub, or a Jacuzzi. Perhaps it was silly, but she could never shake the fear— why, hadn't a psychic warned her of danger only a few weeks ago?

It almost seemed as if Death were stalking her.

She slipped out of her blue-and-red silk caftan and removed all her jewelry, except for the cherry pearl studs Kevin had given her for Christmas. She donned a pair of sweats to ward off the night chill, and slipped her feet into her well-worn scruffs. After a few moments' consideration, she crossed to her husband's closet and pulled one of his down vests out and slipped it on, then rubbed her arms. Damn, what she wouldn't give for a drink right now! But that would entail returning to the main cabin and rejoining the others—and she had other more important things to do.

She could hear the soft murmur of voices as she tiptoed past the main cabin, and risked taking a quick peek. Marshall Connor and Buck Tabor were huddled in one corner, talking, while her husband and his admin, Patti Simmons, were on the divan. She saw the way Patti's hand roved possessively across her husband's arm, and Lola felt the warm color rise to her cheeks—then she steadied herself and moved swiftly down the corridor, past the kitchen, where the captain was seated, enjoying a brandy, and made her way toward the guest staterooms.

If she ever had a shot at finding out the truth, it was now or never.

A half hour later Lola perched on the edge of her king-size bed. Her hands were clammy, slick with sweat, and her whole body shook with suppressed—what?

Anger? Fear? Rage?

No . . . panic.

Her fingers roved restlessly across the envelope she'd taken from one of the cabins. What was it her dear departed friend Laura Charles used to say?

An eavesdropper rarely hears anything good about themselves.

Well, she hadn't been eavesdropping, but she had been snooping. And she'd found just what her source had said she would . . . which certainly explained a lot. Now she knew the reason behind her husband's recent foul mood swings, his often irrational irritability, the time he'd spent away from home. It was completely understandable, if what she'd found out was indeed true.

Even though Kevin hadn't been completely honest with her, one thing she knew. No one threatened her family. No one.

She wished she could talk to Laura Charles. Her friend had always been so sensible, so levelheaded. She would have known just what to do—but Laura was dead. There was only one other person she could depend on now.

She reached for her Dooney & Bourke, rummaged inside for her iPhone. She clicked it on, opened up her directory, scrolled down—and yes! She had put it in. She clicked on the number, let out an agitated sigh when it went into voice mail.

"Hi, it's me. You were right. I found it hidden just where you thought it might be. I can't believe Kevin kept this from me . . . it's no small matter. Why, it could put me in danger! I'm so mad at him . . ." Her voice began to shake and she paused to take a deep, calming breath. "Listen— I'm going to have a showdown. Kevin will probably kill me, but—this can't go on. Thanks for all your support. I won't forget it." She rang off, ran her hands through her hair. A showdown might be considered a foolish move, but she didn't care. All she knew was she no longer wanted either herself or her husband played for fools. She sighed. It would probably be best, though, to confront Kevin and tell him just what she intended to do. Maybe her assertion would awaken some courage in him—she hoped so. She really didn't fancy facing down the enemy alone.

Thump. Thwack. She raised her head as the sounds from the side deck got louder. Damn dinghy's rope had probably come loose again. She thought about calling Kevin or the captain, then decided against it. The dinghy was something she could take care of herself—hadn't she retied it a million times? She turned her attention to the prize she'd found earlier. Her fingers closed around the manila envelope, and she looked around for a safe place to put it until she could confront Kevin. Her lips curved in a half smile. Oh, yes, she knew just the place! Her little secret hideaway. No one knew about it; her little treasure would be perfectly safe there . . .

A few minutes later she stood on the deck, picking her way carefully toward the dinghy. As she drew nearer, she stopped and cocked her head, puzzled. The thumping sounds had stopped. Now that was odd. She started to turn, and then she saw the shadow, out of the corner of her eye. Lola shoved her hands into the pockets of the down vest and took a bold step forward.

"I know what you're trying to do," she yelled. "You coward, come out and face me. I know what you're doing, and it stops now! I found your little stash, and I've taken care of it. I won't let you hurt—"

Her voice stilled as something heavy crashed into the back of her skull. Everything started spinning, and she lashed out with her arms at her unknown assailant. She whimpered as something struck her across her left side, and then she felt herself being pressed against the side of the boat. Terror rammed through her and she tried to cry out over the pain that was radiating through her side, but her throat was so constricted, she could do no more than whimper. She felt a slight pricking at the base of her skull, and then found herself descending into a pool of blackness, a pool as relentless as the dark waters she'd feared all her life, as she felt herself drift down . . . down . . .

ONE

"From printer's ink to pastrami. I guess it's quite a change for you, eh, Nora?"

I smiled as I sliced the pastrami sandwich in half and arranged it on a paper plate. I'd gone to high school with Lance Reynolds, even dated him while in college, but our romance was just not meant to be—and not just because he dated four girls at one time, either. Whereas he was content to remain in the old hometown and go into business with his brother, I opted for the exact opposite—I got as far away from Cruz, California, as I could get. Armed with my trusty BA (major in journalism, minor in English) I moved to Chicago, where I was lucky enough to land a job on the *Tribune*, working my way up the ranks from small articles to my own column—*Crime Beat*—with my very own byline—*by Nora Charles*. I'd thought I'd spend the rest of my days reporting on big crime bosses and their related activities, until life threw me a curve.

Life's funny that way. And no, my decision didn't have anything to do with a broken romance (although I'd had my share) or malicious coworkers (a few, but not too many, thank God). My decision to return to my roots had been dictated by something much more simple: family loyalty.

I added a kosher dill and a side of coleslaw and wrapped it all up, slid it inside a brown paper bag. "Well, you know what they say, Lance. All good things must end."

I rang up his purchase, and he removed a ten-dollar bill from his wallet, passed it across to me. "I bet your mother's happy, looking down from heaven. She was proud of you, for sure, but she wasn't crazy about you trailing criminals and mobsters around."

Quite true. My mother had counted on the fact that cooking, as much as writing, ran through my veins. "She knew I'd step in," I agreed. Had I declined ownership, the shop would have passed to my sister—who, no doubt, would have wasted little time in selling it. The last thing Cruz needed was another fast-food eatery—or an empanada stand. We had three now.

I handed Lance his change. He slid it into his jacket pocket and then, almost as if he'd read my mind, asked casually, "So how is Lacey these days? Have you seen much of her since you came back?"

I knew Lance had always harbored a crush on my younger sister, even while we were dating, but I couldn't help breathing a sigh of relief that things had never worked out between them, mainly because my sister is, first and foremost, a flake. "She's okay. We spent a few days together after the funeral, but then she took off for Carmel."

"Carmel?"

"Yeah. She's gotten it into her head she wants to study art, and there are a lot of artists' colonies and good instruc-

tors out there. Our Aunt Prudence has a spare room, so . . ."
I shrugged. "Lacey's still trying to find her bliss, as they
say, and one day she'll succeed. Art is one of the few pro-
fessions she hasn't sampled yet." At last count my sister had
been everything ranging from secretary to short-order
cook to gas station attendant—plus a few select jobs we're
better off not mentioning.

"You were always the grounded one," he agreed. "It
must be hard for you, doing something so different from
what you've been used to."

I pushed the bag toward his outstretched hand and
leaned across the counter. "To be perfectly honest—I
haven't given it up entirely. I started writing some short
stories for an online crime magazine last month. Ever hear
of *Noir*?"

"Louis Blondell's magazine? I read the first issue. It
wasn't bad. He mentions it whenever he's in the Poker Face
to anyone who'll listen, though. Sometimes he even buys
rounds of drinks, trying to get folks to order subscrip-
tions." He chuckled. "He's definitely an acquired taste.
How on earth did you hook up with him?"

I laughed. "The same way I meet most people these
days. He came in for lunch, and we got to talking about
writing. I got to talking about the articles I wrote in Chicago and that I'd always wanted to try my hand at fiction
and—wham! Next thing I knew I had a part-time job."

Lance nodded. "Louis knows a good thing when he
sees one. Not only are you a local girl, but your prior experience will lend an air of credibility to the magazine. I
imagine his circulation will jump."

I thought of Louis—early forties, just a tad older than
me, overweight, and balding—and had to agree. He could
definitely be overbearing and demanding, but I had a

feeling his pompous attitude was an attempt to cover up his basic insecurity. "He just wants to make a success of *Noir*," I heard myself defending him. "And in this economy, who can blame him?"

"Not me. As a matter of fact, I'm going to make sure I have the next issue sent to my Kindle." He tapped two fingers on my counter. "Well, it's been swell catching up, but I'd better get back to work. Stop by Poker Face one night. The drinks are on me."

"Thanks."

He left and I turned my attention to Hot Bread's new menu—my attempt to attract a younger, hipper crowd while still retaining the old, faithful customers. I ran my finger down the listing of over twenty different kinds of specialty sandwiches, named after cities, places, and people: The Parisian Fling. The Siena Sub Sublime. The Lady Gaga Special. The Michael Buble Burger. There were even some homages to literary characters: The Sherlock Holmes Humdinger, Miss Marple's Magnificent Chef Salad, The Richard Castle Club—and my own personal favorite: The Thin Man Tuna Melt.

Hey, with a name like Nora Charles, it was inevitable, right? Plus, lots of people over the years had told me I bore an uncanny resemblance to Myrna Loy. How could I go wrong?

I was immersed in reviewing the listing when a hand dropped on my shoulder. I jumped, the menu falling to the floor. "Good God!"

"Oh, I am sorry, *chérie*. Did I startle you? I didn't mean to—you always say you can hear me coming a mile away."

I frowned at my intruder. Chantal Gillard has been my best friend for the past twenty-eight years, ever since we were ten and she'd rescued me from Leonard Goldie, the class bully, attempting to tie my shoelaces to the cafeteria chair in the fourth grade. Such an event can really bond two people, and Chantal and I had been thick as thieves ever since—so thick, in fact, that people usually took us for real sisters, even though we were nothing alike. My friend was somewhat of a dreamer, which she claimed enhanced her latent psychic abilities (which to date, I've really seen no concrete evidence of, other than that she is very good with tarot cards). I, on the other hand, prided myself on being levelheaded and practical to the point of being anal. What can I say? At thirty-eight, I'm pretty set in my ways and not likely to change anytime soon.

My gaze dropped to Chantal's feet and the flat-heeled ankle boots on them. "I can—then again, you're usually wearing five-inch Manolos."

Chantal slid onto one of the high-backed stools behind the counter and raised one foot up. "My feet are still recovering from the Psychic Fair. So much walking. Who knew?"

Chantal's California born and bred, but both her parents hail from Paris, France. Since she grew up thinking English, not French, was her second language, she likes to emphasize her heritage through her mannerisms and speech—although her affected accent can get a little dicey at times. She has a definite flair for fashion, although many would say it borders on the quirky—today her slender figure was enveloped in a voluminous blue caftan that matched her eyes, a scarf of the same color wound through her cap of tight, black curls. The Psychic Fair, an event held in Parsons, a town about five miles south of Cruz right on the coast, was heralded as a "major event"—supposedly renowned psychics from the world over attended. "Ah yes, the big excursion. So how'd it go?"

She shrugged. "Not bad. I got to meet a lot of interesting people there." Her hand dipped into the pocket of her caftan and she whipped out a small card, which she extended toward me. "I almost forgot—Remy had these made up for me. I gave some out yesterday."

I looked at the purple-tinted card and read the bold script:

LADY C CREATIONS ONE OF A KIND JEWELRY
CHANTAL GILLARD 504-555-5578

Below the embossed lettering were drawings of a necklace, bracelet, and two rings. I pushed the card back and applauded. "Going public? About time, I must say."

"It was more Remy's idea than mine." She took the card and shoved it back in her pocket. "The flower business is slow, and there aren't that many people in Cruz interested in a good psychic reading. He thought I might as well turn my little hobby into something profitable."

Chantal and her brother, Remy, ran Poppies, a flower shop located on Main about three blocks from my store. Chantal had a little cubbyhole set up in the back where she served tea and gave psychic readings, but thanks to the recent economic downturn, both businesses were suffering. Chantal had a degree in art from UCLA, and lately she'd taken to designing and creating necklaces, earrings, and bracelets—more for relaxation than profit. Now it appeared her brother wanted to turn it into something more.

"He's making up a catalog, can you imagine? And yesterday I heard him on the phone with his buddy Raj. They were talking about signs, website design . . ." Chantal rolled her eyes. "He's putting more energy into this than the flower arrangements in the window."

"Remy knows a good thing when he sees it. Your jewelry is beautiful," I said. "I've always said you should sell it."

She wrinkled her pug nose. "I don't know—it's kinda like putting your children out for sale. But Madame Michelau read my cards yesterday, and said my new venture would be profitable, so . . ." She shrugged expressively. "Why not, right?"

Chantal removed a purple velvet pouch emblazoned with silver stars out of the tote and shook it. Her tarot cards slid out and across the black-and-white-checkered tablecloth. She gathered them up, began to shuffle them. "Odd thing—yesterday Madame Michelau said a friend of mine was about to undertake a dangerous mission. I thought of you immediately."

I shot her a look of mock innocence. "Me? Why?"

"Don't play dumb with me, Nora Charles. You know exactly what I mean." When I remained silent, she raised both eyebrows. "I saw what you were looking at on your laptop yesterday. Lola Grainger? You are researching her for some sort of article for Louis, right?"

Lola Grainger had been the wife of one of Cruz's premier businessmen, and a faithful customer of my mother's, having her cater events at her palatial mansion at least once a month. About a week after my mother's death, Lola had gone on a weekend cruise with her husband and a few of the members of his staff. Long story short, there had been some sort of accident and poor Lola had drowned. The story piqued my interest for more than one reason. For one, details on the incident were sketchy at best, and the people on the yacht all seemed very reluctant to talk about it. One could excuse that, perhaps, but the manner of death truly disturbed me, since I distinctly remembered my mother telling me on more than one occasion of Lola's deathly fear of water. Twice monthly yachting excursions aside, Lola never ventured alone into any sort of water—she'd even confided to my mother the only water she felt comfortable in was bathwater. The case had been ruled a "horrible accident" and closed rather quickly—a little too quickly, I'd thought, but chalked it up to the husband's standing in the community, as half the population of Cruz were employed by his company, KMG Incorporated. "The thought did cross my mind," I admitted.

Chantal made a little sound deep in her throat. "For goodness' sakes, why? The case was so open and shut—what possible story could there be?"

"Open and shut—maybe so, maybe not. Personally, I'd have liked to see our police department put a bit more effort into the case," I said. "Although I can guess why they didn't. Mrs. Grainger was one of Mom's best customers, both on a business and a personal basis. They really liked each other. Mom always said Mrs. Grainger seemed to be a lonely soul." I shut the refrigerator door and leaned against it. "Call me crazy, but I'd kinda like to give Lola's soul the peace it deserves."

Chantal's hand fluttered in the air. "You know I do not think you are crazy. Oversensitive, perhaps . . ."

"Gee thanks."

"Anyway, one of the psychics yesterday told me a friend of theirs read Lola Grainger's fortune at her last fundraiser. She told Lola she saw a fatal disaster in her future. Can you imagine?"

I stood up, mainly to ward off the chill that was inexplicably making its way along my spine at Chantal's words. "Honestly—no. How did Lola react, did she say?"

"Not well. She got all pale and left without waiting to

hear any more." Chantal shuddered. "Frankly, if someone had told me that, it would have taken a small miracle to get me to go out of the house, let alone on a boat in the middle of the ocean."

I nodded in agreement. "It gives me the creeps, and it's not even my fortune. Who wants to hear they're walking headlong into disaster?"

"Not I, that's for sure. I'd much rather let the universe surprise me."

"Speaking of surprises . . . what else did your psychic friend say about me?"

Chantal looked at me from under lowered lashes. "Ah, so now you are curious. I thought you did not believe in psychic impressions."

"I don't—but I do believe in intuition. I guess it's pretty much the same thing, when you get right down to it."

My friend cut me an eye roll, a sure indication she thought I was full of, as the French would say, *merde*. "The only other thing she saw was that this mission had to do with something that was switched."

I wrinkled my nose. "Something switched? Like what? That's not much of a clue."

Chantal shrugged. "What can I say? Sometimes the images come over a bit . . . clouded, shall we say? We have to interpret them the best we can." She hunkered over the pile of cards before her and flipped over the one closest to her. "Well, well," she murmured. "On a much better note, it looks like there is love in your future, *chérie*."

I let out a squeal and gave her arm a playful punch. "So now you're reading my cards? Please don't. I do so hate when you do that."

"That is because you do not open yourself up to the universe."

"I wouldn't say that. I'm very open. Just not to portents and omens."

She shook her curls. "You are practical to a fault. Just once I'd like to see you let yourself go—believe in the unbelievable. The world is a wondrous place, if you only open yourself up to all the possibilities."

"Tempting, but I can't afford the luxury. I'm a businesswoman now. I've got to keep my feet planted firmly on the ground and a level head."

"You know, if I didn't know you, I'd think you had no adventure in your soul at all. Now, are you certain you don't want to hear it?" She tapped the cards. "Trust me—it's good."

I hesitated, and then shrugged. "Oh, what the hell. Hit me."

She plucked a second card from the pile. "The King of Swords crosses your card," she said. "That means a dark, handsome stranger will shortly enter your life and sweep you off your feet."

I rolled my eyes. "You can tell that from one card?"

"Not just from the card—the vibe. And this is a strong vibe, very strong indeed."

Uh-huh. I'd heard all this before from my friend, in many ways, shapes, and forms, and a handsome stranger, dark or otherwise, had yet to make an appearance in my life. "Well, when he shows up, you'll be the first to know. I'm not holding my breath."

Chantal glanced at the clock on the wall and jumped up. "*Oh, zut*—I am late for my shift at the flower shop. Remy will kill me." She swept her tarot cards into their velvet pouch, tucked them inside her tote, and ambled toward the front door. Her French accent slipped a bit as she said, "Try not to work too hard, willya? You've been looking a little peaked lately." She opened the front door and stopped still. "Well, well," she murmured, accent back in full force as she shot a swift glance over one shoulder. "Come quickly, *chérie*. This will teach you to have more faith in my predictions. There is a dark, handsome stranger out here who wants to see you."

"You're kidding." I moved forward and looked over Chantal's shoulder. The street outside was deserted. I cocked a brow at my friend. "There's no one here."

Her tongue clucked against the roof of her mouth. "You are not looking in the right place."

Chantal pointed down. I followed her finger and beheld her dark, handsome stranger.

A stocky, black-and-white cat.

TWO

The cat squatted square in front of my door. He lifted his head, and large, unblinking golden eyes bored into mine. The stare was so intense that for a moment all I could do was gape. The portly fellow chose that moment to rise and walk inside, his black plume of a tail swishing regally behind him.

"Hey, wait a minute, you can't—" I stopped, bit my lip, and whirled to Chantal. "He can't come in here."

"Too late. He is already in." Chantal snickered. "After all, what's stopping him? You do not have a sign that says NO PETS on the door, *chérie*. He might not be a paying customer, but there are other ways he can earn his keep. Take that storeroom of yours, for instance. I am positive I saw mouse droppings in the far corner the other day."

"Mouse droppings—there better not be," I grumbled. "I just paid two hundred for an exterminator—you're kidding, right?"

She didn't answer, merely inclined her head toward my kitchen. The cat had leapt up onto one of the counters and was calmly washing himself. I sighed and whirled back to Chantal. "Come clean. Are you behind this? Did you go to the animal shelter and—"

She placed one fist on a slender hip, made an exaggerated sign of the cross over her heart with the other. "Cross my heart and hope to die—I've never seen this cat before today."

I eyed the animal, who'd finished his bath and now lay sprawled across the counter next to the sink. "Well . . . I like his coloring."

"I do, too." Chantal gestured toward the cat's plump belly. "I think they call that type of black-and-white cat a tuxedo. With their white bib and paws, they look as if they are ready for an evening on the town. And he does look ready to step out to a black-tie event, doesn't he?"

I had to admit the cat did cut an elegant picture. And then he flopped over on one side and started licking his privates.

Chantal's voice rumbled with suppressed laughter. "Nothing shy about him, is there? I think you've finally met your match."

I shrugged. "He must have wandered off. He looks too well cared for to be a mere stray. He's got to belong to someone."

"True," Chantal agreed. "Or perhaps his owner died, and he is now all alone in the world. He could use a friend." She gave me a sidelong glance. "Admit it—you've always had a soft spot for cats."

Well, I couldn't deny it. Out of all types of animals, cats did appeal to me the most—probably because I identified with their independent spirits. Caring-wise, though, my track record stank.

The cat stretched out full length, paws dangling over the side of the counter. His wide, golden eyes were fixed directly on me. He looked almost pleading—appealing even.

Dammit.

I shook my head. "Oh no, you don't. I like cats, but you know I'm not good with pets. Just ask my sister about the goldfish I let starve to death, and the chameleon I got when I was in fourth grade. Poor thing lasted a week."

"What happened to him?"

"I—ah—accidentally flushed him down the toilet." I saw my friend's lips start to twitch, and I added defensively, "Well, he was really small . . . what do you want from a ten-year-old?"

"You cannot compare a reptile to a cat. I doubt you *could* flush him down a toilet."

I studied the cat's girth. "That's for sure. He'd probably break the plumbing on the way down."

Chantal pressed her finger to her lips. "Ssh—you will insult him. Why not keep him? If nothing else, you can use him as a mouser."

I gave the cat another once-over. "I don't know how good of a mouser he'd be. He doesn't seem to be the athletic type. The mice would probably outrun him."

Chantal clapped her hand over my mouth. "Ssh, *chérie*. Animals are very smart. And look at him. He's listening to us."

I glanced over at the cat. Damned if his head wasn't cocked to one side. He did look as if he was very interested in our conversation, which, of course, was impossible.

Chantal squeezed my arm. "Take a chance on him, Nora, who knows? Give him a week. And then, if the two of you aren't *sympathique* . . . well, then ask me again. He seems far too fine an animal to end up in a shelter, trapped in a cage."

A loud purr emanated from the cat's throat. Dammit, could he understand us? I found that thought particularly unsettling, to say the least. Still, there was something about him that touched me. I couldn't explain it and I wasn't sure I would if I could. "Why don't you take him now?" I suggested. "I know how you love animals, and you really seem to like him."

Her finger wagged under my nose. "Nice try, but you know Remy would have a fit. My brother thinks he's allergic to every animal on the planet, and cats top his list."

"We both know it's all in his head. You could convince him to adopt the cat, Chantal. I know you could."

Chantal tapped her chin with one long nail. "Probably," she conceded at last. "But I think you should at least make an attempt with him, Nora. He would be good company for you and who knows? Perhaps you can discuss the Lola Grainger case with him. Who knows, he might have some good ideas."

The cat's head lifted, bobbed up and down. "*Meowww-www.*"

I started, then shook my head. "Come on Chantal, I haven't got time for this. Admit it—this is one of your practical jokes, right?"

Her chin lifted. "Do not insult me, *chérie*. I would have selected a purebred. A Siamese or a Persian."

"*Grrr.*"

We both turned. The cat was up on his haunches, upper lip peeled back displaying a good amount of fang, wide golden eyes trained straight on Chantal.

I slid my friend a glance. "Now *you've* insulted him." I

slapped my forehead with my palm. "Good God, what am I saying?"

Chantal moved over to the cat, bent down, and scratched him under the chin. "Ah, handsome, do not take any of this personally. I did not mean to insult you. You are obviously a stray of great quality. Play your cards right, and I shall make you a beautiful jeweled collar for your neck." She snapped her fingers. "Say, you know, that's not a half-bad idea. Collars for cats and dogs. People love to pamper their pets, right, handsome?"

The cat's growling turned into a satisfied purr as Chantal continued to stroke his chin. I shook my head.

"Chalk up another male who's succumbed to your charms." Guys had always found her appealing, and apparently the cat was no exception.

"What can I say? Men of all types adore me." She rubbed her fingers across the cat's head. "Oh, come on, Nora. Look at him. He's so adorable—how can you possibly turn him out?"

The cat flopped on his side and lay looking up at me, his golden eyes wide. I sighed and threw both hands in the air. If there's one thing I've learned, it's not to fight city hall. Or a cute kitty.

"Fine. I'll keep him until I can locate his owner. I'll make some inquiries tomorrow."

"Good." Her eyes twinkled. "You could name him Nick, you know, after those movies you love so much?" She cocked her head to one side. "He even looks like a Nick, don't you think?"

The cat purred louder, as if in agreement. I felt definitely tempted, but shook my head.

"Hmm. I'm not sure about naming him. That's too much of a commitment."

"So you say—now," Chantal chuckled. "But I have a feeling this could be the beginning of a beautiful friendship."

I cut her an eye roll. "I do so hate it when you quote *Casablanca*—or any classic movie, for that matter."

Chantal blew me a kiss, and then she was gone, leaving us alone. The cat jumped from the front counter to the rear one, and it only took me a minute to figure out why—he'd smelled the leftover tuna from today's special. I could hear slurping sounds as he pushed his face hungrily into the bowl.

In spite of myself, I had to admit he was cute—but cute enough for me to abandon my resolve of "no pets"? Well, maybe, especially if he earned his keep. Even though I greatly doubted there were mice in the storeroom now, it was a well-known fact that the scent of a cat often kept the rodents at bay. "You'd be cheaper than the exterminator," I murmured, and I moved closer to him, reached out my hand, and stroked his black fur. It felt soft and . . . nice. The cat raised his head, leaned back, and bumped it against my hand. I scratched him behind his ears and he purred, his whiskers streaked with flecks of tuna.

"I'd like to help you out and give you a home, Ni—cat," I corrected, my hand absently stroking up and down his back, "but to be perfectly honest, I'm terrible with pets. Aside from the whole chameleon incident, I just don't have the patience. I'm not even good around other people sometimes." I paused, and then added, "But you can finish the tuna. You must be hungry."

He stopped purring and stared at me, gold eyes unblinking. At length he turned back and buried his head in the tuna bowl again. I sighed, locked the door, and switched the sign from OPEN to CLOSED and returned to the kitchen, where I pulled my laptop out from under one of the cabinets. I carried it over to the table near the kitchen entrance, settled myself comfortably, and called up the file I'd started on Lola Grainger. I opened the document labeled ORIGINAL ACCOUNT and followed the link to the *Cruz Sun* story:

SOCIETY MATRON FOUND DROWNED

Cruz, Calif—The body of socialite Lola Grainger was found floating Monday morning in a shallow lagoon off the Cruz coastline. County lifeguards and sheriff's deputies said Mrs. Grainger, 47, drowned accidentally. The Graingers were on a weekend cruise with friends and members of Mr. Grainger's staff, celebrating their fifteenth wedding anniversary. According to witnesses, Mrs. Grainger had been drinking rather heavily and was thought to have gone to bed. It is suspected that she got up in the middle of the night, slipped, and fell in. Her body, clad in sweats and a down vest, was found floating in the cove waters around 5 a.m. Her husband identified her body and is unavailable for comment.

I jumped as something soft wound itself around my legs. I looked down. The cat was stretched comfortably out at my feet. I bent over and lifted him onto my lap. God, he was heavy!

"You must weigh twenty pounds at least. Probably more. I guess a lot of people take pity on you and feed you, eh? If you did live here, I'd have to put you on a diet. If you're too fat, you won't be able to catch any mice."

The cat opened his mouth in a wide, unlovely yawn. I caught a whiff of his breath and set him back on the floor.

He pinned me with another golden gaze and jumped back on my lap in one fluid motion. Rearing up, he raised one white paw, placed it on my shoulder, and swatted at a stray curl. I tucked the strand behind my ear and ran my hand along his soft fur.

"Okay, okay," I murmured, letting my fingers tangle in the cat's ruff. "You win. We'll do as Chantal suggested, a trial thing—test each other out, see how we get along. And if things work out . . . but I'm not making any promises, okay, Ni—ah, cat?"

His mouth opened, almost as if he were going to answer me. And at that moment the phone rang. I reached over, shut off my laptop, and then got up, unceremoniously dumping him from my lap, and went over to the phone.

"Hot Bread."

"Hey," the voice of Louis, the owner of *Noir* and my online editor, boomed out. "I just thought I'd let you know I got the story you sent in. It's great, Nora. I'm going to feature it on the cover."

"You're kidding," I cried. "Louis, that's . . . that's wonderful."

"You've done a remarkable job in the short while you've been with *Noir*," he continued. "So much so that I wondered if perhaps you'd like to move on from the fiction end, maybe try your hand at something more realistic."

"You must be reading my mind," I said. "As it happens, I had an idea for a series of articles on cold cases."

A loud laugh. "That sounds terrific, Nora."

"I'm glad you think so. I've been doing a bit of research, and I thought I might start out with Lola Grainger."

I heard a sharp intake of breath, then a moment of silence during which you could hear a pin drop all the way back in Chicago. Finally he cleared his throat. "Lola

Grainger? That's not an unsolved crime—that was ruled an accident."

I twined a stray auburn curl around my finger. "I know it was, but—I've been going over every newspaper account I can find—which isn't much—and something just doesn't hit me right. I thought maybe—"

"I can sense your frustration," Louis cut me off mid-sentence. "As a former true crime reporter, I can see where this type of story might appeal to you, but to be frank, I think it'd be better if you concentrated on less sketchy topics."

I bit down hard on my lip. "What if I could prove there was some substance to it—that it wasn't just a 'sketchy topic'? What would you say then?"

His sigh was audible. "I'd probably say run with it, but you're not going to find anything, so it's a moot point."

Hah. He had no idea whom he was talking to. If there was anything I loved in this world, it was a challenge. "Don't bet on it."

"I try not to take bets that aren't sure things, and with you, anything's possible." He paused, then said, "How about your own column, you know, like you had in Chicago? People love 'em. It's kinda natural, too, for an online magazine. Maybe you could do a sort of advice column—you know, for wannabe detectives? We've got lots of readers who fancy themselves in that category. They devour every crime show on television and think solving crimes is easy."

A pang of disappointment arrowed through me. "It's an interesting concept, but I'm not a detective, Louis."

"You were a true crime reporter, right? That's kind of the same thing. Besides, a little birdie told me you once had a secret yen to be a detective for real—did you ever get a PI license?"

I sucked in my breath. I'd confessed that long-ago dream during my first meeting with Louis—but only because I thought he was more than half-drunk and really wasn't paying attention. "That's all true, about my wanting to be a PI," I stammered. "But all it's ever been is a dream. There's no way I could do that now, not with running Hot Bread."

He interrupted, "Just because life's thrown you a few curves doesn't mean you should give up, especially if it's something you really want. Why, if I'd done that, *Noir* would still be a couple of scratched pages in the back of my notebook." He cleared his throat. "Anyway, I haven't worked out all the details yet." He paused. "You know, the bigger the readership we develop, the more money we take in, which would mean a nice raise for you. You can always use more money, right?"

Leave it to Louis. He knew just how to appeal to someone—right in the old wallet. "Of course. I'm just not certain I could devote enough time to it. And as I've said, I really don't have PI experience."

"I'd be willing to work around your schedule," Louis assured me. "As for the PI stuff, we could call your column *Notes from an Aspiring PI*, or something like that. How about we get together for lunch, say, one day next week and brainstorm? That idea's not cast in stone, you know. I'm open to other suggestions you might have."

I had the feeling he was just paying lip service to my qualms—but I was still intrigued by the idea. "Sure. I'm agreeable to a meeting, but I can't do lunch. That's my busy time, Louis."

"Oh, right. How about a drink at the Poker Face, then?" I could hear him flipping pages over the receiver. "How would next Monday work for you? Around six thirty?"

"That should be okay. It's a date. And Louis—thanks."

"No problemo, Nora. Thank you. Don't worry—I'm confident we can work something out."

I was hopeful as I hung up the phone. Okay, maybe Louis had all but shot down my unsolved crimes idea, but the alternative he'd proposed signified a huge step forward not only for his magazine, but for me as well. Maybe, just maybe, my luck was changing.

"Sure, why not," I murmured. "Nora Charles, former investigative reporter turned sandwich shop entrepreneur slash private eye. I could do it."

I turned back to the table and stopped at the sight of the cat, squatted in front of my laptop, his eyes glued to an article displayed on its screen. I frowned. I'd been certain I'd shut the computer off when I'd gone to answer the phone. I moved closer and peered over the cat's shoulder. An article from a sister paper, the *California Sun*, rehashing the details of Lola's unfortunate "accident." I made a move to shut off the laptop when Nick's paw lashed out, the tip of his nail grazing the bottom of the screen. I tried to press the power button again—and once more his paw tapped insistently at the monitor.

"What do you want me to see?" I squinted at the screen. At the very bottom of the article, no bigger than a footnote, was one line: *"The deceased's sister was unavailable for comment, other than to say her sister's death was a travesty that bears further investigation."*

I frowned. I hadn't realized Lola Grainger had any relatives. That in itself was interesting, and compounded with the fact it appeared her sister also thought there was something off about Lola's untimely demise . . .

I leaned over, switched off the laptop, and closed the cover, still wondering just how that article had popped up on a computer I'd have bet my last nickel had been shut off. I shook my head, determined not to obsess. Chantal would have called it Fate, and maybe it was.

Sometimes you just had to believe things just . . . happened. For a reason.

"Hm," I said. "Two and two make four, right? Lola's sister—whoever she is—thinks there's something off about that 'accident,' too. I bet my hunch is right. I smell foul play—meow if you agree."

The cat meowed without hesitation. He sat up on his haunches and cocked his head at me.

"Okay, it's settled then. Lola's death might not have been accidental. It could have been . . . murder."

The cat looked up at me, ears and whiskers back, and I could swear the corners of his mouth tipped up, just a tad, in a sort of half smile.

I took that as a yes.

THREE

"So, Nora, I see you have a new friend?"

Rita Robilliard smoothed her tight, gray chignon and smiled at me over the rim of her tortoise-framed glasses. She'd managed the local Century 21 office in Cruz for years and had always been one of my mother's best customers—and now, by extension, one of mine. She tugged at the lapel of her mustard yellow jacket as she leaned across the counter, her gaze fixed firmly on the cat who lay by the back door, head on paws, quiet as a mouse.

I looked up from the hot turkey sandwich I was preparing—hot turkey had always been my mother's Tuesday special, and I saw no reason to change a best-seller—and gave a quick glance over my shoulder. I hollowed out the thick kaiser roll and spooned a generous amount of turkey gravy into the opening. "Oh, yeah. He wandered in last night, and I just didn't have the heart to turn him out."

Rita chuckled. "He's certainly watching you. Probably hoping you'll drop some of that turkey on the floor, where it's fair game. He can smell quality stuff."

That was for sure. Like my mother, who would have balked at the idea of using processed meat, my hot turkey was real and sliced fresh from the bird; maybe I didn't bake my own bread, as she did, but the kaiser rolls were from Lassiter's Bakery, the best in the county, and my mashed potatoes wcrc farm grown—no instant mix for me!

"Well, when one gets up at four a.m. to start preparations, one expects a quality product," I chuckled. "I imaginc thc cat is no exception. He ate all the tuna I had in stock."

"Yes, he looks well cared for. Probably someone's pet."

"That's what I thought." I sliced the sandwich in half, spooned a generous amount of potato onto the plate, added a pickle, and set it on Rita's tray. "I'm going to put up flyers later. I took a picture of him with my phone last night—I've just got to get it printed out. I was hoping Max down at Staples would help me."

"I'm sure he would." Rita reached into her oversized purse for her wallet. "A male, right? He probably just wandered off, you know, looking for love." She winked.

I took the twenty she offered me and rang up her purchase. "You could be right. I've got a feeling he might belong to someone who either lives right here in Cruz, or not very far away. I'm sure whoever owns him must be missing him."

Rita nodded. "He is a nice-looking animal. If he were mine, I'd be frantic."

The bell above the shop door tinkled and Chantal breezed in, a large grocery bag clutched in her arms. She nodded at Rita, then slipped behind the counter and set the

bag down. "Good afternoon, *chérie*. I got some pet supplies down at the RediMart for you and Nick—well, mostly
for him unless you've taken a shine to catnip and Fancy
Feast."

Rita took the change I offered her and glanced over at
Chantal. "Nick?"

I started to answer, but Chantal cut me off. "That's what
we named him. Nick, after those movies Nora loves so
much, you know, the ones about the alcoholic detective
and his society wife."

"Oh, yes, Nick and Nora Charles. *The Thin Man*." Rita's
thin lips quirked upward slightly. "I loved them, too. They
were such a charming pair." She sighed. "They don't make
movies like that anymore. Well, good luck finding his
owner." She picked up her tray and moved to a table for
one in the back.

Chantal strolled over to the cat. She chucked him under
his chin. "Hello, Nick. Is Nora treating you well?"

A contented purr escaped his lips, and he wiggled his
rotund, furry body closer to Chantal.

I brushed a stray curl out of my eyes and ignored the
quick stab of jealousy that pinged at me. "See, he likes you
better. You should have taken him."

"Oh, pish." Chantal waved one hand. "You're doing
fine." She moved closer to me and squeezed my arm. "I bet
he even slept in the bed with you last night, no?"

"No," I said firmly. "But it wasn't for lack of trying, I
assure you. He's got really strong forepaws. He kept nudg-
ing the door open, so I finally had to shove my Queen
Anne chair up against it. He slept out on the rug in front of
the fireplace."

Chantal shook her head and turned her attention back to
the cat. "Don't worry, Nicky, she'll come around. She

wasn't always this mean. It comes from working the crime beat in Chicago, reporting on all those murders, mob bosses, and crime—it hardens the heart." She pounded her fist lightly against her breast. The cat's head jerked up at mention of the words *murder* and *crime* and his eyes narrowed into golden slits.

"*Ew-erow!*" he growled, lips peeled back revealing his sharp teeth.

I wiped my hands on a dish towel. "I swear he can understand you. It's spooky." I gave a mock shudder. "And I haven't named him, by the way. I told you, naming him made it too much of a commitment—and I intend to find his owner before this week is out."

Chantal winked at the cat. "She's such a meanie. But don't worry—it's all an act. I bet she does not try as hard as she says she will. She'll be calling you Nick before the week is out."

"And you would be wrong," I sang out.

"We'll see, won't we?" She dipped one hand into her tote, pulled out several pieces of paper, and waved them under my nose. "I was inspired last night. What do you think?"

I took the papers and riffled through them. They were rough sketches of collars, different designs, colors, and styles, and not half-bad. I passed the drawings back. "Designer collars. You said you were thinking about it."

"Well, I thought I might try to make a few this weekend, and I'm hoping Nicky will still be around to model for me. I want to take some pictures to put on the site Remy designed for me."

We heard a soft *grrr* and turned our heads. The cat's head shook emphatically from left to right.

I laughed. "I don't think Nick is thrilled by the

possibility of being your cat model, Chantal. Either that or he doesn't like being called Nicky."

"Ah—see, I win!" Her finger shot up in the air. "You called him Nick."

I sighed. "So I did. Okay, fine. His name is Nick—for now. I only hope when we find his real owner, he doesn't have an identity crisis."

"Nora, dear. I can't decide what to order. What's on that Lady Gaga again?"

I turned my attention from Chantal and Nick to the petite, gray-haired woman standing before the plate glass case. Ramona Hickey was an indecisive soul, but she'd been one of my late mother's best customers for years. "The Lady Gaga is Genoa salami and pepperoni on marble with German mustard—very hot, very spicy. Not something you'd like, Ramona." The woman was always complaining of one stomach ailment or another—most of them imagined, symptoms courtesy of *WebMD*.

She patted her flat stomach with one carefully manicured hand. "I do like spicy foods," she admitted, "but with all the stomach troubles I've been having lately . . . I'd best stick with something bland. Just give me the Father Knows Best."

"An excellent choice." The corners of my lips twitched. Ham and Swiss on rye, lightly toasted, a dash of mustard with a pickle on the side. Traditional, bordering on boring and—need I say it—unquestionably the perfect sandwich for Ramona Hickey.

I removed two slices of rye from the bread box and saw Ramona's gaze swivel over to where Chantal stood cooing over Nick. She raised one brow questioningly and gave a mock shiver as her eyes darted around. "A cat, Nora? You don't have mice in the shop, do you?"

"None that I'm aware of, Mrs. Hickey."

"Thank goodness." She gave me an anxious look. "Is it wise, though, to have him back there—you know, so close to where you prepare the food?"

I opened the glass case, withdrew ham and Swiss, sliced it thinly, and then piled it on the fresh rye bread, smearing one side gently with mustard. I sliced the sandwich in half, transferred it to a paper plate and placed a kosher dill beside it, and then added a small side of coleslaw. I wiped my hands on a towel and handed her the plate. "Nick doesn't get anywhere near the food, Mrs. Hickey. If he did, I wouldn't allow him in here."

She took the plate, passed me a ten-dollar bill. "Well, that's good to know, dear. I just thought I'd bring it to your attention."

Her tone irked me and I snapped, "Nick is very clean, Mrs. Hickey. As a matter of fact, I think he's even cleaner than some of my customers. You can rest assured his being here isn't against any health violation—if anything, his presence would be a help in keeping rodents at bay. He doesn't get into anything he's not supposed to, and his manners so far have been impeccable—for a cat."

Mrs. Hickey's eyes widened at my outburst. She shoved her change into her jacket pocket and mumbled, "I didn't mean to insult you, Nora. I know you treat this shop with as much care and respect as your dear mother did. I was merely making an observation."

"Thank you for your concern," I said, teeth clenched, "but it really isn't necessary. I have things under control."

"Yes dear," Ramona said, her lips drawn into a rictus of what was probably supposed to be a pleasant smile. "That's apparent."

As she moved away, Chantal squeezed my arm. "Good

for you! I'm so glad you defended Nicky. It just proves what I thought originally—the two of you are getting to be fast friends, no?"

I shrugged. "I just didn't like her attitude, although I should know that's just the way she is. She's such a gossip, though. I don't need her questioning the cleanliness of the store."

Chantal's lips curved upward. "That's what you say. I think you didn't like her insinuating *Nicky* wasn't clean."

I shoved my hands into my apron pockets. "Does it matter if I was defending my store or Nick? He's not mine to keep, remember? His owner is out there, somewhere, missing him."

"Maybe," Chantal grumbled. "Maybe not. Whether you want to admit it or not, Nora Charles, this cat is growing on you. You can't fool me. Deep down, you're hoping his owner can't be found."

I had no chance to respond because the shop bell tinkled once again and Lance ambled into the shop. "Hello, Nora. Hey, Chantal." He leaned against the counter and grinned at me. "Got anything for a hungry man? Pedro's gonna be late, and I'm starved."

Chantal shot him a wicked grin. "Tell the truth, Lance. You don't want that finger food you serve up at the Poker Face. You've got a hungering for a real meal."

He wiggled his eyebrows and wagged his finger. "Can't fool a psychic, can I?" He shot me a wide grin. "So? Since your friend's predicted I'm after a real meal, how about rustling me up one of those Buble Burgers I've heard so much about?"

I grinned back and headed for my freezer. "One extra-thick burger with Black Forest ham coming right up."

Lance's gaze settled on Nick and his eyes widened. He

looked from the cat to me and back to the cat. "Whoa—who's this? Since when did you get a cat? I thought you swore off pets after that chameleon episode."

I made a face at him as I removed a thick slab of ham from the case. "Apparently I've been given a second chance. He wandered into the shop last night, and Chantal talked me into keeping him until I can locate his owner." I set one of the burgers I'd taken out earlier on the grill and listened to it sizzle.

"Yes"—Chantal grinned mischievously—"and don't believe her when she says she wants to locate the owner. Why, she's already named him Nick after the detective in *The Thin Man.*"

I was about to correct her on just who'd done the naming when I caught sight of the expression on Lance's face. "What's the matter?" I asked, waving my spatula. "Is something wrong?"

Lance scratched at his ear. "No, it's just funny, but I thought he looked familiar, and when Chantal said his name is Nick—I think I might know who owns him."

I almost dropped the spatula, and tried my best to ignore the sinking feeling in the pit of my stomach. I hesitated, surprised at my own reaction, and then asked, "You do? Who?"

He barked out a short laugh. "That's what made me laugh. I think his owner's name is Nick, too. Nick Atkins. He used to come into the Poker Face a lot, but I haven't seen him in weeks. Now, I could be wrong but I could swear I saw a photo of that cat in his wallet once."

I cocked a brow. "He had a photo of the cat in his wallet? That's odd."

Lance shook his head. "Anybody can tell you're not a pet person, Nora. Lots of people carry around pictures of their pets. Why, I have one of Brutus on my digital key ring." Brutus was Lance's half pit bull/half Lab. He treated the dog as if he were a human—last Christmas he'd bought the dog his own featherbed.

Chantal let out a low whistle. "I think it's odder that the owner's name is also Nick. Now that would be quite a co-incidence indeed—if it is true."

I pressed the spatula down on the sizzling burger and then moved back to the counter. "It's certainly worth look-ing into. Atkins, you say?"

"Yep." Lance cleared his throat. "And while we're on the subject of coincidences, you said you named the cat after a detective? Well, Atkins is a PI, too. The best in all of California, according to him."

I chuckled. "That's quite a statement. This Nick Atkins sounds like a bit of a braggart."

Lance shrugged. "If you knew him, you'd know he wasn't bragging. This guy really believes he's the best PI in all of California, and to tell you the truth—he might be." At my look he went on, "Okay, maybe not the entire state. But definitely in Cruz, and maybe even up as far as the San Francisco area. Listen, don't take my word for it—Google him." He pointed at Nick. "But I'll bet a month's receipts that's his cat."

I turned away to finish preparing his burger. No way was I taking that bet, because *my* gut told me that Lance just might be right.

Once the lunch crowd had dissipated and Lance and Chantal had departed, I put the CLOSED sign in the door and pulled out my laptop. I typed "Nick Atkins" into the search engine. To my surprise, a plethora of sites came up.

I clicked on a few. Some were murder investigations, others involved missing persons, and they'd all been successfully solved by one Nick Atkins. One of the sites had a photo of Nick, standing beside a young girl he'd found. I studied the tall, handsome man with eyes the color of a fine aged whiskey, lantern jaw, and Pepé Le Pew streak in his jet-black hair.

"Well, Nick Atkins, I'll say this—you are one good-looking PI. The ones I worked with in Chicago sure didn't look like you."

I jumped as something furry rubbed against my arm. Nick purred like a motorcar as he rubbed against me, his head butting my chest. I looked into eyes the color of moonlight and absently stroked the thick black fur. Suddenly I stopped and frowned.

"That's funny," I said. "Nick Atkins has a small white streak in his hair right behind his ear and so"—I ran my fingers across the white fur shaped almost like an angel's wing—"do you. Odd I didn't notice this before. Now there's another coincidence, huh? You seem to be full of 'em."

Nick's lips peeled back in what I imagined was a cat version of a grin. I gave him another quick pat on the head and set him down on the floor.

"Okay, Nick. I must admit, you've been pretty good company—you know, for a cat. But—you can't stay here if you truly belong to someone else. I've got some store business to deal with today, but tomorrow, right after closing, you and I are going to go to this address I found"—I waved the paper in my hand—"and return you to your rightful owner. Okay?"

Nick looked at me for a full minute, then turned around and stalked off, tail and head both held high. "Yeah, okay, it's true," I said as his rotund bottom slunk underneath the damask tablecloth. "Chantal might have been the one who initially wanted you to stay but . . . if it does turn out Nick Atkins is your owner . . . I'll be the disappointed one."

He turned around, trotted back to me, rubbed against my leg. I leaned down to chuck him under the chin and he raised his head and closed his eyes. I heard a purr rumble deep in his chest as he accepted my ministrations. As I pulled my hand away, he turned toward me and yawned.

"Phew." I waved my hand to and fro. "One thing for sure—if you end up staying here, Nick, we've gotta get you some breath mints."

FOUR

The next day right after the lunch crush ended, I closed the shop and hopped into my SUV. Since I'd had no luck finding a working phone number, I took out the paper where I'd printed the address I'd found online for Nick Atkins and propped it on the dashboard in front of me, then programmed it into my GPS unit. I'd barely turned the key in the ignition when I heard a slight rustling behind me, and a second later Nick hopped from the rear of the car into the passenger seat in front, his plumelike tail swishing to and fro double time.

"How did you—never mind." I waved my hand. I'd been fairly certain I'd put him upstairs, but apparently—as with the laptop incident—I'd been mistaken. "It doesn't matter. Maybe it's best if you come along. If you do belong to this Nick Atkins, it'd be best for us to make a clean break, y'know." I cleared my throat. "It's been great having you—bad breath and all—but as you know, I'm not a pet person, and I'm sure you'll be much happier back where you belong. I mean, he carried your picture around with him, for goodness' sake. He has to be missing you."

Nick looked down his nose at me, then turned his back and devoted his time to staring out the passenger window at some birds in the tree overhead. I swallowed the lump that had arisen suddenly in my throat and backed out into the road. About fifteen minutes later I pulled up in front of a small brownstone apartment building in the neighboring town of Cragmere.

I peered out the window at the number emblazoned on the front door. "Okay—427 Peach Street." I tapped the paper with my nail. "This is where your master lives—or at least, it's the most recent address Google has for him." I opened my door and swung my legs out. "Come on, Nick. It's time for you to go home."

Nick sat perfectly still, his back ramrod straight, his tail curled under his forepaws, and blinked twice.

I fisted my hands on my hips. "What? You don't want to come in? You're not anxious to get back to your home, your toys, the nice little fleece bed I'm sure you have?"

He blinked again and turned his head in the other direction.

I sighed as I exited the SUV and shut my door. "Okay, fine. Wait here. Play hard to get." I walked around to the passenger side and tapped my fingertips against the window. "What happened? Did you and your owner have some sort of falling-out?"

Still no response. I straightened. "Well, no worries. Whatever may have happened, I'm sure once Mr. Atkins knows you're out here, he'll rush right out. I'm positive he's missed you, and I'm sure you've missed him."

Nick's black nose twitched, and one ear flicked forward.

Other than that, he gave no response, showed no enthusiasm whatsoever at the prospect of going home. I had to admit, I wasn't exactly thrilled at the idea, either, and no one was more surprised by my reaction than me.

I walked up to the front door and pushed it open. I found myself in a small, fairly dark vestibule. I glanced upward, noted the overhead light, which had, apparently, burned out, and turned my attention to the bells that lined the wall next to the door. I ran my finger down the list of names—Atkins was nowhere to be found. I found the bell marked SUPER, and pushed it once, twice, three times before the intercom just off to the side of the row of bells blared to life.

"If you're a salesman, you can just get your behind back outside. No one here wants any."

I leaned forward. "I'm not a salesman. My name is Nora Charles. I've come inquiring about one of your tenants."

A moment's hesitation and then, "Which one?"

"Nick Atkins."

There was complete and utter silence for at least a minute—possibly longer—and then the voice said, "Okay. Come on in. I'm downstairs."

The buzzer sounded and I found myself in a dark, dingy anteroom with one dimly lit bulb overhead. The stairs were only a few feet away, and I hurried down them into an even darker, cubelike area lit by an even dimmer bulb. A door at the far end of the room opened, and a stout woman wearing a dark blue terrycloth bathrobe, hair in curlers, approached me. I fought back a sudden urge to giggle. All she would have needed was a green mineral mask on her face and a pointy hat, and she could have passed for the Wicked Witch in *The Wizard of Oz*.

Her snappy black eyes looked me up and down. "I'm

Mrs. Rojas. Please tell me you are here to pay the dead-beat's rent."

Deadbeat? That didn't sound good. "No, actually, I came here because I believe I have something of Mr. Atkins's I'm sure he'd like back."

Beefy arms crossed over her ample chest. "Yeah? And what might that be? Something salable, I hope."

"Hardly. I believe I have his cat."

"His—aw heck!" She made an impatient gesture with her hand. "I wondered where he'd gone off to. Frankly, I was going to call the shelter or Animal Control, but as long as you've got him—" She shrugged. "I won't bother."

Shelter? Animal Control? It was my turn to make an impatient gesture. "I'm sorry, I don't understand. Doesn't Nick Atkins live here? The Nick Atkins who is supposed to be a private investigator?"

"He did live here. But I ain't seen him for going on six weeks now. He's three months behind in his rent, and I got responsibilities. My no-good husband ran up gambling debts larger than Texas before he ran off to Costa Rica with my hairdresser, and I've got to support myself and three teenagers, so . . . I ain't making money on an empty three-room apartment. I rented it, packed up all his stuff, and what I couldn't sell I'm waiting for Goodwill to show up and take away. You might tell him that, if you run into him."

I shook my head, trying to process what Mrs. Rojas had just said. "He's been missing for six weeks? Didn't you report it to the police?"

She snorted. "Why? I could probably tell you what happened." She held up one large hand and started to tick off on her fingers. "A, he probably shacked up with some broad. I've seen some of the women he hung out with, and let me tell you, they had 'loser' written all over 'em. B, he's probably off following up some lead on some case. He told me, right before he disappeared, he had a real doozy he was workin' on—thought it would bring him, now what's the word he used? Oh, yeah. Notoriety. He thought it might make him famous." She let out another snort. "Yeah, right. If I had a nickel for every time he said that—well, he'd be flush with me."

I licked at my lips. "But throwing him out on the street—isn't that a bit drastic?"

She sighed. "Honey, drastic is deliberately letting a perfectly good apartment sit vacant because you don't know where the tomcat ran off to when I could be getting over a thousand a month on it. Besides, he's not exactly homeless. He's got his office space. Worse case I'm sure he can shack up there until he gets new digs."

"Oh"—I breathed a sigh of relief—"he does have an office, then? I wondered, because when I Googled him, the only address that came up was this one."

"Yeah, well, that's probably because the space is rented in his partner's name." Her tongue clucked against the roof of her mouth. "Another poor, trusting sap Nick Atkins took advantage of, if you ask me."

I looked up sharply, positive the surprise I felt was plainly visible in my expression. "Partner? Atkins had a partner?"

"Yep. Ollie was a good investigator in his own right, till he got divorced, and then his son tried to kill himself. Poor soul—he tried to drown his troubles in drink, until—and this is about the only good thing I can say about Nick—he took him under his wing. They went in business together, and Ollie's been dry for two years now. Out of the two, Nick brought in most of the business, so if he's down for the count, Ollie's on tough times again. I just hope he can keep it together, 'cause—you see where I'm headed with this, right? Kinda hard to keep up with your bills when you don't have payin' renters."

"Must be," I murmured. "If you could just tell me . . ."

"Anyway, their office is in Castillo, on Clement Street, number 634. Tell Ollie—that's short for Oliver, by the way—Norma sent you, and if he sees that no-good scum of a partner of his, he better not show his face around here unless he has the three thousand in back rent he owes—or else he can tell it to the judge."

I started to retrace my steps back up the hallway. "I'll give him the message. Thanks."

"Wait!"

Mrs. Rojas disappeared into her apartment and emerged a few minutes later with a large box, which she summarily thrust into my arms. "Here you go."

I looked down at the box and the jumble of items jammed inside. "What's all this?"

"The few things I didn't pack for Goodwill. The cat stuff, of course, and I think there were some journals of Nick's in there—Ollie might want 'em." She chuckled. "The journals, not the cat. I have a feeling you're gonna be stuck with him."

The offices of Sampson and Atkins were located in downtown Castillo, a town about a mile and a half south of Cruz. They were tucked into the basement of a converted firehouse that looked as if it had seen better days, although the neighborhood surrounding it bordered on—for want of a better word—upscale yuppieville. I pulled my Hyundai SUV into the asphalt parking lot behind the building and parked in the spot farthest away. I turned around and looked in the backseat. I'd folded it down and laid out all the toys from the box Mrs. Rojas had given me. Right now Nick looked content nibbling at a catnip mouse tucked between his toes, and I sincerely hoped he would stay that way. I locked the SUV and walked briskly to the building, then down the flight of stone steps to the lone oak door bearing the placard SAMPSON AND ATKINS INVESTIGATIONS. I noted as I rang the bell that someone had attempted to scratch out AND ATKINS. A few minutes later a buzzer sounded, and I pushed through the door into the dimly lit interior hallway. There were three doors, all unmarked, and I stood there uncertainly, doing an *eenie meenie miny moe* in my head, when the door on the left suddenly swung open and a tall, muscular frame filled the doorway.

"Oliver Sampson?" I asked.

Both eyebrows rose. "Uh-oh. You're not the Pizza Hut delivery person, are you?"

I shook my head and took a minute to study the brooding hulk of a man who loomed over me. I placed his age as somewhere in the late forties, early fifties. He wasn't what one would call handsome—certainly not in a conventional way—but his features had a certain amount of Humphrey Bogart charm, from the crooked nose right down to the firm jawline and the slightly buck teeth. His mocha skin had a leathery look to it—no doubt the result of years of alcohol consumption—and his eyes were a pale, pale blue, almost a washed-out gray. He was huge—built like a linebacker— and I got the impression he could be intimidating if the need arose. His eyes flashed and he gave me a quick once-over as he cleared his throat loudly.

"I'm Oliver Sampson, all right, and you're not from Pizza Hut. Who are you? If you're a bill collector, you want my ex-partner. And all I can tell you, lady, is there's a long line ahead of you of folks looking for that good-for-nothing Atkins."

He started to turn away and I found my voice. "I'm not a bill collector, Mr. Sampson, but I was hoping to have a word with you about your, ah, former partner?"

His gaze raked me head to toe. "What about him? If you're another disgruntled girlfriend—although I must say, you don't look like his type—sorry, I can't help you. If he's been working on something for you, well, I can't help you there, either. Nick had lots of cases he worked on alone, and he wasn't one to share details."

"I'm not one of his lady friends, and I'm not here about a case. I'm here about the cat."

He stared at me blankly. "The cat?"

"Yes. The black-and-white tuxedo. Someone told me they thought it might be his."

Sampson's pale eyes lit up, and he stroked at his chin with his long fingers. "Oh, you found Sherlock? That's great. I wondered what happened to the little fellow."

I frowned. "Excuse me—Sherlock?"

"Yeah. My boob of a partner got a huge kick out of naming the cat after the only detective he considered smarter than himself—fictional, no less." He scratched at his ear and grinned. "So where did you find him?"

"Actually, he found me."

He stared at me a moment, then pushed the door all the way open and made a motion with his hand. "Why don't you come in? We can have a chat."

I moved past him into a small room that held a single desk, a scarred file cabinet tucked into a corner, and two worn-looking leather chairs. Along the walls were several pictures that looked as if they'd been bought at bargain basement sales—a flower arrangement, a wooded hillside with a church and lots of fluffy clouds, a lake scene—there were also some framed photographs as well, and even though I only took a quick glance, I thought I recognized Nick Atkins in some of them. Oliver Sampson walked around to sit in the leather chair behind the desk, and motioned me to take the other chair. I slid onto the well-worn cushion and heard the chair hinges squeak.

"Sorry." He granted me a small smile. "Redecorating is on my long-term agenda, but it's not a priority right now. Can I get you some coffee, or water?" He inclined his head and I saw a low-slung cabinet, which apparently also doubled as a mini-fridge. A small black Keurig coffeemaker sat on top of it. I took note, too, of the small pile of Pizza Hut boxes stacked off to the left of the cabinet—apparently it was Sampson's food of choice. A photograph of a good-looking young man wearing a cap and gown was tucked behind the coffeemaker—I wondered vaguely if this was the son whose attempted suicide had prompted Sampson's spiral to the bottle. I shook my head and leaned back a bit in the chair, and the springs squeaked. I'd be damn lucky if they didn't poke me in the ass.

Sampson steepled his hands beneath his chin. "So you found little Sherlock."

"As I said, he found me. He happened to wander by my shop."

"Your shop?"

"I own a little sandwich shop—Hot Bread—in Cruz."

"He wandered two towns over, eh? Well, well." Sampson

leaned back in his chair. "Honestly, I'm not surprised. That cat could always smell a good meal—or a free one—a mile away—like his owner."

"Yes, Nick is very enterprising." At his swift look of surprise I added, "I've been calling the cat Nick—after Nick Charles, the detective in *The Thin Man*. I had no idea his owner's name was Nick as well."

Sampson nodded. "Good movie. Nick never cared for Bill Powell, though." He frowned. "What did you say your name was?"

"Nora. Nora Charles."

His eyes widened a bit, and he chuckled. "Ah—your renaming Sherlock makes a bit more sense now."

I cleared my throat. "I stopped by Mr. Atkins's apartment first—it was the only address I could find for him."

"Sure, sure." He drummed his fingers absently on the desktop. "Meet his landlady? She's a real piece of work."

"That she is. She's also rented his apartment and had his stuff shipped off to Goodwill."

"Really?" He let out a gigantic sigh. "Well, I suppose it was bound to happen, sooner or later. It's not the first time he's stiffed her on rent. Not everyone's as easygoing as me. I know I owe him a lot but—even saints have limits." He raised his gaze to mine again. "Sorry, I didn't mean to digress. Now, you are here because . . ."

"I wanted to return Nick—or Sherlock—to his rightful owner," I said over the lump that had suddenly risen in my throat. "He looked so well cared for, I knew he had to be someone's pet. Someone in town thought they'd seen your partner with a picture of him in his wallet, so I Googled him and"—I spread my hands—"here I am."

"Sweet. You're not a bad detective yourself, little lady."

"Thanks. They say investigative reporting is the next

best thing to being a detective, although I do confess I've always had a secret desire to be a female Paul Drake or Sam Spade."

"For what it's worth, I think you've got what it takes." He leaned forward, rested both elbows on the desktop. "Want to know why Nick kept the cat's photo in his wallet? He thought it was a good way to attract chicks—you know, show his sensitive side, caring for animals, all that."

"Really." I sighed inwardly. I was almost glad Nick Atkins was missing because, in truth, after hearing all these details from Ollie and the landlady, I'd have been loath to give the cat back to him. The guy sounded like a real jerk.

Oliver leaned forward. "Yep, but to tell the truth, he really didn't need any gimmicks. My ex-partner had a way with women. It was depressing, really." He slid me a glance. "He'd have charmed you, too—then again, maybe not. Like I said, you're far from the type Nick usually went for. I mean, look at you. You've got class." He barked out a short laugh.

I cleared my throat. "Thanks. So—do you want to keep the cat until your partner returns?"

He eyed me. "You mean *if* he returns. And no, I don't. I like the little fellow but"—he rubbed at his nose with the tip of his finger—"I'm allergic. I took antihistamines when Nick brought the cat around." He leaned forward. "Why don't you keep him? You sound like you've grown fond of him."

I fidgeted a bit in the chair. "I thought about it but I've never been very good at taking care of animals."

He waved his hand carelessly. "Oh, if that's your only concern, I wouldn't worry. That cat can take pretty darn good care of himself. Took good care of Nick, too. Plus, he's got personality—grows on you after a while. Smart, too. I mean, he found you, didn't he?"

I laughed. "That sounds like a compliment, Mr. Sampson."

"It was, and you can call me Ollie. Anyway, Nick used to say Sherlock was just like a dog—maybe even smarter. He even taught him a few tricks—why, he was even teaching the damn cat to play Scrabble. Cat wasn't half bad, either." He croaked out a chuckle. "Anything to impress the ladies, after all."

"Scrabble? Really? Now that I've got to see." A sudden thought occurred to me. "Do you think he might have taught him to turn a computer on and off?"

He shrugged. "Probably. It's simple enough. Wouldn't surprise me, either, if he taught him to surf the Net."

"Me, either," I muttered under my breath. Well, at least now I knew I wasn't losing my mind. "I suppose I could take care of him until Mr. Atkins returns."

Ollie's hand dropped back to the desk, his fingers beating a swift tattoo against the wood. "I wouldn't count on that. As much as I'd like to get my hands on Nick—he owes me half rent for two months, too, and people aren't exactly beating down my door with investigative jobs—I'd be surprised to ever see him again."

"Why do you say that?"

He sat silently for a minute, then abruptly raised his gaze to meet mine. "I'm sorry—you said your name is Nora Charles?"

"Yes."

He half rose out of the chair. "You wouldn't originally be from Chicago, by any chance?"

I looked at him, surprised. "I was born in Cruz, but I lived in Chicago for twelve years. I moved back here to take over the family business."

He snapped his fingers. "You were a reporter, right? True crime?" At my nod, he slapped his palm facedown on the desk and laughed loudly. "Yeah, I remember you now. You came up in some articles Nick Googled. He was looking up some info about Chicago crime families. You were quite the reporter."

"I had some success, yes."

"Some?" He barked out a laugh. "Two national journalism awards suggest otherwise."

I waved my hand. "I might have had a bit of luck. I'm curious. Why was your partner looking up mob families in Chicago?"

"To be honest? He didn't say, and I didn't ask. Where Nick was concerned, it could have been about anything. He had lots of balls in the air at one time, and he operated mainly on gut and hunches."

"And you have no idea what might have happened to him? Where he is?"

"Oh, I've got an idea, all right," Ollie said. "I'm pretty sure it might have something to do with this last case he was working on. I wanted no part of it, and I told him he was a damn fool for taking it, but—that was Nick. He was certain he could solve anything. The deuce of it is, he usually always did." Ollie let out a giant sigh. "This time, though, I'm afraid he might have gotten in a bit over his head."

"Really? How so?"

Ollie looked all around the room, almost as if he expected someone to come crashing in at any moment, and then he got up, walked around the desk, and leaned over so he could put his lips close to my ear.

"I'll tell you," he whispered, "but you can't breathe a word. Nick took this last case because he was convinced it would make him famous. You see, he was hired by Adrienne Sloane—Lola Grainger's sister. Right before he disappeared, he told me he suspected Lola's death was no accident—that it was murder, and he was this close to proving it.

"And now . . . I'm afraid he may be dead, too."

FIVE

After a few seconds, I found my voice. "You really think Nick Atkins is dead?"

Ollie cleared his throat. "Of course, I'm not one hundred percent certain, but considering what he was working on, it's a very good possibility."

I pursed my lips, my thoughts in a whirl. "I have to admit," I said slowly, "that I myself read all the accounts of Lola's . . . accident, and I also feel something just doesn't add up."

"Ssh!" Ollie's eyes went wide, and he put a finger against his lips. "I wouldn't voice that opinion too loudly if I were you."

"Okay." I paused. "It is possible he's undercover somewhere. Gathering his facts. I witnessed a lot of that in Chicago."

"I'm sure you did, and of course it's a possibility, but somehow I don't think so. Six weeks is a long time not to hear from Nick."

"Six weeks is a drop in the bucket when you're under-cover."

"Yes," Ollie laughed, "but trust me, undercover or not, if Nick were still able to, he'd have communicated with me in some way, I know he would." He waved his hand. "I know what you're thinking—I called him a deadbeat and all, but—what can I say? We were best friends as well as partners. I know Nick as well as I know myself. If he were alive, even if he were in deep cover, he'd have gotten word to me somehow. That's what makes me think I've seen the last of him, dammit."

Ollie's eyes glistened with sudden moisture and I squeezed his arm. "Have hope, Ollie. It's never over till the fat lady sings, right? You never know, Nick could walk through that door tomorrow."

"Yeah, and I could get hired as one of Cher's backup singers, too. Hey, it's always been a secret dream of mine." He grinned. "Or maybe Lady Gaga. I like her style."

The thought of this two-hundred-something-pound black man in one of Lady Gaga's outrageous outfits made me want to laugh out loud. I resisted the impulse and asked, "You said that Adrienne Sloane hired him. Have you tried to contact her, see if she possibly knows any-thing?"

"No, I haven't."

"Why not?"

He made a clucking sound, deep in the back of his throat, and mumbled something so low I had to lean over and ask him to repeat it. "Because it's possible she might be dead, too."

I half rose out of my chair. "*What?* How can you pos-sibly make a statement like that?"

"I can't be absolutely certain, any more than I can be certain Nick is dead. But the last time I saw him, he was on his way out that door to meet Adrienne Sloane. He said she had something to tell him that could change the direction of the entire case."

I frowned. "That's all? He didn't tell you any more than that?"

"I was lucky to get that much out of him. Anyway, a few hours later my phone rings. It's Nick, but we had a real bad connection—static all over the line. He was whispering into the phone, too, so it was hard to make out what he said, but it sounded like he'd seen a body lying under the docks, and he thought it looked like Adrienne."

I sucked in a breath. "Oh my."

"Yep," he continued. "Next thing I knew, the phone went dead. I hightailed it right down to the docks, but I didn't see hide nor hair of Nick—or any bodies, either."

My brow lifted. "So then what makes you think they might be dead?"

He licked at his lips. "Right before our connection was broken, I heard something—it could have been a car backfiring—or it could have been a gunshot. I'm still not sure." He reached out and laid his hand over mine. "Listen, Nora, I don't want to think the worst, but I knew Nick like a book, I worked with him for years. I knew the types of cases he got involved with, and the Grainger case was a disaster waiting to happen. If it was murder—and I'm not saying it was—then there is more there than meets the eye, much more. There's something brewing there people will kill to keep secret."

I nibbled at my lower lip. "I know you're trying to discourage me, Ollie, but I'm afraid all this is having the opposite effect on me. It's making me, as the White Rabbit would say, 'curiouser and curiouser.'"

"Actually," chuckled Ollie, "it was Alice who said that, not the rabbit. And it's a trait that makes a great ace reporter, but could ultimately place you in grave danger." He rose and took my arm. "Listen to me, Nora. Go on home, and give little Sherlock—or Nick—a pat on the head for me. Tell him I'm glad he finally found himself a good home with a good person. If you need anything—you know, like advice on caring for cats or the services of a pretty good investigator?" One eye closed in a broad wink. "Feel free to call. My dance card ain't exactly full. I'll be here."

I gave Ollie a small smile. "I just might take you up on your offer. I told you, I'm not really that good at caring for animals."

He held up both hands. "Nora, the cat found you, remember? Animals have better instincts about what's good for them than most humans. Believe me, he knows exactly what he wants, and it happens to be you."

"Well," I said, "I suppose I can keep him—at least, until his real owner turns up."

"Yeah, well, that might be a while. Quite a while."

That prospect pleased me, although I hated to think how I'd feel if Atkins returned to claim his little roommate. I squared my shoulders, deciding I'd cross that bridge when—or if—I got to it, and then added, "I'd really like to keep calling him Nick, but if he's used to the other name . . ."

"You should call him whatever you like," Ollie said. "I doubt it'll matter much to him, as long as he has somewhere soft to sleep and three squares a day." His hand shot out to cover mine. "Nick's your cat now, and you couldn't ask for a finer companion. The poor thing had to listen to all of Nick's stories about his women and his investigations. If you decide to go back into investigative reporting or even detective work someday, who knows? That cat might be more of a help to you than you think."

I laughed. "And just how would he help? Cats can't talk, after all."

"He doesn't have to." Ollie tapped his forefinger against his chin as he walked me to the door. "Believe me, cats have plenty of tricks to make what they're thinking known, and Nick has more than most. You just wait and see."

I retraced my steps back to the SUV and hopped inside. Nick lay curled up on the backseat, head between his paws. I'd thought he was asleep, but his head jerked up as soon as I shut the door. I twisted around in the seat to look at him.

"Well, Sherlock. I understand that's your name. It seems your master is MIA—for now."

He blinked twice.

"If it's okay with you, I'm going to keep calling you Nick, at least until your master shows up to reclaim you. I think you're a bit more Nick Charles than Sherlock Holmes, don't you?"

He sat up, stretched his forepaws out, then jumped over into the front seat. He laid his paw on my arm, rubbed against my shoulder, and began to purr.

I chuckled as I guided the car into the steady stream of rush-hour traffic. "I'm glad we agree."

"*Meow.*"

"Ollie said you could be a big help to me," I said thoughtfully. "That you had plenty of tricks up your sleeve—or paw."

Nick gave me a solemn nod. "*Er-ow!*" he said emphatically, waving his paw in the air.

"Uh-huh," I said, making the turn on the road back to Cruz. "That's just what I was afraid of."

SIX

Back home, I dug up some fresh salmon leftover from the salad I'd prepared for tomorrow's special and put it in a bowl for Nick. As he chowed down, I dragged the box Mrs. Rojas had foisted upon me onto the counter and began unpacking it. There were lots of cat toys—several catnip mice, some socks, a few soft balls—and a warm-looking fleece blanket I assumed had been Nick's bed. There were a few cans of Fancy Feast as well, although I had an idea that after sampling my leftovers, Nick would turn his nose up at any food of the canned variety. My fingers closed over the well-worn Scrabble board and the vinyl pouch of letter tiles and I chuckled.

"We'll have to play one night," I tossed over my shoulder at Nick, and held up the board. "I've been told you're pretty good."

Nick glanced up from his bowl, licked some salmon from his whiskers—and yawned.

I laughed. "Sorry to bore you, pal."

I fished out three rolls of breath mints and chuckled. "Well, well—seems your former master had a breath problem, too. Either that or he had stock in Life Savers."

The cat ignored me and continued pushing his face into the bowl.

In the bottom of the box were three large fat notebooks. I hit my forehead with my palm. Mrs. Rojas had mentioned she'd put Nick's journals in the box. I'd forgotten all about giving them to Ollie.

Oh, well, I thought, picking one up. *No harm in just looking through them, right?* Tomorrow I'd call Ollie and ask him if he wanted me to drop them off. While Nick was still slurping up salmon, I carted the book over to the table, propped my feet up on one of the chairs, and started my perusal.

The first book was dated several years ago and contained accounts of several different cases—a philandering husband, a kidnapped girl, a guy who'd embezzled funds from a local charity. Nick wrote his accounts in great detail, sometimes belaboring a point, and while his grammar could stand a good going-over, his narrative style was compelling. I was almost finished with the first book when I felt a tug on my skirt. I looked down.

Nick lay underneath my chair. Tucked under his paws was another of the notebooks.

"Hey!" I wagged my finger at him. "You are a rascal. How on earth did you get that down from the counter without me hearing you?"

Nick stretched out his paws and pushed the notebook closer to my chair. "*Eeower*," he said, rubbing one paw against the notebook's cover. When I didn't react, he gave the book another push. "*Eeower*," he beseeched, louder this time.

"What are you trying to tell me? You don't agree with my choice of reading material? You think I should read the notebook you've selected?"

I reached down and pulled the journal from underneath his rotund belly. I flipped to the first page and started. Written in a bold hand was:

Lola Grainger CaseDetails/Interviews

I looked down at Nick, who lay on his side, one of the socks clamped firmly in his paws, his back feet clawing at the air as he sniffed the catnip contained within. I shook my head and flipped to the first page, where I read with great interest what Nick Atkins had written down:

When I first read the account of Lola Grainger's accident, I have to admit, I was immediately suspicious. Something sounded off—at first glance it reeked of a domestic dispute gone badly awry, and I ought to know—I've been involved in enough of them. Anyway, I was in my office one evening after Ollie'd gone home, going over some bills, when the phone rang. It was a woman who identified herself as Adrienne Sloane, Lola Grainger's sister. She wanted to hire me to investigate her sister's murder—note she said murder and not accident.

I checked her out, of course—one can't be too careful these days—and then I went to the house she was renting and met with her. A very nice woman—not a beauty like her sister, but she had a quiet charm—very soft spoken, ladylike. She and her sister hadn't spoken in years, she said, and they were just starting to get to know each other again. Lola confided a few things to her that led her to believe things weren't all so hunky-dory in her marriage—such as the fact Kevin Grainger liked to drink, but couldn't hold his liquor well. Apparently there were many arguments that resulted in Lola getting the short end of the stick—and considering hiring a divorce lawyer.

"Hm." I looked up from the journal. "Now that is interesting. From what my mother used to tell me, Lola and her husband always got along. She never mentioned the d word to Mom."

At my feet, Nick let out a resounding "*Yowl.*" I continued reading:

Adrienne wasn't certain her sister would have actually gone through with a divorce. She did think, though, that going through the motions might make him straighten out. The night of the accident, Lola called her sister from the ship. Adrienne didn't have her cell on her, so she didn't get the message until she got home. She said Lola seemed very upset. She'd found out something about her husband and needed to talk to her sister—she needed her help figuring out what to do. She ended the conversation with, "Kevin will probably kill me." And shortly thereafter . . .

I stroked my chin. "That's pretty thin. Lots of people say stuff like that in the heat of an argument, but they don't really mean it. And why would Lola confide marital problems to a sister she hadn't spoken to in years?" I read further:

Adrienne supplied me with a lot of information that never made it into the papers, or the original police report, for that matter. For one, Grainger didn't make the initial ID, like the papers reported. He left that detail to his controller, I believe. There were also a few bruises on the body. Of course, those could be explained as injuries from when she fell, but . . . it just raised more questions in my mind.

"Mine, too," I murmured. I kept on reading.

To my mind, the crime scene was handled all wrong. PI 101—no one should leave the scene, whether it's in a limo, a plane, or on horseback. Everyone knows the first twenty-four hours investigating a homicide are crucial. Any hopes of fact finding rode away the minute they let Grainger and company walk. Gave him a chance to lawyer up, to get his story straight, and make sure all the others matched.

I set the journal facedown on the table and leaned back, lacing my hands behind my head. No doubt in my mind that Nick Atkins was correct in this assumption—the lead detective blew it. Although, to be perfectly honest, it might not have been his fault. His superiors had probably told him to go easy on a man of Grainger's stature. I knew, of course, what should have been done, just as I was certain Atkins had known, too: Even if there was no reason to suspect foul play, Grainger and all the others should have been hauled in for questioning immediately. If nothing else, proper police procedure would have been adhered to. The crime scene should have been protected from possible disturbance, the event reconstructed, a timeline organized.

Why hadn't that been done?

I wondered what the other people on the boat had said. If any of them deliberately covered for Grainger, that would make them just as guilty, make them accessories after the fact. It seemed a large chance to take just to prove loyalty—particularly since that charge carried a hefty prison sentence. The witnesses, in this case, had all claimed to have been in their staterooms and not heard a thing.

Two years ago I attended a seminar on criminal investigation at the Hilton in Beverly Hills, and Grainger happened to be at the same hotel on business. I was at the bar, and he came in with some of his colleagues and sat near me. I've got to tell you, I wasn't impressed. Even then I got a strange vibe from him—like he was hiding something.

I went down to the marina shortly after Lola's death and nosed around. The consensus there was Lola Grainger was a saint, hubby is the second coming, everyone is rallying behind him in his time of need, and of course it was a tragic accident. How could it be otherwise? Bottom line: Everyone I talked to sympathized with the grief-stricken husband. Grainger couldn't—wouldn't—didn't—murder his wife. And that in itself struck me as odd. Out of all those people, not one person had a bad word to say about Kevin Grainger. You expect most people to stick up for him, but there's at least one or two who will pull you on the side to dish the dirt. Not in this case, though. Frigging weird.

I chuckled at that and continued.

*At first, I thought it could have been an accident—
she was drunk and did slip and—fall in; however, recent events have forced me to reassess. There is
something much, much bigger afoot here. The more I
dig, the more certain I become.*

I nodded in silent agreement so far with everything
Nick Atkins had written down. I flipped the page and bit
back a cry of disappointment. There were flecks of paper
caught along the spine's crease, as if other pages had been
torn out. One page remained, with only one line written
there.

*Tonight I received a text from Adrienne. She wants
me to meet her at the docks—she believes the wrong
Grainger might have been killed.*

There were no more entries in this journal. I closed the
book and leaned back. "The wrong Grainger," I murmured. I looked down at the cat, who was now sitting next
to my chair on his haunches, watching me through slitted
eyes. "What in heck does that mean?"

A sound emanated from deep in Nick's throat, a cross
somewhere between a gurgle and a sigh. "*Yurgle!*"

"True. There was only one other person named Grainger
on that boat," I said. I dropped my hand down, rubbed
Nick between his ears. He let out a deep purr and flopped
to one side. "Did she mean Kevin was supposed to die? But
how on earth could she have known that?" I drummed the
fingers of my other hand against the journal's cover. "I
wonder—could she possibly have been setting your former
master up? Telling him that to deliberately have him meet
her at the pier?"

Nick's head jerked up and he blinked his golden eyes.

"But why would she do something like that? I mean, she hired him, right?"

Nick sat up on his haunches. "*Yow*," he said again.

I pushed my chair back and stood up. "You know what I think, Nick? I think the police did a damn awful job. I think they need to reopen this case."

His paw shot straight out and his nails caught in the fabric of my pants. He gave a little tug. I leaned down and gently disengaged his claw. "What, Nick? You think I should investigate? I have to admit, I'm considering it."

Chantal's words rang in my ears: *A friend of mine is going to undertake a dangerous mission.* I recalled how nervous Oliver Sampson had been, recounting the case to me. While I couldn't deny I found the whole affair fascinating, I'd put investigative reporting behind me, determined to live a normal life. Did I really need to get involved in something that had the very real possibility of becoming very dangerous?

I could almost hear my mother's voice, ringing in my head. *Lola got a rotten deal, Nora. You're good at solving puzzles. You can solve this one.*

"Maybe so," I muttered. "But there seem to be so many unanswered questions and variables. Finding out if Lola was murdered won't bring her back, right? And then there's Adrienne. What happened to her? Not to mention Nick's former owner. If it should turn out all three of them were murdered—then it must be to cover up something really, really huge."

Nick cocked his head and blinked twice. Then he raised a paw, almost as if he were gesturing toward the journal.

"You think your former master was on to something, I can tell." I sat back down and pulled my laptop in front of me. I called up the original article I'd read on Lola Grainger's death and read it slowly. Then I reread what Nick Atkins had written.

"Critical things were overlooked. Grainger's status in the community got in the way of the police investigation."

Nick hopped up on the chair beside me and sat on his haunches, his paws skimming the tabletop.

I pointed at the screen. "It says here her blood alcohol level was only point oh-four. That means she was only slightly intoxicated. It doesn't make sense that she fell in the water in a drunken stupor. The coroner said her down vest weighed her down and her intoxicated state contributed to the fact she couldn't think clearly in an emergency situation. Yet she should have been able to, at only point oh-four."

I drummed my fingers on the tabletop. Something didn't add up. According to the statement given by Kevin Grainger, Lola had retired ahead of him to their stateroom. When he entered about an hour later, she was gone. He checked outside and found the dinghy missing. The consensus had been she'd slipped and fallen into the water attempting to retie it. The dinghy had been swept into the ocean by the heavy winds, and since she never managed to climb back into it, she eventually contracted hypothermia, sank beneath the waves, and drowned.

All tied up, neat and tidy. Yet something just wasn't right.

"It makes no sense," I mumbled. I closed my eyes and leaned back, trying to visualize the scene in my mind's eye. A slightly inebriated and frightened Lola, slipping, falling into the dark waters, clutching at the dinghy, hanging on for dear life as it got swept out into sea, trying to put one foot aboard it, and getting knocked back by the weight of her down vest . . .

"That's it!" I cried and sat bolt upright, my eyes wide. Nick, startled at my sudden outburst, slipped off the chair and landed right on his plump bottom on the floor.

He rose, shook himself in a doglike manner, then hopped back up on the chair, cocking his head at me as if to say, *Okay, human. What's so important you had to scare the crap out of me?*

I reached over and gave him a quick pat on the head. "Sorry, Nick. It just occurred to me. Ducks."

Nick lay down, rested his head on his forepaws. "*Ewwr?*"

"Okay, I'll tell you. My sister tried to wash her duck down comforter a few months ago," I murmured. "She called me, all worked up. Seems down is very buoyant and floats high on top of the water—it doesn't like to get wet. It took her two and a half hours to finally soak the damn thing. When you think about it, it makes sense. Ducks float, right, so Lola's down vest wouldn't have pulled her under. It would have kept her afloat, and if that was the case, she could have called for help—she should have called for help. She should have driven herself hoarse calling. It was a clear night—there were boats docked nearby. Why didn't she call out? I can only think of two possibilities.

"Either she was unconscious when she went into the water—or she was already dead."

SEVEN

I made dinner for myself and Nick, and then stayed up till after midnight researching various articles on Lola Grainger. It was obvious that as little time as possible had been allotted to the investigation—the dearth of information was astounding, and it only served to pique my interest more. There was some sort of cover-up going on, I could just feel it. Why? What had been covered up? And did it have anything to do with Lola's statement to her sister: *Kevin will probably kill me.* What was she supposed to have known? It had to be something really, really big—explosive. The coroner's report stated conclusively the cause of death was drowning—but if some sort of cover-up was going on, did it extend to the coroner? Could he have been persuaded to falsify the cause of death? Or continuing to think along those lines, Lola could also have been unconscious when she went in—then the coroner's report would be correct. To a point.

If the drowning occurred as a result of some sort of inflicted physical injury, it would still be . . . dare I say it? Murder. Taking the scenario one step further, perhaps Kevin had been the intended target, and Lola found out. From everything I'd heard about the woman, she'd be just the type to confront the murderer. Had she been disposed of before she could tip her husband off to what was in store for him? In which case, he'd still be in danger. If Kevin were the intended target, why hadn't the killer struck again? There were a lot of loose ends that needed to be connected, and it seemed the only way to get answers was from those either deceased or MIA.

So many questions, so little time. I wondered if the pages torn out from Atkins's journal were missing because they could shed some light on the puzzle.

After writing down a good ten pages of notes, I shut off the lights and saw Nick curled up in a ball next to my non-working fireplace, snoring away. I undressed, brushed my teeth, and tumbled, exhausted, into bed, where my dreams were scattered between visualizing Lola Grainger fall into the water, her husband standing on deck watching her, his hands tied in front of him, and Nick running around the boat deck chasing his tail. Talk about strange. Well, it's my own fault for mixing cilantro and hot pepper—the combination gives me nightmares every time. I'd finally drifted back into a dreamless sleep when the ring of my alarm shrieked in my ear. Four thirty, good grief! I reached out, shut it off, and rolled over on my side, intending to just catnap (excuse the pun) for ten more minutes. I kept shifting my position, unable to get comfortable for some reason until I realized why I couldn't feel my left foot. I tried to wiggle my toes: nothing.

Alarmed, I sat bolt upright, and instantly saw the cause of my foot problem. Nick's hefty body was spread over the bottom half of my bed, his large head planted squarely on my left foot. I poked at him with my other foot, and he just rolled over on his back, paws in the air. With a sigh I threw my covers back, leaned over, and jabbed him in the ribs. He twisted his body over, stretched out his front paws.

"*Yower!*" he rumbled and squeezed both eyes.

I perched on the bed's edge, my arms thrust into my bathrobe. "My bad. I forgot to prop the chair in front of my door last night. Oh, well." I slid him a smile. "Until we find out for sure what happened to your owner, you're here to stay, so . . . I imagine, like most cats, that includes giving you the run of the house."

Nick looked at me, gave a loud purr, and raised one paw to my knee.

I finished buttoning my bathrobe and gave him the eye. "I see you must have picked up some pointers on charming women from your former owner. Although—that was a pretty nice fleece blanket in that box. I could make you a nice little bed of your own in front of the fireplace. You wouldn't have to share."

In answer, Nick burrowed his furry body deeper into my bedspread. Apparently he preferred my down comforter.

I leaned over and chucked him under his chin. "Okay, okay. We'll be bedmates—for now. But try not to hog all the space, will ya?"

I got an indifferent stare in return. Of course.

I usually opened for the breakfast crowd at seven a.m. sharp. Mollie Travis, a high school junior who lived up the block, came in three days a week to help out. I didn't serve anything real fancy, just the usual: bagels, muffins, ham and eggs for an occasional special, but I usually got a pretty good crowd. This morning Mollie left a message on the store phone: She was sick with a twenty-four-hour bug, so she wouldn't be able to come in either today or tomorrow. Great. And, of course, it seemed as if every working person in Cruz felt the need to stop in for something this morning, so by the time nine o'clock rolled around, I was pretty much about done in. Once the last customer had departed, Nick emerged from underneath the counter and planted himself square in the middle of the floor.

I chuckled. "I know what you're looking for."

I retrieved a plate of leftover bracciole and set it in front of him. As he pushed his face into the bowl, making little slurping sounds, I checked the messages on my cell phone. A former contact of mine from Chicago (I hate the word *snitch*), Henry "Hank" Prince, had come through with some useful information, thanks to the wide range of contacts he'd amassed over the years that spanned our fifty states and beyond. Besides confirming what I already knew, he was also able to verify that Marshall Connor identified Lola's body and did most of the talking to the police. Patti Cummings, Grainger's majordomo, never left his side. As for the bruises, he couldn't confirm any on the body, but there was one near the base of Lola's skull. Lott, in particular had seemed very nervous. According to Hank, a reporter from one of the L.A. tabloids tried to approach him a few days later and got the cold shoulder for her trouble. He'd also learned that the coroner who performed Lola's autopsy had left his position for a cushy teaching job at Quantico—three guesses who was responsible for that, and the first two don't count.

Snapping my phone shut, I decided that if I were going

to try and get some answers, the captain might be a good starting point. Hopefully the passage of time had loosened his tongue somewhat. Before I did that, however, I thought I'd give the police the courtesy of a visit—give them an opportunity to exchange useful information. The policeman who answered the phone was brusque to say the least, and not very willing to help after I explained the purpose of my call. I imagined if I ran the local donut shop, things would have gone much more smoothly. I was summarily informed that the detective who had been in charge of the Grainger case was, unfortunately, out on medical leave. The good news, though, was his replacement agreed to give me a few moments of his oh-so-valuable time.

I had a one o'clock appointment with Detective Daniel Corleone.

Chantal was more than willing to watch the store—and Nick—so I could keep the appointment. "Do not worry about a thing, *chérie*," she assured me. "This will give Nicky and me a chance to get better acquainted, *non*?"

Nick purred loudly and rubbed his furry body against her legs.

"It will give me a chance to tell him about my new jewelry line—and the pet collars I am designing," Chantal went on. "Ooh, it is going to be *magnifique*! How would you like to be my catalog model, Nicky?"

Nick abruptly stopped winding himself around Chantal's ankles. All purring halted—his neck jutted forward, his head snapped up, and he bared his teeth, affording us both with an excellent view of his sharp fangs. "*Ffft*," he hissed, and then promptly dove underneath the back table.

"Well, for goodness' sake! What did I do?"

Chantal leaned over and tried to coax him out. All she got for her trouble was more *fft*s and some spitting.

"I don't think he likes the idea of wearing a collar," I chuckled as I reached for my car keys. "Either that or he really doesn't like to be called Nicky. Did I tell you Ollie Sampson said his real name is Sherlock?"

"Sherlock? *Ewww.*" Chantal wrinkled her nose. "I'm glad you decided to keep calling him Nick. Being named after *The Thin Man* seems to suit him much, much better."

"I agree," I chuckled, "even though the 'Thin Man' doesn't refer to the detective Nick Charles at all."

Chantal frowned. "It doesn't?"

I shook my head. "It's a common mistake. The 'Thin Man' is the man that Nick is initially hired to find, Clyde Wynant. During the investigation they find a skeletonized body they assume to be that of a much heavier man because of the clothing, but it's just a diversion. They manage from a war wound to identify the body as being that of a 'thin man'—Wynant. The whole thing was a setup—the murderer had stolen a great deal of money from Wynant and was trying to frame him for murder."

"Wow—guess I'll have to catch up on my Turner Classics." Chantal went over to the back counter, shook some cat treats into her hand, and then knelt by the table. She carefully picked up the edge of the tablecloth. Nick lay, crouched far in the back, his ears flattened against his skull, his back raised, attack fashion.

"*Ffft,*" he spat again. Chantal offered him a treat. He blinked, and the tail bristled. "*Ffft.*"

I chuckled at the woebegone expression on my friend's face. "Give him time. He'll get over it. Nick has very definite ideas on what he likes and doesn't like—I swear, at times he seems almost human."

"*Yowwwl,*" came from underneath the table.

Chantal waved her hand. "Ah, he will come around. Just wait and see. I bet you I'll have him modeling collars before you get this article on Lola Grainger finished for *Noir*."

The damask tablecloth wiggled slightly, and then we heard a loud growl.

I chuckled as I reached for my purse. "I'm not a gambling woman, but I do believe I'll take that bet."

Chantal grabbed my arm as I walked past her. "Is it so very wrong of me to hope this Nick Atkins never shows up, *chérie*? That we can keep our Nicky with us forever and ever?"

I looked down. Nick stuck his head out from underneath the tablecloth and I could swear the corners of his lips tipped up, a feline grin.

"*Meow*." One paw rose and lightly grazed his forehead, as if in a kitty salute.

I couldn't stop the grin that spread across my face in return. "Nope," I answered. "I find nothing wrong with that train of thought at all."

EIGHT

Police Headquarters were tucked into a skinny, two-story brown building located on the south end of Cruz. I pulled into the parking lot behind the building, locked the car, walked up the flight of stone steps, and pushed through the plate glass door and into the wide reception area. It looked as if the station was hopping this afternoon—apparently Tuesday was prime time for crime. A policeman stood in one corner, taking down a report from a girl in jeans and a tight sweater. Off to my left I recognized another cop, Henry Whittle, from high school. He was talking to an elderly woman in a flowered dress who kept twisting her hands as if greatly agitated. As I passed them, I heard Henry say, "So, he's got white fur with two brown spots, one over his left eye?"

The woman nodded, and I thought I saw tears glistening in her pale blue eyes. "Yes, my Frederick looks just like that terrier from those old Bill Powell movies—you know the ones I mean, right?"

I did indeed, I thought as I passed them. When I was younger, I'd always wanted a dog like Asta.

I made my way over to the wide, walnut wood reception desk, where a bored-looking woman wearing a starched denim blue shirt, long dark hair pulled back into a braid that hung over one shoulder, sat. She eyed me warily as I approached.

"Nora Charles," I said. "I'm here to see Detective Daniel Corleone."

She shot me a sharp look. "I'm not certain he's around," she snapped, "and if he is, he's very busy. Do you have an appointment?"

"I made an appointment," I began, and then a shadow fell across the desk.

"No need to screen her, Margaret. I've got it." A hand shot out. "I'm Detective Daniel Corleone. You must be Ms. Charles."

I had to bite back a gasp as I turned to the man behind me. I'm five-ten in my two-inch heels—he was easily six-foot-two. Burnished blond hair, cut a bit shaggy, stood out against tan skin and clear blue eyes. The slight stubble of a five o'clock shadow covered an otherwise strong jaw. I let my gaze trail a bit lower, taking in the broad shoulders and narrow waist that nipped down to what appeared to be firmly muscled thighs encased in a pair of straight-leg dark denim jeans.

I didn't recall any detective in Chicago looking half this sexy. Seeing this guy who could easily be a *GQ* model was more than a bit disconcerting.

Well, Danny Corleone was most definitely not Don Vito. Not Kojak or Columbo, either.

But he was most definitely HOT. H-O-T in flashing neon red letters.

I dragged my gaze upward with supreme effort. "Detective Corleone. So nice to meet you in person." I took the proffered hand, felt strong fingers close over mine in a steely grip. "Thank you for seeing me on such short notice."

His full lips twisted into a wry grin. "Well, I have to admit you certainly piqued my interest." He stood aside and motioned to a door across the hall with his hand. "Won't you please come into my office? We'll have privacy in there." He turned to the woman behind the desk. "Margaret, hold my calls. Don't buzz me unless it's Captain Rogers."

"Sure, Detective Corleone." He brushed past her, and I could swear I saw a bit of red creep up her neck and color her café au lait skin. Her gaze on him bordered on worshipful—as it shifted to me, I could almost swear a hint of green tinged her chocolate brown eyes.

Apparently I was not the only one affected by Detective Corleone's looks.

I followed him into a small room that held a single desk, a scarred file cabinet tucked into a corner, and two worn-looking leather chairs. The pale beige walls were dotted with framed citations. It seemed a serviceable office, and yet in spite of the few homey touches, something seemed off.

"Is something wrong, Ms. Charles?"

I glanced up to see him looking at me. I shrugged. "No. I was just taking a quick peek around." And then, before I quite realized it, I blurted out, "This office is so not you."

One eyebrow quirked. "Pardon?"

I felt color dot my cheekbones. "I'm sorry. It's just"—I waved my arms to encompass the space—"everything seems disjointed, like it's been thrown together. You don't impress me as being either careless or disorganized."

"Do tell?" He smirked.

I let my gaze rove over his polished appearance and said, "Someone well organized, who thrives on order, both personally and in business."

He regarded me in silence for a moment, and then finally smiled. "Well, you're right. This office isn't my regular one. I'm here for a few weeks on loan, so these are just temporary quarters. And I am a stickler for order."

I'd have bet anything he was the type who laid out his clothes for the week on a Sunday night, making sure everything was coordinated, from the shirt to the socks to the boxer briefs. I bit back the urge to smile and say, "I knew it," so all I got out was a lame-sounding, "Okay. So, um . . . you're not from around here?"

His features settled into an amused expression. "No."

Ah, a man of few words. I gave him a bright smile. "I bet you must get a lot of remarks, right? Hear a lot of jokes?"

The amused look segued into a quizzical glance. "Pardon?"

"Your last name, you know—Corleone, *The Godfather*, you being in law enforcement and having a last name that's usually connected with—well, those who are not."

The puzzled expression cleared, and he shook his head. "Not really. And now that's settled, please have a seat."

Okay, no sense of humor. I put one check in the minus column for Detective Hunk.

He walked around to sit in the leather chair behind the desk and motioned me to take the other chair. I was dying to ask him just where he was from, but figured I'd best quit before I made an even worse impression. I settled myself in the chair and folded my hands in my lap.

"Before we begin, can I get you anything?"

I shook my head. "I'm fine, thanks."

"So." He leaned back in his chair, bright blue eyes trained on me, obviously studying me. "Furnishings of my office aside, you wanted to discuss the Lola Grainger case, Ms. Charles?"

"Nora," I piped up.

He paused. "Pardon?"

"I'm sorry." I shifted in the chair, crossed my legs at the ankles, and pulled my skirt hem down a bit lower. "It's just that calling me Ms. Charles makes me sound like my late mother. I'd much prefer Nora."

"Okay, Nora." He waited a beat, and then said, "You said on the phone you wanted to discuss the Lola Grainger case for a possible article?"

I cleared my throat, which felt suddenly dry and scratchy. "That's correct, Detective."

One eyebrow crooked. "As you may or may not know, I wasn't actively involved in the case, Detective O'Halloran was. I'll do what I can for you, although I can't imagine what someone could possibly find interesting. The Lola Grainger case is closed. It was an open-and-shut accident."

"As far as paperwork is concerned, maybe," I said. "But to an investigative reporter, there are plenty of unanswered questions. Details that appear unclear."

He shifted position in his chair, steepled his long fingers beneath his chin. "Unclear, you say? How so?"

I reached into my tote bag and removed a pad and pen, which I balanced on my knee. "Well, for starters, there's the way the crime scene was handled."

Another quirk of his brow. "What about it?"

"Normally all the witnesses would have been segregated, would they not, and questioned separately back at

Police Headquarters? That didn't seem to happen in this case."

Corleone was silent for several seconds, then nodded. "You're correct, that's what usually happens when we suspect foul play, but from O'Halloran's account, there was no reason to suspect wrongdoing. O'Halloran clearly states Grainger was in bad shape, that he could barely pull himself together. The man was near to tears, kept saying that his wife was gone; he wasn't quite sure just what had happened, but that nothing would bring her back. I expect O'Halloran did the humane thing and left a grieving husband to his sorrow."

I shifted my pad on my knee. "It's one thing to act humanely, Detective, and quite another to be incompetent."

One brow rose. "Incompetent? That's a mighty serious accusation."

"Oh, don't misunderstand me—I'm not making any accusations. But I've read the newspaper accounts of how the case was handled, and I've got to tell you, there are quite a few things that don't hit me right."

Now the other eyebrow followed suit. "Such as?"

"Well, for starters, doesn't it seem strange to you that out of the five other people on board the *Lady L*, not one of them heard anything? Not even a splash when Lola supposedly fell overboard?"

"Supposedly?"

Heat seared my cheeks and I tossed my head. "Lola Grainger had a fear of water—dark water in particular. It just seems odd to me that she'd go out in the middle of the night, get in a dinghy, and take off."

He leaned back, ice blue gaze trained on me. "She was upset and she'd been drinking. People acting under those conditions rarely do things that make sense. As for the others not hearing anything, well, Ms. Cummings and Mr. Tabor both admitted to taking a sleeping pill before retiring. And Mr. Connor said he was not only exhausted, he was feeling the effects of alcohol. By his own admission, he's quite a sound sleeper."

"Convenient admission," I muttered.

Corleone laced his fingers in front of him and leaned forward. "You sound as if you suspect foul play, Nora."

I wiggled around in my seat, hoping he couldn't hear the way my heart beat double time at the way he'd lingered over my name. "I'm not certain I suspect anything, Detective. But I have to admit, I've followed similar cases before and they were all handled much differently. The witnesses were separated, sequestered, questioned . . ."

"Apparently the officer in charge didn't see the need." Corleone picked up a pencil and twirled it between long, tapered fingers. "There were no witnesses—no evidence of foul play—nothing to indicate it was anything other than a terrible accident." He tapped the pencil against the desk. "With all the liquor that was consumed, I think Detective O'Halloran thought himself fortunate to get as much detail out of them as he did." His head jerked up and he looked me straight in the eye. "Do you have some reason to question his findings?"

I hesitated, and then blurted out: "She should have called out for help."

Once again, the brows rose. "Pardon?"

"Contrary to your coroner's report, I believe her down vest would have kept her afloat, not sucked her under. She should have been in a position to call for help—I know I would have."

"Who's to say she didn't?"

"Once again, no one heard any cries."

"And once again, she might not have called out because she was either feeling the effects of alcohol impairment or was in shock—or both."

Or unconscious or dead. "According to the coroner's report, her blood alcohol content was very low—point oh-four, to be precise."

"Various levels affect people differently. Actually, all it takes to impair someone is point oh-four to point oh-seven. Using those parameters, Lola drank enough—she fell well within the guidelines where her judgment could be questionable."

"Questionable enough where she'd just surrender to her fate? Not utter a sound to save herself?" I shook my head. "Lola Grainger was a strong woman, even though she was afraid of deep waters. I doubt she'd have succumbed to dying without putting up some sort of fight."

His lips compressed into a thin line. "Once again, alcohol affects people differently. One must take a lot of things into account—the subject's frame of mind, for instance. Mrs. Grainger was upset that evening—that fact was consistently reported by all involved."

I pursed my lips. "I don't recall reading that in any of the accounts."

His broad shoulders lifted in a careless shrug. "Facts get omitted often enough."

"There could have been another reason she didn't call out, you know. She could have been dead when she went into the water."

His supercilious smile faded into a frown. "That's not possible. According to the coroner's report, he did an analysis of single-celled algae, or diatoms found on the body, against those found in the water. The samples matched, which prove she was alive upon entering the water."

"Granted—if the coroner's report was accurate."

The frown deepened, causing a deep V crease in the middle of his forehead. "You have reason to suspect it wasn't?"

"Just a hunch." I didn't think the time was right to share all my inside information with Daniel Corleone. "Then again, she could have been alive—but unconscious. It would explain why no one heard any cries for help from a terrified woman."

"You seem to be very knowledgeable of this case, Nora."

I shrugged. "It's a puzzle. Puzzles interest me."

He was silent for a few minutes, fingers steepled beneath his chin. "You mentioned Mrs. Grainger's fear of water. How did you know that?"

"She mentioned it to my mother on several occasions. I would have thought Mr. Grainger would have brought it up."

"Perhaps he didn't know."

"They were married fifteen years—surely he suspected something."

Corleone didn't even crack a hint of a smile. "Not necessarily. Some women are excellent at keeping secrets."

I gave him a look. "Some men are, too."

He kept staring at me, almost as if he expected me to crack and reveal some of my secrets under his steely gaze. I tapped my pen against my notebook. "I just find it hard to believe a woman with an almost obsessive fear of deep water would go for a midnight excursion in the ocean. And then there's the matter of the bruise at the back of her skull. Did she get that from a fall, or could someone have attacked her?"

He folded his arms across his chest. "And just how do you know about that, Nora? It wasn't made public."

"And I bet I know why," I burst out, deliberately avoiding his question. "It's a prime example of how the Cruz police slipped up. They should have examined the others for bruises, and—"

"What makes you think they didn't?" He was silent a few more moments, then said, "You seem inordinately passionate about this case, and I can't help but wonder why. You're not related to the deceased, are you?"

"No, I'm not related."

"I'm sorry, but I'm not quite making the connection here. If you're not related—"

I hesitated, then added, "Mrs. Grainger was a good customer of my mother's sandwich shop."

Those perfectly shaped lips twitched slightly and he clapped his hands. "Ah, so she liked a good bologna on rye. That explains it then."

"It's not as unusual as you make it sound," I spat. "Besides, I'm not the only one who feels this way. Lola's sister hired a PI to investigate her death."

His expression didn't change, but a strange light appeared in the depths of those impossibly blue eyes. "Lola's sister? Did she now? A PI, you say?"

"Yes. Adrienne Sloane. She was trying to get the case reopened."

He leaned forward. "Was trying? She stopped?"

I shifted uncomfortably in the chair. "I—I'm not sure what happened to her."

He tossed me a look that spoke volumes before asking, "What about this PI? Who is he? Have you spoken to him?"

I swallowed. "I tried to get in touch with him but— apparently no one's seen him for several weeks."

He leaned back, eyes closed, and tapped the pencil against his knee. "I see." His tone clearly indicated he didn't. He sat up and fixed me with another piercing stare. "I'd love to know who your pipeline is," he said at last. "Who's feeding you this information?"

I shifted in the chair, crossed my legs at my ankles. "I was an investigative reporter for years," I replied. "I have my sources."

"Chicago, right?"

I nodded. "Yes, but how—"

"Google is a wonderful thing, Nora. I looked you up. You wrote a very popular column in Chicago; you won a couple of awards. Makes one wonder why you'd give it up to come back to the old hometown and run a sandwich shop."

His tone clearly indicated he thought a man had been behind my decision, and I felt a swift flash of resentment. Why did people constantly assume a failed love affair was the obvious reason for a move and/or a job change? Well, maybe it was, nine times out of ten, but not in my case. I resisted the impulse to set him straight on that score, and just inclined my head. "Some people have family loyalty," I said, looking him straight in the eye. "Besides, it was time for a change in my life."

He matched my stare with a piercing one of his own. "A rather big change."

"Maybe." I shifted a bit in my chair. Something about him made me feel unsettled—and not just the lingering aroma of Old Spice, either. "Now, getting back to our discussion. This is just a suggestion, but—Adrienne Sloane was renting a house on the outskirts of Cruz. She hasn't been seen in a while. It might not be a bad idea to go out there, ask around, see if you could get a line on her. There must be a reason why she hasn't come forward."

"Are you intimating foul play?"

"I'm not intimating anything—I'm just trying to be helpful."

"I see." His hunched stance relaxed. "So—anything else you'd care to share with me?"

"It's my understanding Lola and her sister were estranged for years. Adrienne came back to try and make things right. And Adrienne didn't trust Kevin Grainger."

He picked up a pencil, tapped it against the desk. "Perhaps he didn't trust her, either. Do you know what precipitated their estrangement?"

I shook my head. "No."

He gave me a look of mock horror. "You mean your source couldn't enlighten you? I'm shocked."

It was on the tip of my tongue to mention what I'd read in Nick Atkins's journal—that Lola had found something out, something her husband would "kill her" over—but I knew it would raise even more questions I didn't want to answer. I bit my tongue, sank back in my chair.

"I just think the witnesses should have been more rigorously cross-examined," I said.

"Ah—and just why is that? Do you think their stories would break down? Differ greatly?"

"Possibly," I shot back. "Since I don't know exactly what their stories were, it's not a question I can answer."

"Their accounts, if you will, were essentially all the same. They all retired long before the incident, and since they'd been drinking a good deal, all fell asleep almost instantly. The only two who remained awake were Mr. Grainger and Shelly Lott, the boat captain. They looked for Mrs. Grainger and placed the call to the Coast Guard. Both their accounts were consistent, down to each detail."

"I don't know about you, but I find that rather odd in

itself. I mean, when stories are too consistent, the word *rehearsed* immediately pops to my mind."

"I'm not certain what you mean. There wouldn't have been enough time between the other occupants waking up and the finding of the body to rehearse too much."

I crossed my legs at the ankles and slouched back in my chair. "Believe me, if someone wants something rehearsed, they find the time. I saw plenty of that in Chicago."

"I'm sure you did." He paused in his pencil tapping. The odd look was back in his eyes again. "So it's your opinion there was some sort of cover-up regarding Mrs. Grainger's death?"

I held up my hand. "I wouldn't presume to make that judgment, not without more facts. All I'm saying is a little more effort could have gone into questioning the sus—the other people on the yacht."

The intercom buzzed just then. Corleone murmured, "Excuse me," and then pressed the button. "Yes, Margaret?"

"The captain is on line one for you. Shall I transfer him?"

"Yes. Give me a minute, please." He disconnected, and glanced at me. "I'm sorry. I have to take this call."

"Of course." I picked up my notepad, stuffed it back in my purse, and rose. "Thank you for your time," I murmured, hoping my jaw wasn't clenching too badly. I was having a hard time concealing my disappointment.

"Wait." He held up one finger. "I'd like to continue this discussion with you, if I may."

That surprised me, since his demeanor had indicated he thought me either incredibly nosy or one step away from a fruitcake. "You would?"

He nodded. "You make some interesting points. I think they may bear some further investigation."

"You mean you'd be willing to recommend the case be reopened?"

"I don't know if we can go that far," he said. "But I agree—certain aspects could have been handled better. I'd like to ask you to postpone publishing anything on this in your magazine until we talk further. Will you agree to that?"

"Why, of course." That was pretty easy, considering I'd never really intended to do a story—yet anyway. "That seems only fair."

"Good." His phone rang. "I'll call you. And remember—don't discuss this with anyone. Do I have your word?"

I nodded. "Sure."

He picked up the phone, and I felt as if I'd been summarily dismissed. His interest seemed vague at best, and I've never held much stock in words without action. *I'll call you* sounded pretty indefinite to me—like something you'd say to appease someone you were afraid might turn into a troublemaking pest.

In the doorway I paused. Something else bothered me about Daniel Corleone—and not just the way his jacket molded to his upper torso like a second skin. Something was off, but I just couldn't put my finger on it. I gave him one last look from the doorway.

"I won't hold my breath for that call," I muttered, and left.

NINE

I drove back to Hot Bread, making one stop along the way. I parked in back of the store and let myself in through the rear entrance. I could hear the murmur of voices coming from the kitchen. Moving quietly, I went over to the door and pushed it ajar, stifling a laugh at the scene before me.

Chantal hunkered over a squirming Nick, a rhinestone-studded bright fuchsia collar halfway around his neck. The cat's fat belly shook as he fought to elude her grasp. He flopped over the edge of the counter and tried to run in the opposite direction. In one swift motion she grabbed him and pulled him back up onto the counter.

I was impressed. I didn't realize anyone, let alone Chantal, could move that fast in five-inch heels.

"Goodness, Nicky," she scolded, her finger slicing the air. *"Mon Dieu!* How do you expect to model for me when you won't even try anything on!"

Nick's lips peeled back. "*Ffft!*" he growled.

I pushed the door all the way open and came into the kitchen. "Hey, I'm back. Everything okay here?"

Chantal brushed an errant black curl out of her eyes. "We are doing just fine, thanks. Getting acquainted. I finished cleaning up, so I thought I'd work on my new line of pet collars." She threw Nicky a baleful glance. "He does not seem to like it much. He keeps trying to pull it off with his claws."

I looked at Nick, squatting there, the pink collar half on, half off his neck, and couldn't resist a grin. He bared his fangs and hissed.

As Chantal bent to remove the collar, I stuck my tongue out at him, then gave my friend's arm a gentle squeeze. "Oh, I think he'd like it fine—maybe in black, though, with some flat, not so shiny stones?"

Chantal considered this. She twined the pink collar between her fingers and held it up. "Too girly, huh?" she said at last.

I turned my head in Nick's direction and closed one eye. "Well . . . yeah. After all, Nick's a macho cat."

She slapped the side of her head with her palm. "Oh, of course. How could I be so stupid? Of course he is a manly cat. He would not want to wear rhinestones around his neck."

"*Er-ow*," Nick meowed from his place on the counter. Chantal's head cocked to one side as she studied the cat. "Black would get lost against his fur," she said at last. "We need a color that stands out—how about red?"

I hefted him into my arms—geez, he seemed heavier than ever—and smiled at Chantal. "I don't think he likes bright colors—how about navy blue?" I looked down at Nick as I said this. He hesitated, then purred loudly.

"Hm." Chantal swept her materials back into their linen

bag. "That might work. Navy with clear stones. I'll give that a try." She slipped the bag into her tote, and then moved over to stand in front of Nick. She bent over and said in an apologetic tone, "Sorry, handsome. I did not mean to upset you."

Nick hung his head and meowed.

I laughed. "And I think that's about as much of an apology as you're going to get."

Chantal gave Nick's head a final pat, then moved toward the door, where she paused, hand on the knob. "How did your appointment go?"

"It could have gone better, but okay."

Her eyes searched my face. "Is everything all right?"

I set Nick back on the counter and brushed a stray curl out of my eyes. "Well, like I said. It could have gone better. Daniel Corleone—excuse me, Detective Daniel Corleone—didn't exactly turn a cartwheel at the thought of reopening the Lola Grainger case."

Chantal suppressed a smile. "Well, you knew going in it wouldn't be easy."

"Yeah, I just didn't realize it would be that hard." I flopped into a chair and kicked off one shoe. "He was polite enough, but not overenthusiastic. I got the impression he was laughing at me."

Chantal shook her head. "That is because he does not know you, *chérie*, or how tenacious you can be."

"Oh, he knows me," I spat. "He Googled me, can you believe it? Maybe it's for the best. Working with him would be like climbing Mount Vesuvius when it's getting ready to explode. No, wait, scratch that. Climbing Vesuvius would be easier."

Now Chantal laughed outright. "Surely you exaggerate?"

I shook my head. "I wish. Basically he told me that because there were no eyewitnesses, there's no reason to

MEOW IF IT'S MURDER   95

suspect Lola's death was anything but a tragic accident. I brought up the fact that if a bit more effort had gone into questioning those aboard the yacht, perhaps their carefully matched stories might have crumbled a bit."

Chantal nodded in approval. "Good point."

I rubbed absently at my forehead. "One thing I found odd—he didn't seem to know about Adrienne Sloane, or care too much after I informed him. He did want to know where I got all my information." I chuckled. "I told him I had my sources—that seemed to satisfy him."

"So, what was the outcome? Is he going to help or not?"

"He did agree certain aspects of the case might bear further investigation. We were interrupted, but he did say he'd like to discuss it further."

"So he's going to try and get the case reopened?"

I shrugged. "He said he'd call."

"And you do not think he will," she prompted as I lapsed into silence.

I gave my head a quick shake. "I'm not sure. I got the impression he considered my presence a nuisance, that I'm just another reporter out after a sensational story, out to exploit Kevin Grainger's grief."

"Perhaps you should have told him the truth—that you only do this part-time now."

"It wouldn't have mattered. Anyway, I told you—he Googled me. He knew all about me." I sniffed. "As far as I'm concerned, I don't think Detective Daniel would be of too much help. He's the kind of guy who thinks he knows it all, and they can be particularly frustrating, because, well, half the time they do . . . know it all, that is."

"I see." Chantal's lips twitched slightly. "Tell me—what does this Detective Daniel Corleone look like?"

"Tall—six-two I'd guess—blond hair, not golden blond,

but kind of an ash-blond, dirty blond, shaggy around the neck, no bangs, high forehead. Eyebrows that match his hair, and blue eyes—sort of a cross between sky blue and cornflower blue, and really bright. Tanned skin, like he spends a lot of time outdoors in the California sun. Probably hits the beach each weekend, chasing down beach bunnies. Broad shouldered, narrow waisted—man, he must spend a lot of time in the gym, too, to get those muscled thighs and his waist—what's the matter? Why do you have that silly grin on your face?"

Chantal shot me a look of mock innocence. "No reason."

"Oh yes, there is." I lunged forward and gripped her wrist. "Out with it, missy."

She laughed. "It's just that—well, it's written all over your face. You've got a crush on this guy!"

Nick's eyes narrowed and his upper lip curled back, exposing his fangs.

Chantal leaned back and crossed her arms. "See—even Nick agrees."

"The two of you are nuts, then," I growled. "Why would you think that?"

Chantal rolled her eyes. "*Chérie*, if you have to ask the question . . ."

"Fine," I grumbled. "While he might be physically attractive, his personality leaves a lot to be desired—or haven't I mentioned the man seemed very full of himself and condescending?"

Chantal just looked at me and shook her head. Ditto Nick, squatting at my feet.

I let out a nervous giggle. "You guys are too much. I have one meeting with the guy and you've got me engaged already."

"Oh, not engaged, *chérie*. It is too soon for that. Going steady maybe."

I cut her an eye roll. "Trust me, I have no interest, romantic or otherwise, in Detective Daniel Corleone—other than possibly proving him wrong about the Lola Grainger case, that is. The good detective doesn't interest me in that way. Not at all. No sir." I pushed a hand through my curls. "Besides, something just doesn't jibe."

"Doesn't jibe? In what way?"

"That's the problem, I don't know. Couldn't tell you anything specific, but something just seemed—I don't know—off about him."

"Besides the Mafia surname? You didn't sound like you thought anything was off when you were describing him." Chantal laughed. "As a matter of fact, if you ask me, you sounded pretty darned excited over him."

"Excited? Hardly," I snorted. "And I didn't ask you."

"Fine. Be in denial." Chantal turned to leave, then abruptly paused. "Something you should know, though, *chérie*. Before I started working on Nicky's collar, I pulled out my tarot cards and did a reading for you."

"And?" I asked as she hesitated. "Don't tell me—the Death card came up?"

"That would have been better. The Death card refers to transformation and a total change in life cycle, not one's demise. No, the card that concerned me was Strength."

"Strength? I would think that would be one of the better ones."

"You have to take it in context. In the reading I did for you, it indicated you would soon find yourself in a situation over which you have no control. It was sandwiched in between the Tower and King of Swords. That indicated to me the situation could have dangerous overtones, but the King of Swords would help you overcome the obstacle."

I gave her a look. "You do know one way not to creep yourself out is to refrain from reading cards for people who aren't right there with you."

Chantal stuck her tongue out at me, turned on her heel, and with a quick wave was gone. I had to admit, I'd felt an uncanny chill slice right through me at her words. One thing I definitely did not need was to get involved in a dangerous situation.

That King of Swords stuff, though—now that didn't sound half-bad—even if the King should turn out to be one sarcastic detective.

I felt a tug on my skirt and looked down to see Nick regarding me with a steady, golden stare. I bent down and gently disengaged his claw. He turned around twice, and motioned with his paw toward the back table. I saw Scrabble tiles lying on the floor and let out a little cry.

"How did you get those? I could have sworn I had them in the pouch in the drawer!"

I bent over to scoop them up and noticed they were an F, an I, and a B. I chuckled.

"FIB. Very appropriate. Of course, I wouldn't come out and call Daniel Corleone a liar, but I just get a strange vibe from him. Like he's hiding something. Oh, I don't know." I made a motion with my hand, swept the tiles up, and deposited them back in the drawer. I looked at Nick.

"Like I was saying, I doubt Detective Corleone is going to be of much help. If I'm going to get to the bottom of all this and find out what happened to Adrienne and your owner, I'm going to have to do some digging on my own. Besides interviewing the captain, I need to know more about the other people who were on the yacht that night. If

I can figure out who had the most to gain from Lola's death, I can narrow down the field."

I leaned down and gave Nick a quick pat on the head. "I picked up something on the way home that should prove extremely helpful. Come on. We're going to do something I haven't done in quite a while—make a murder board."

I set the board up in the center of my den. Nick hopped up on the divan and watched as I opened my new package of markers and started to draw boxes on its surface.

"Here we have the victim—Lola Grainger." I drew a box and wrote Lola's name inside. "And here we have the people who were on the yacht the night of her death." I drew five boxes underneath Lola's name, with lines running from her box to each of the others. "First, her husband, Kevin Grainger.

"Next there was the boat captain—Shelly Lott. And then the other three were Kevin's employees."

I consulted the listing I'd made earlier. "Marshall Connor—the controller of KMG, and one of Kevin's key people."

I pointed to the next box. "And then there was Buck Tabor—VP of Accounting, I believe. He went to the same college as Kevin—there were some rumblings when he was hired. Lots of other employees thought Mike Shale should have gotten the job, instead of Buck." I tapped the marker against my chin. "Maybe Buck had something on Kevin. Blackmail's always a good possibility." I started to write on the board again. "Last but not least, Patti Cummings, Kevin's administrative assistant slash majordomo."

I made a face. "I know she's pretty, but I just hate to think of Kevin cheating on Lola. Of course, from all accounts, Patti is devoted to Grainger—maybe a little too devoted. Unrequited love is another possible motive. Get rid of the wife and you've got the husband all to yourself."

"*A-rowr!*" Nick made a guttural sound deep in his throat. He turned in a semicircle in front of the board.

I beamed. "Ah—so you agree. Good."

I stepped back to survey my handiwork. "Back in Chicago, I was involved with lots of cases where the police messed up, overlooked important facts because they were in a hurry, or they thought something wasn't relevant. Sometimes the most obvious answer isn't always the correct one."

I flopped down on my couch and ran my hand through my tumble of curls. When I worked the true crime beat, the biggest thing I'd found police messed up was looking at suspects. Lots of times they tried to make the evidence fit the obvious choice.

Except in this instance, there were no suspects, obvious or otherwise. It'd been written off as a tragic accident—owing in large part, I was certain, to Grainger's standing in the community.

"Police tend to gravitate toward the most time-efficient solution. Rather than cast a wide net and see if they can locate who might have committed a crime, they tend to focus on a few likely suspects and build their case against them. It makes sense, of course, but it's not always the best way," I muttered, tugging absently at a stray curl. "There's got to be some sort of connection somewhere. What I've got to do is determine the weak link in the chain and snap it."

Nick clawed at the carpet, another kitty sign of approval. I set down my marker and paused. Something still nagged at me, something I couldn't quite define. As I started for the kitchen, I suddenly stopped, snapped my fingers.

"He knew an awful lot about this case," I cried, startling Nick, who'd been trotting right beside me, no doubt anxious for a more substantial afternoon meal. "Danny Corleone. He's only here filling in, he's not even from around here, and yet he seemed to know an awful lot of details about the Grainger case. What's more—he did it all from memory—never even opened a file folder. He knew so much and yet—he didn't seem to know about Adrienne Sloane. Very, very odd."

"*Yargle*," Nick gurgled.

"Glad you agree," I chuckled. "I think we've done a good job today, don't you?"

Nick looked me right in the eyes and inclined his head in a nod.

I riffled his fur. "Come on—I think there's some salmon with your name on it. Tomorrow I'll start narrowing down our pool of suspects."

We went into the kitchen, where I spooned out a generous portion of salmon for Nick, unable to escape the gnawing feeling that there was more to Detective Corleone than appeared on the surface. It might be wise to keep an eye on him—a task I doubted I'd find *too* hard to take on.

TEN

I had to start somewhere, and I figured my best bet was Captain Shelly Lott. Adding in the fact that Hank had tagged him as "nervous," he appeared to be the only one so far with ties to both Lola and Kevin. Plus, I had a niggling suspicion Lott might also have been the one feeding Adrienne Sloane information. If so, she'd gotten him to talk—now I just had to figure out what buttons to press to get him to open up to *me*.

Since I had some time in between my breakfast crowd and the lunch rush, I did a quick Internet search and came up with Lott Cruises, located right in the Cruz Marina. Lott himself answered on the third ring. I introduced myself, explained that I was writing an article on the Lola Grainger accident for *Noir*, and was greeted with thirty seconds of complete and utter silence. Finally he rasped out, "That? It's old news. What on earth do you want to write about that for?"

"Lots of reasons, Captain. This case was closed before the right questions were framed, let alone answered. I think we owe it to the public—and to Lola—to ferret out the truth about what really happened that night."

"I can save you the trouble. Lola Grainger's death was an accident. End of story."

"Is it?"

More silence. Then, "Just what good do you think writing a story about this would do? Authorities don't like to reopen cases, especially open-and-shut ones involving high-profile figures. Why would you want to embarrass yourself like that, miss? 'Cause asking questions that are none of your business is all that will do."

"I'm of a different mind. I believe asking questions is the best way to get at the truth."

He sniffled. "Are you insinuating that we all lied?"

"I believe you weren't asked the right questions."

There was a pause and then, surprisingly, Lott let out a gravelly laugh. "Maybe so. But it's over. Take my advice, little lady, and let it be. Find something else to write about."

I sensed he was about to hang up so I interjected quickly, "Adrienne Sloane wouldn't let it be, though, would she?"

The note of surprise in his tone was evident, at least to me. "Adrienne Sloane?"

"Lola's sister. You've spoken with her, haven't you?"

"Absolutely not. I wasn't even aware Mrs. Grainger had a sister."

Somehow I doubted that, but I pressed on. "She did. They'd been estranged for quite some time." I paused and then added, "She believed her sister was murdered."

He snorted. "Where'd she get a crackpot idea like that?"

"From an inside source. You wouldn't know anything about that, would you?"

"Are you intimating I'm her source?" A moment of stunned silence, and then Lott barked out a nervous laugh. "I don't know where *you* get your information, lady, but it's all wet. I never Fed anybody anything, least of all a woman I never met."

Prying information out of Lott was akin to pulling out a wisdom tooth. No wonder Grainger trusted the man. "Look," I said in a gentler tone, "all I'm asking for is a half hour of your time. One half hour, and I promise I'll never bother you again."

He sighed. "One half hour, and then that's it? Fine. I've got an afternoon cruise leaving in fifteen, but I'll be back in my marina office at five."

Perfect. "I'll see you then."

I hung up the phone and caught a swish of black out of the corner of my eye. A second later Nick hopped up onto my lap. I ran my hand along his soft fur.

"It wouldn't surprise me if he was making a call to Grainger right about now," I murmured. Nick's head moved up and down, as if in agreement. I laughed and pushed my chair back. I'd planned to see how I did with Lott before deciding on a plan of attack for the others. Patti Cummings was a possibility—admins usually had a good handle on lots of details others weren't privy to. I'd run into a few in Chicago who knew where their bosses' bodies were buried—literally. But if she and Grainger were indeed warming the sheets together, I doubted she'd want to do anything to upset that arrangement. And if all there was between them was the usual employer-employee relationship, well, then I had to hope he'd screwed her out of something big, like a raise or promotion. No one gave up a cushy job like that without incentive. Although here the incentive should be fairly obvious—staying out of jail as an accessory to murder.

Hell, it would work for me.

* * *

I was knee deep in my lunch rush when I glanced up and saw none other than Detective Daniel Corleone standing in Hot Bread's doorway. Several ladies in line graciously moved out of the way, allowing him a clear view of the large sign listing the various sandwiches, and there was no mistaking the rapturous looks on their faces as he smiled and thanked them ever so graciously.

Must be nice, I thought, to have such charm. And charisma. And sex appeal. And . . .

"Nora!"

I jerked to attention, realized that I held a cup of ketchup in my hand instead of the side of coleslaw Minnie Hopper had asked for. I apologized, made the switch, and rang up her Reuben. As I waited on my next customer, I saw Daniel sit down at a table at the rear of the store. Our gazes met and held for a minute—then he raised one hand in greeting. I nodded, wiggled two fingers in response. The blue shirt he wore under his tan jacket set off his coloring and accentuated the color of his eyes. His hair was slightly mussed, a curl falling down over one eyebrow, and he looked almost as if he'd just gotten out of bed. That thought sent a nice, warm feeling arrowing through me down to my very toes as I thought of the good detective, his muscular body tangled between satin sheets, wearing only a pair of boxer briefs and a smile . . .

"And I'd like it on rye instead of pumpernickel, if you don't mind."

"Huh—what?"

Ramona Hickey pinned me with her steely gaze. "Didn't you hear me? I said, I'll have the *Joe Piscopo*, but on pumpernickel instead of rye. You might go a bit easy on the mustard, too."

"Oh, yeah, right. Coming right up."

I quickly prepared her sandwich, and then two more before the good detective faced me across the counter. "Well, hello again, Ms. Charles—sorry. Nora," he said.

"Detective." I could feel heat rise to my cheekbones and self-consciously wished I'd done something nicer with my hair. "How nice of you to visit my shop."

"I pass it all the time and I've been meaning to stop by." He paused and then added, "And I definitely didn't mean to brush you aside yesterday. I hope you understand."

"No problem." Since Daniel Corleone was the last customer in line, I allowed myself to relax a bit and eased one hip against the counter. "I know what it's like to have your boss on your back. It's part of the reason I became my own boss."

He smiled, showing off those picture-perfect teeth. "I didn't want you to think I was dismissing you. It's just your request was unexpected."

"I realize that. No offense taken."

"Good." His eyes searched my face, then met my gaze and held it. "I thought you'd like to know, I went over to the house Adrienne Sloane's been renting. It's locked up, and some of the neighbors saw her leaving with suitcases."

I frowned. "When was this?"

"About seven weeks ago."

Right around the time Nick Atkins had gone missing. "Do you have any idea where she might have gone?"

He pulled his notebook out of his pocket. "As near as we can tell, she purchased a one-way ticket to Bermuda."

"Bermuda!"

"I hear it's lovely this time of year." He slipped the notebook back in his pocket. "It looks like she abandoned her investigation."

"Looks can be deceiving," I mumbled. It made no sense. Why would Adrienne hire a PI, then text him with a cryptic message and disappear?

Daniel's voice broke into my train of thought. "Listen, I really would like to discuss the case with you in greater detail. You made a lot of good points."

I raised one eyebrow. "Will that help get the case reopened?"

"I can't make you any promises. As I said, I'm just here filling in. But if there turns out to be enough evidence that the investigating officers dropped the ball, and there's new evidence to consider—then yes, there's a good shot the case would be reopened." He smiled, and the dimples at either end of his lips deepened. "I don't mind admitting I'm curious as to your source. Whoever it is, they're remarkably well informed. Is this person a reporter as well?"

I clucked my tongue, biting back a pang of disappointment. Apparently my source's identity was the focus of his interest in me, and not my all-American good looks or sparkling wit—or even my culinary expertise. "Now, Detective, surely I don't have to tell you a good reporter never reveals their sources."

"Confidentiality is important. It's nice to see you respect that. Many don't." Something in his tone made me glance at him sharply, but his expression was bland. "Well. I don't have to be on duty tonight till six, so perhaps I could hang around and we could talk after you close?"

I groaned inwardly. He would pick today. The bell above my shop door tinkled, and I cast a quick glance over the detective's shoulder. Chantal stood there, eyes wide, giving me *that look*. I turned my attention back to Daniel.

"Ah—I'm sorry, but today's really not good for me.

Perhaps we could make it for tomorrow? Or some other day when you have free time?"

His expression darkened for an instant: Disappointment? Suspicion? I might have imagined it, because the next second his oh-so-handsome face was wreathed in a smile. "No problem," he said at last. "My bad. I should have called first, and not just assumed you'd drop everything to have that discussion. After all, you were so gung ho yesterday—but that's neither here nor there, is it?"

Wow, talk about making someone feel guilty. "I *am* sorry," I assured him. "Trust me, if there was any way I could reschedule my appointment, I would, but unfortunately—"

"Hey, it's okay, really." He pulled out his iPad, consulted it for a few moments. "Barring an emergency, I have Thursday afternoon free, if that works for you."

I gave him my most winning smile. "I'll make it work. Do you want to meet here, or at the station, or—"

"How about I call you Thursday morning and we can work out something that suits us both. And I promise I *will* call you," he said.

"Fine."

"Great." His gaze strayed to the giant placard listing of sandwiches right above the counter. "Did you think up all these yourself?"

"Most were my mother's," I admitted. "But some of the newer ones—like the Lady Gaga and the Michael Buble Burger—were my idea."

He chuckled. "So you aren't responsible for the Thin Man Tuna Melt?"

My smile widened as I answered, "I love those movies, but they were a little before my time—sorry. My parents were huge Bill Powell and Myrna Loy fans, though. And I've got the entire set on DVD—Blu-ray."

"Spoken like a true fan." His eyes roved over me for a long moment before shifting back to the menu. "I'm almost afraid to ask—what's in the Ricky Gervais?"

"Tongue on rye with extra-hot mustard," I said, and that elicited a big grin.

He whipped out his wallet. "I'll take a Thin Man. Extra cheese."

I pulled out two slices of rye and the container of tuna salad from the refrigerated case. Daniel leaned against the counter and turned to gaze around the shop. "You do a brisk business," he noted. "Almost every table's full."

"I do okay," I answered as I spread tuna liberally on the bread. "Most of the clientele are my mother's loyal customers. They like my cooking enough to stick with me."

"You do everything yourself?"

"I have a high school girl who helps out in the morning before her first class, and occasional afternoons. But if business keeps picking up, I'm going to have to think about hiring more help."

"Well, in this economy, that's a good thing. Maybe soon you won't need that second job. Sandwich making is a lot safer than crime reporting."

"Maybe not. You should see my knife drawer."

He laughed, and then suddenly reached inside his jacket pocket. "Excuse me." He whipped out his phone, said, "Daniel Corleone," and listened for a few minutes, his eyes slitted. He shook his head a few times, then said, "On my way," and slipped the phone back into his pocket. He looked at me apologetically and pulled out his wallet. "I'm sorry, I gotta run. Can I get that to go?"

I wrapped the sandwich and placed it in a bag as he slid a ten-dollar bill across the counter. "I'll call you Thursday."

He snatched up the sandwich, turned on his heel . . . and was gone.

I frowned. My stomach rumbled, reminding me I hadn't had anything except a cup of yogurt at 6 a.m. I pulled out some more rye bread, tuna, and cheese, and had just slipped the sandwich into the toaster oven when a hand dropped on my shoulder. I jumped.

"Will you stop doing that," I cried, turning and gazing into Chantal's twinkling eyes.

"You have no excuse for not hearing me, other than the look of love." She laughed, pointing to her impossibly high heels. "So—who is he?"

I thrust my hands into the pockets of my apron. "Who's who?"

She gave a snort of disgust. "Don't play coy with me, *chérie*. The tall, blond, and handsome man who just left— oh, wait!" She slapped her forehead with the palm of her hand. "Of course, I should have known. So that is your Detective Corleone?"

"That's him." I gritted my teeth. "But he's not my detective. He's the community's."

Chantal let out a low whistle. "Well, he's even yummier in person. I would not mind being investigated by him. He does not look as if he belongs on the Cruz force. Most of them resemble Dennis Franz—this guy has Pierce Brosnan written all over him."

"Maybe because he's really not a member of the Cruz force. He's here on loan, remember?"

She wiggled her fingers. "Whatever. It looked as if you two were having quite a nice conversation."

"Yeah, well, looks can be deceiving," I mumbled.

The toaster gave a soft *ding*! I pulled my tuna melt out of the toaster oven and carried it to a table in the back, Chantal right behind me. She watched me as I sat down and spread my napkin on my lap, a silly grin plastered across her pretty face. I took a bite of the sandwich, and frowned at her.

"I can't eat with you watching me with that cat-ate-the-canary grin, so out with it. What is it you're just dying to tell me?"

"Isn't it obvious? I said it the other night. You've got a crush on him, but it's more than that. Yet another prediction of mine has come true. You have met your King of Swords."

I wagged my finger. "Oh, no. You said tall, dark, and handsome. Detective Corleone is a blond."

"First off, I do not recall 'tall' being part of the equation. Second, description is nothing but a mere detail." She cocked her brow. "Mark my words. He is your King of Swords—your champion."

I took another bite of my tuna melt, which was delicious, even if I had to say so myself. "So he's the one who's gonna sweep me off my feet, eh?"

"More than that." Chantal leaned forward, all seriousness. "He is the one who is going to lead you out of danger. As I said—your champion."

Ah, yes. I'd forgotten about the addition to her original prediction. "Very romantic," I chuckled. "Right now, the most danger I'm going to be in will be from the electric company shutting me down if I don't pay the bill this month."

Chantal shook her head. She reached into her bag and pulled out her trusty deck of tarot cards. "He is going to help you out of a dangerous situation. I saw it in the cards, *chérie.*" She tapped the deck with one long nail. "And the cards . . . they never lie."

Had I any idea at that moment just *how* dangerous a situation we were talking about, things might have been very, very different. But you know what they say.

Ignorance is bliss.

ELEVEN

Five o'clock on the dot found me down at the Cruz Marina. A sleepy-looking teenage girl directed me to the Lott Cruises office, located at the end of the pier in a ramshackle building that looked as if a good strong wind might blow it away at a moment's notice. I tapped on the door and, getting no response, tried the knob. The door swung inward at my touch, and I found myself in a rather large room with many nautical embellishments—a ship's wheel hung low on the wall behind a cherrywood desk, and framed pictures of ships and sea scenes dotted the walls. A glass case off to one side of the office next to a scarred file cabinet held a collection of scrimshaw, carved objects made originally by North American whalers from the teeth and bones of whales, in various shapes and sizes. This collection looked pretty extensive—there were pieces in the shapes of animals—turtles, foxes, a large grizzly bear. There was a money clip with a clipper ship square in the center, and a pocketknife with a deer. Off to one side lay a man's large signet ring. The ring had a scrimshaw inlay as well, an odd-looking design. It was obvious Lott took a great interest in his hobby. I'd just bent over the case to get a closer look when the distinct creak of a floorboard alerted me to the fact I was no longer alone.

"Interested in scrimshaw, are ya?"

My head snapped up. "Captain Lott?" At his nod, I smiled and continued, "I've always admired the workmanship. You've got some unusual pieces there—the clip, the knife. And such an unusual ring."

"Ayuh." He took my elbow, steered me away from the case. "It's a hobby that can get expensive, especially when you invest in the quality pieces." He looked me up and down. "I'm guessing you're Nora Charles?"

At first glance Lott struck me as nondescript. He was shorter than me—around five-five or five-six—and thin, almost scrawny. He had a thick shock of gray, curly hair that was swept back from his high forehead, and what I could see of his complexion screamed "outdoorsman." A good portion of the lower part of his face was covered with a thick beard, well trimmed, the same iron gray shade as his hair. His lips were thick, as were his eyebrows, and his squinted eyes were gray-blue, like the sea on a storm-tossed day. His hand shot out and gripped mine, and his handshake was firm. After a moment he released my fingers (which I immediately flexed) and motioned to me to take a seat in one of the high-backed chairs that flanked his desk. He moved with some difficulty, shuffled rather than walked. He leaned heavily on a thick, ebony walking stick as he moved around the desk. Once he'd eased his thin frame into the leather chair, he leaned back and reached inside his shirt pocket for a pack of Kents, which he held out to me.

"Smoke?"

I shook my head, and he proceeded to light up. He exhaled the smoke in one long breath, watched it curl upward toward the high-beamed ceiling before turning his attention back to me again.

"So? What is it exactly you think I can do for you, Ms. Charles?"

I leaned forward a bit, not too close as the air in the small office was a bit cloying and overloaded with cigarette smoke. "It's more like what I can do for you, Mr. Lott," I said.

One shaggy eyebrow lifted. "I don't understand."

"I thought you might look upon this interview as a chance to free your conscience of any burden it might be under in the Lola Grainger matter."

His eyes narrowed, and he barked out a short laugh. "Now, where did you get an idea like that? I'm not under any burden, Ms. Charles."

"Are you sure?"

The ruddy cheeks got a bit ruddier. "Look, I don't know where this is coming from, but you're definitely barking up the wrong tree. I told the police everything just as it happened that night—I'm not hiding anything."

I decided on a bold move. "Adrienne Sloane would disagree."

Something flickered in the depths of those gray eyes, and then his face turned into a stone mask. His hand curled into a fist and he slammed it down hard on the desktop, enough to make the phone and pencil cup shake. "Like I told ya on the phone—I don't know any Adrienne Sloane.

If you're here on account of something she said, well, you're wasting your time—and mine."

I sensed a shift in his attention, so I decided to switch gears. "I'm merely here to check the facts for my story. Make sure I have them down correctly." I pulled my notepad and pen out of my tote and set them on the edge of the desk. "Surely you've no objection to that."

He laughed mirthlessly. "Would you care if I did? Okay—" He slapped his palm against his thigh. "Let's get on with it. What do you want to know?"

"I'd like you to reiterate the facts for me, Captain Lott, just as they happened that night."

He took another drag on the cigarette. "You know, you can read the account in any old newspaper."

I shifted my notepad on my knee. "I'd rather hear it firsthand. From you."

"From me. Okay." He ground out the cigarette then leaned back in the chair, lacing his fingers behind his neck. "Mr. and Mrs. Grainger were celebrating their fifteenth wedding anniversary. Mr. Grainger wanted to cruise out a bit, out to Pelos Island. There's good restaurants and some shops there. He'd invited some of the people who worked for him. There were two men and his admin."

"Had you ever met any of them before?"

"Neither of the men, but I'd seen his admin before. She's been working for him about six months now—four at the time of the accident. She'd come aboard once or twice with papers for him to sign." He snorted as I raised my eyebrow. "I know what you're thinkin', and no, they weren't havin' an affair. Not that she didn't want it—but Mr. Grainger only had eyes for his wife."

"What made you think Patti Cummings's interest in Mr. Grainger was anything other than professional?"

He snorted. "A woman comes aboard, dressed to kill, smelling all soft and pretty like she did—they're hopin' for more than just contracts signed. Plus, there was the way she looked at Mr. Grainger—her eyes lit up, and she got that sappy smile on her face—heck, she had it bad. Has it bad," he amended. "Even now, she don't leave him alone. She's always around now. Funny thing, too. Before the accident, he never gave her the time of day, never really looked at her. Now he's all over her, too. It's like a switch got thrown, or something."

Or his wife got launched overboard. "So they're an item now?"

He pursed his lips. "I don't know as I'd go that far," he said at last. "But he's sure showing a heckuva lot more interest in her than he ever did before."

I nodded. "Okay, let's continue on with what happened that day."

"Right. Anyway, I'd done a lot of shoppin' for the trip— laid in some filet mignons, lobster tails, champagne, the works. We were goin' to have a real feast Sunday night— the night of their anniversary." He paused, a catch in his throat. "We never got to that, though," he said softly.

"Well, we spent Saturday anchored just off Pelos Island. Everyone went out in the dinghy on a shopping trip, all except Mrs. Grainger. She said she didn't feel well— thought she might have a migraine coming on. She stayed on board the ship."

My ears perked up with interest. "How long were the others gone?"

He stared off into space. "Lessee—they all went out in the dinghy to grab a bite of lunch and walk around—so they were gone from twelve o'clock till around three thirty."

"You weren't with them?"

He shook his head. "I was fixing things for dinner, plus I had some cleaning to do."

"And Mrs. Grainger stayed in her stateroom the entire time?"

He shrugged. "I suppose. I had chores to do. I wasn't about keepin' tabs on her. She had a headache. When she got one of those headaches, she usually laid down and took a nap in her stateroom." His lips puckered. "Now, she coulda been wanderin' around the yacht, I dunno. Like I said, I had some things to do down in the hold and the galley. I had music on, so I didn't hear anything."

"Okay. Then the others came back at three thirty. Then what?"

"Then they headed straight for the bar. They were all feelin' pretty good already, if you ask me. They all wanted to continue the party. Mr. Grainger asked me to mix some drinks—I make a mean margarita and Bloody Mary—and there was wine and beer all over the place."

"Did Mrs. Grainger recover enough to join in these festivities?"

He nodded. "She came out around four thirty. She was dressed to kill, too—man, it looked as if she'd put on every piece of jewelry Mr. Grainger had ever given her. I made her a Bloody Mary and then she sat in the main cabin with the rest of 'em. They were all discussing some new work contract, but Mrs. Grainger looked pretty bored to me."

"Kind of an odd way to spend one's anniversary, don't you think?"

He shrugged. "Not really. They didn't have many friends. Mr. Grainger didn't have any, and Mrs. Grainger might have one or two, but no one real close. They didn't have kids, or relatives."

"Except Mrs. Grainger's sister," I prompted. "And since

they'd apparently been estranged for years, what did they do on holidays?"

"Spent 'em together, or else they went abroad. Sometimes Mr. Grainger would schedule business trips and they'd both go. They went to Rome last Christmas—stayed through New Year's."

How sad, I thought. I could see where Lola might have wanted to reconnect to her sister. "Go on," I said to Lott.

"Well, they all kept drinkin' and talking shop. Around seven I called 'em all into the main dining area. We had grouper for dinner. Afterwards they all went back to the main cabin to continue drinking."

"And this was around what time?"

"Eight o'clock." He shifted in his chair. "They all had after-dinner drinks—that was when things started to get a little dicey."

My ears perked up. "Dicey? In what way?"

He shifted his gaze away from mine. "Maybe dicey ain't the right word. Uncomfortable? Awkward?"

"In what way?"

He half rose from his chair. "Look, are all these questions necessary? They won't bring her back, ya know. Nothing will. Besides, I told all this to the police already."

"Yes, but I'd much rather hear it firsthand from someone who was actually there, rather than have my article just be a rehash of old news." I parted my lips, gave him my most disarming smile. "Humor me."

"Fine." His fingers drummed a swift tattoo against the smooth surface of the desk. "The alcohol was starting to get to 'em—all of 'em—and tempers were a mite short, shall we say? Miss Patti spilled a drink, and I thought Mrs. Grainger was gonna have a stroke—started goin' on and on about the silk cushions. Then the topic changed to

politics, and she and the shorter guy—Buck somethin'—
got to arguing over the election. The others joined in, and
it was pretty loud for a bit, and then I served port and des-
sert, and it quieted down. Ms. Patti and Buck, they excused
themselves around ten thirty and went to their rooms, so's
it was just the four of us—me, Mr. and Mrs. Grainger, and
the Connor guy—and Mrs. Grainger and Mr. Connor, they
was having a conversation on one side of the room. Around
eleven o'clock he interrupted 'em—pretty loud, too—and
he told his wife that she didn't have to overdo it—pretty
much his exact words. And she says, 'No, I don't, but at
least one of us should be honest around here. One of us
shouldn't try to be somethin' we're not.' And then he says
to her, 'Just what does that mean?' and she says, 'You
know damn well what it means,' and then she got up and
just left. Then Mr. Grainger, he and Mr. Connor talked for
a few minutes, real civil-like, and then Mr. Connor went to
his room—that was around eleven fifteen."

"And Mr. Grainger? Did he retire as well?"

"No, ma'am, he had another drink. I sat with him. He
raised his glass and said to me, 'To women, Shelly. Can't
live with 'em, can't live without 'em.' And I agreed, naturally. And then . . ."

"And then?" I prompted as Lott fell silent.

He nibbled at his lower lip. "And then, he says, 'Ya
know, Shell, sometimes they make it damn hard to live
with 'em.'" He cleared his throat. "Then he said good night
and went down to his cabin. I started clearing up the
glasses and plates. Next thing I know, he—Mr. Grainger—
is grabbin' my arm, and he's all wild-eyed and nervous
like. 'Shel,' he says to me, 'help me. Lola's gone.'"

I stopped writing in my notebook and looked at Lott.
"What time was this?"

He scrunched up his lips. "Around eleven thirty, maybe a few minutes later."

"So at that point you and Mr. Grainger started looking for Lola?"

His eyes darted around the room, settled at a point beyond my left shoulder. "Yeah. Yeah, that's what we did. We went all through the boat, and then Mr. Grainger noticed the dinghy was gone. Then he seemed to relax a bit. 'That fool woman,' he says. 'She just took the dinghy out, probably wants to piss me off. She thinks I'll go lookin' for her. Well, we'll show her,' he says. So we waited about a half hour and she didn't come back. So then he started to get real nervous like. He thought she was just havin' a hissy fit, ya know? But then it was like, he realized somethin' was wrong, very wrong. So we called the Coast Guard."

I held up my hand. "You said this was around midnight? The news account said the Coast Guard wasn't called until three a.m."

"Oh, yeah. That's right." His hand swiped at the back of his neck. "I might be a bit off on the time. He mighta waited over an hour for her to come back in the dinghy. And then he took the small cruiser out, lookin' for her, but couldn't find nothin'."

"He went out on his own to look for her? That wasn't in the news account."

"Hey, what can I say? The reporters slipped up. If you get the police account, it'll be in there." Shelly pulled a handkerchief from his jacket pocket, wiped it across his forehead. "Anyhow, the Coast Guard finally found her around five a.m. She'd drifted into a small cove. Guess that's why Mr. Grainger didn't see her when he went out in his boat."

"And where were all the others during this time frame?"

"All in their rooms, sleepin'." His fingers tapped the side of his desk. "We knocked on their doors," he said at last. "We wondered if Lola might have gone inside one of their rooms, but their doors were locked. No one answered."

I frowned. "Did you knock really loudly, bang really hard? Or didn't you have a master key? Even if they were sleeping, you could have opened their doors, just in case—"

"Mrs. Grainger wasn't in any other room," he barked. "And no one else was up," he added, almost as an afterthought. "Now, that's what happened. Satisfied?"

Hardly. "You've been captain of their yacht for how long, Captain Lott? Years, right?"

"Ten years. Well, actually nine. I was in a bad car accident—I was laid up almost an entire year. Mr. Grainger—I don't know what I'd have done without him. He paid for all my surgeries, all my medical bills, even kept paying me my salary—and then once I got a clean bill of health, he took me right back, bless his heart."

So that explained the limp and walking stick—and the unswerving loyalty. Grainger certainly was a generous employer. "So you mean to say that in all that time, you never knew Mrs. Grainger had a fear of deep water? That she was afraid she'd die by drowning?"

The tongue came out again, swiped over his lower lip. "We never really had personal conversations, miss. We just talked about stuff relatin' to whatever cruise they were takin'."

"Regardless, do you really think it's a plausible explanation for a woman with a deep-seated fear of water to suddenly take off in a dinghy in the middle of the night?"

He lowered his gaze. "She had a lot to drink," he mumbled.

"Not that much. You only made her one Bloody Mary."

"It mighta been two," he said defensively. "Now I think

of it, I'm pretty sure she did have two." He paused. "And some wine."

I tapped my pen against the edge of the desk. "By your own admission, Mrs. Grainger wasn't one to get carried away with drinking. Not only that, but don't you think a woman who was just getting over a severe headache would have enough presence of mind to limit her alcohol intake, let alone mix drinks?"

He thrust his lower lip out. "She might not have wanted to appear ungracious in front of company. All I know is, that's what happened."

"Can you answer me this? If Mr. Grainger thought she took the boat out for a spin, then why did he tell the police she must have slipped while trying to retie the dinghy?"

"We didn't know what happened for certain. It could have been either scenario. Either she took the boat out, got disoriented, and fell in, or she went to retie the dinghy, slipped, and fell in."

"Slipped and fell in. Is that how Mr. Grainger accounted for the bruises on his wife's body?"

His tongue snaked out, rubbed over his lower lip. "Bruises?"

"There were bruises on the body—her legs, across her left side, her chin, the base of her skull."

He studied the floor. "I don't know what you're talkin' about. I didn't see no bruises."

My eyebrows rose. "So you did see the body, then? After it was pulled out of the water?"

His eyes darted around the room. "I—ah—went with Mr. Grainger to view it. He was in no shape to look at it alone."

"Really. Because I thought you and Marshall Connor were the ones who ID'd the body. Grainger was in no condition to look at her."

A thin sheen of sweat broke out on his wide forehead. "Well, now, let me think . . . yes, that's right. He wanted to, but he just couldn't bring himself to do it. So me and Mr. Connor, we ID'd her." His face took on a dreamy look. "She looked beautiful—just like she was sleepin', not dead. I kept hopin' she'd open her eyes."

"I see. And who noticed the bruises?"

His head snapped back. "Will you stop harpin' on bruises? I didn't see any, I tell ya."

"An eyewitness insists there were."

I saw a blush start to creep up his neck. He reached out, grabbed the walking stick, and clutched it, knuckles bled white. "That—that's—" He shook his head. "An eyewitness, you say? Who?"

"I rather hoped you'd tell me."

His finger shot out, jabbed at the air under my nose. "What is this? An inquisition? You're tryin' to trip me up, aren't you?"

My heart beat double time as I scooted to the edge of my chair and met his gaze head-on. "If you're telling me the truth, Captain Lott, then there's nothing to worry about."

Lott abruptly scraped back his chair and rose, splayed both his palms across the desktop. "I think this interview's over. I've said all I've got to say. You need more information, you read the news accounts. Or you ask Mr. Grainger himself. You newspeople are all alike. Try and sully the memory of a good person just to sell a few papers."

"That's not what this is about. I think you know that." I paused. "Were you aware Lola called her sister from the boat?"

His head jerked up, eyes narrowed. "She did? No, ma'am, I did not know that."

"Well, she did. Furthermore, she told her that she'd found out something Kevin might kill her over, if he were aware she knew."

His lips compressed into a thin line. "Fool talk, that's what that is. How do I know you're telling the truth?"

"You don't," I admitted. "But I assure you I am." I leaned forward. "If you know something, Captain Lott, anything at all that would shed some light on this—"

He drew back abruptly and hunched his shoulders. "Sorry. I'm not sayin' another word, hear me? Not another word. I said too damn much already." He fumbled in his pocket, pulled out the pack of Kents, and scissored one between nicotine-stained fingers. "Lola Grainger was a good woman who wouldn't harm a fly. I can't think of a person on earth who'd want to see her dead."

I nibbled at my lower lip, then blurted out, "What about Kevin Grainger? Could you think of anyone who might want to kill him?"

Lott paused, the cigarette midway to his lips, and tapped it thoughtfully against the desk. "Kill Kevin Grainger? Where'd that come from?"

I shrugged. "Just a theory I'm toying with. Could you think of any reason why he might be a target?"

His eyebrows formed a perfect V. "No. I don't know where you dreamt up this crazy theory of yours, but that's what it is—damn crazy." Lott jammed the cigarette between his lips, floundered in his pocket for a match, scraped it into flame. He exhaled a thin stream of smoke right into my face. "Crazy," he muttered again. "Next you'll be telling me some mobster put a hit out on him. And I'm not saying a damn thing. Not another word."

I waved my hand, trying not to choke on the cloying smell of nicotine and roses, stuffing my pad and pen back into my tote. "I just have one last thing to say. You seem a decent human being to me. You know as well as I do there's more to what happened that night than Grainger's let on to the press, or the police, or anyone else. Adrienne Sloane knew it, too.

"You're probably the only one who can give Lola Grainger's spirit the peace she deserves, Captain. Think about it. And when you're ready to talk, here's my number. Thank you for your time. Oh, and I think it might be best for both of us if what was said here today remained just between us."

He grunted in assent.

I pressed one of my business cards into his hand and turned on my heel. When I got to the door, I turned my head slightly. Lott was slumped in his chair, my card clutched in one hand, glowing cigarette in the other, staring off into space.

I'd touched a nerve, I felt sure of it, as sure as I knew there was some sort of cover-up going down. I'd gotten the distinct sense he was lying when he said no one else on the yacht was up at the time Lola had presumably disappeared. All I could do was hope I'd gotten through to him in some way, because I had the definite feeling the others would be much, much harder to crack.

TWELVE

I finished slicing the onion for my salad and carried the bowl over to the table in my little dining nook. Nick was busy eating leftover burger from this afternoon's lunch crush out of the blue-and-white ceramic bowl Chantal had picked up at the Pet Palace. HEAD CAT was emblazoned in large letters along the side of the bowl. I thought it oddly appropriate. I seated myself and picked up the oil and vinegar, poured it over the salad, then tossed it and heaped a large pile on my plate. Nick, done with his burger, hopped up on the chair opposite mine and rested his forepaws on the table. He eyed my dinner warily.

"Sorry, pal. No steak tonight, I'm afraid."

"*Ewwr*," Nick rumbled. He turned around twice and arranged himself comfortably on the chair.

I popped a slice of tomato into my mouth. "I know Lott's hiding something," I said as I chewed. "Right now it seems a bit pointless to try and drag it out of him. He's just going to have to open up to me at his own pace, I guess."

Nick watched me spear another slice of tomato. I held the fork out. He took a sniff and then sat back on the chair. I popped the slice into my mouth, chewed. "He's my best guess on being Adrienne's informant," I said after I'd swallowed. "He's also got my vote for the weak link in the chain. He certainly acted uneasy enough, as if there were something to hide. I don't think he likes being part of a deception. I wonder how Adrienne got him to tell her the little he did."

Nick hopped off the chair and walked away, wiggling his rotund bottom like a gal wearing a too small miniskirt. I watched him sashay over to the corner, give his behind a final shake, and then ease himself down, watching me over one shoulder all the while in sort of a feline pinup pose.

"Ah. You think maybe Adrienne used her feminine wiles to influence him?" I tapped my fork against my chin. "Maybe you've got something there. It wouldn't be the first time sex was used to gain information."

I looked down at my own attire, faded blue denim jeans and Cal sweatshirt. "If I thought it'd help me get some cooperation out of one taciturn detective, I might even break out a leather miniskirt myself." I let out a huge sigh. "That is, if I owned one. Maybe it's time to rethink my wardrobe choices, eh?"

He hopped back up on the chair and his paw darted out and speared a piece of lettuce that hung over the side of my bowl. I bit out a laugh and pushed my chair back. "Right. Why bother. After all, it's not as if the good detective expressed any interest in me personally, right? And that's his loss."

Nick blinked. "*Ew-owr.*"

The corners of my lips tipped up a smidge. "Glad you agree."

I picked up the dishes and carried them over to the counter. "Lott told his story as if it's one he's rehearsed many times before," I murmured. "But if I go on the assumption he's telling the unvarnished truth, Lola had little or no interaction with anyone else on the yacht, save for a possible flirtation with Connor. I wonder—do you think it's possible they were having an affair?"

As soon as I'd said the words, I rejected the idea. From the little I knew of Lola Grainger, she didn't seem like the type who'd cheat on her husband. I recalled my mother describing her as class personified, an assessment I agreed with. Although if there was one thing I'd learned over the years: In affairs of the heart, all bets were off. What was that old saying? *The heart wants what it wants.*

What had Lola's heart wanted?

I sighed. "I guess, just to cover all my bases, I should investigate a possible love connection between Lola and Marshall Connor. If there was one, then maybe Grainger found out about their affair, confronted Lola, maybe killed her in a drunken rage, and tossed her body off the boat in a panic."

It sounded more like the plot of a B-grade thriller than a plausible explanation.

I stared off into space, the wheels in my head turning even faster. My thoughts kept reverting to the mysterious last line in Nick Atkins's journal: *Tonight I received a text from Adrienne. She wants me to meet her at the docks— she believes the wrong Grainger might have been killed.* Assuming Adrienne was on to something, who would want Kevin dead—and why?

Lott had blown me off when I asked if he knew of any reason why Kevin might be a possible target. Recalling his smart-ass remark, I got up, rummaged in my purse for my cell. A few minutes later I had Hank Prince on the line.

"Wow, Nora," he greeted me. "Twice in one week—I didn't realize you missed me that much—or is it just Chicago and all our crime you're craving?"

"Don't miss those Chicago winters, Cruz has its own share of crime, but I do miss you." I laughed. "I was wondering if you could check into something for me."

"My plate's pretty full right now, doll, but you know I'll squeeze your request in ASAP."

"Thanks. See if you can pick up any ties between Kevin Grainger and any mob families in the L.A. area. I'll text you the particulars."

"Sure. You know, for someone who wanted to get out of the crime reporting field and go into business for herself, you seem to still be pretty interested in your old stomping grounds."

"What can I say? Old habits die hard."

Hank laughed. "True that. So, how's the new career coming?"

"Very well. Next time you're in California, look me up. If you're good, I might even name a sandwich after you."

We exchanged a few more pleasantries, and then I hung up. I finished washing the few dishes, set out some dry food for Nick, and then switched on my laptop. I typed in Lott's name and the word *accident*, and a few seconds later several news articles appeared. I clicked on the first one and read it eagerly. He'd said it had been a bad accident—that seemed an understatement somehow. The car brakes had failed, and he couldn't get himself free and out of the vehicle in time. The car crashed through a guardrail and went down a steep ravine. Lott finally managed to free himself, but his leg was badly injured, impeding his escape. As a result, he'd gotten pretty badly burned when the car exploded.

The second article offered much of the same information. At the very end, however, was an interesting note: The car Lott had been driving was registered to his employer, Kevin Grainger.

"Hm. Well, that could explain why Grainger paid all Lott's medical bills. More out of guilt, perhaps, than kindness?" I said to Nick, who'd finished his dry food and had hopped up on the table next to the laptop. "Maybe Grainger was the intended target, and not Lott. I wonder if the police ever investigated that angle?" My gaze wandered across the room, over to the table where Nick Atkins's journals lay. "Or if your former master ever did?"

I thought again of the pages ripped from the journal and turned back to the computer. I looked up the office number for Sampson and Atkins Investigations and then reached for my cell. A few seconds later a voice, sounding as if I'd just awoken him from a deep sleep, rumbled across the line.

"Sampson and Atkins Investigations. Oliver Sampson here."

"Hey, Mr. Sampson. It's Nora Charles. Do you remember me?"

He laughed. "It's Ollie, Nora, and of course I remember you. How could I forget Sherlock's new owner? I must say, I didn't expect to hear from you so soon. Is everything all right with the little fellow?"

"Oh, he's just fine. I just remembered there were a few things in that box Mr. Atkins's landlady gave me that she thought you should have."

"Really?" Ollie sounded dubious. "I can't imagine what."

"Journals. Three thick ones. One of which contains his notes on the Grainger case."

There was dead silence and then, "I see. And the other two?"

"Look to be notes on various cases he worked on through the years. Mainly disgruntled spouses, as near as I can tell."

Ollie barked out a laugh. "Yes, disgruntled spouses were his specialty. But seeing as all those cases are closed, I doubt I'd need them. Feel free to keep them or throw them out, whichever you want."

I cleared my throat. "As long as I have you on the phone, Ollie—did Nick ever share any of the details of the Grainger case with you?"

"Not too many—of course, to be fair, I never displayed too much interest in it. Dynamite, remember?" He clucked his tongue. "Why—is there something in particular you need to know?"

"I've been doing a bit of research, and I'm curious about the accident Captain Lott had right after the incident. One of the accounts I read said the car he was driving belonged to Kevin Grainger, so—"

"You wondered if Grainger were the intended victim and not Lott," Ollie finished. "I remember wondering about that myself," he admitted. "Apparently there wasn't enough left of the car after the explosion to draw a conclusion. The police seemed satisfied Lott was the intended victim, however, due to the fact he owed a certain loan shark a ton of money. The possibility someone might have been after Grainger never entered the picture."

"I see. Well, thanks, Ollie."

"Nora." His tone was sharp. "I don't know why you want to get involved in this, but I feel compelled to offer you the same advice I did Nick. You'd do well to steer clear and let sleeping dogs lie. I know you worked that crime beat in Chicago, but—"

"Thanks for your help, Ollie, and for your concern. But I can take care of myself—and little Nick, too. Don't worry."

"A little late for that," he grumbled, and hung up.

I put the phone down and leaned back, laced my hands behind my head. The key to all this, I felt certain, was finding someone willing to come clean about what really happened on the yacht that night. From my experience, there was no way all those people were telling the truth. One— or maybe more—was lying.

What I needed to do was figure out who and, more important, why.

I stood up, stretched, and put down the top on the computer. Nick watched me with his unblinking golden eyes.

"My next move should be to question the other three, see what they have to say about that night. That's going to require some thought. After all, it's not like we hang out in the same circles, or that they even frequent Hot Bread for lunch. I can't just run into them, you know."

Nick jumped up on the counter. His plume of a tail swished, knocking over the plastic case containing my catering menus. They scattered to the floor like autumn leaves. I sighed, bent to retrieve them, then suddenly straightened. I hurried over to the old rolltop desk in the corner, jerked open the bottom drawer, where my mother's impeccable catering records were kept. I thumbed through the folders, and a little cry of triumph escaped my lips as I pulled out one marked KMG. Sure enough, inside were two neatly drawn contracts, bearing both my mother's signature and that of Lola Grainger, for Hot Bread to cater two of their upcoming company events. I glanced over at Nick, sitting calmly on the counter, licking one paw.

"I get it," I murmured. "Good point. Now that Lola's dead, what happens with these contracts?"

I shoved the file folder under one arm and patted Nick on the head. I figured now was as good a time as any to find out.

THIRTEEN

I got a one o'clock appointment for the following after-noon, and Chantal was only too glad to mind the store—and Nick. I patted his head in farewell and received a plaintive "*meow*" for my trouble. He trotted right along be-side me as I walked up to the door, and looked a bit of-fended when I shooed him away. I chuckled. No doubt he'd have found a ride in the car preferable to trying on more of Chantal's collars. Oh, well.

KMG's plush corporate offices occupied three separate buildings located right off Route 19 on the outskirts of Cruz. I drove up the winding road and saw a guard shack off to one side, with a large sign reading: ALL VISITORS MUST CHECK IN FIRST. Off to the left, there were two lanes outfitted with card readers and automatic gates. I pulled over to the guard shack and parked. As I exited my SUV, I saw a Lincoln Continental drive up to the gates, the driv-er's side window roll down, and an arm reach out, swiping a badge against the reading device. The gate rose, allowing the car to enter the grounds, and immediately lowered once the car passed through. I could see the reason for the security, though. KMG had recently acquired several lucrative government contracts; it was only natural they'd want to keep a close eye on things.

I entered the guard shack. A sleepy-eyed, olive-skinned blond woman wearing a starched navy uniform looked up at me from behind a plate glass enclosure and motioned to me to come forward.

"Can I help you?" she asked. Her voice was thick with an accent I couldn't quite place. Spanish maybe? I felt for a minute like I was at the Cineplex in the mall, buying tickets for the afternoon show. I leaned forward so I could speak directly into the microphone. "Nora Charles. I have an appointment."

The guard's expression didn't change one iota, but I was certain I saw one eyebrow twitch ever so slightly. She ran her finger down a typed sheet. "Ah, yes," she said at last. "Ms. Charles. You're here to see Ms. Cummings, Mr. Grainger's admin."

"Yes, that's correct." I nodded. "Patti Cummings."

She picked up the phone and dialed a number. I strolled over to the plate glass window that took up the entire west wall and peered out. A lone guy on a bicycle had just entered the grounds. I thought for a moment he would come directly to the guard shack as I'd done, but instead he turned toward the gates and pedaled right on through, completely bypassing the automatic card readers.

I turned back to the guard. "Did you see that? That guy just rode his bicycle right past your security gates."

The guard looked up, frowned, and then swiveled her chair around to a computer monitor. She hunched over it for several seconds before turning back to me. "Oh, that was Barry Gray. He always rides his bike in."

"He's an employee?" At her nod I frowned. "Shouldn't he have swiped his badge, though? I mean, so you know he's not a terrorist, or anything?"

Her lips compressed into a thin line. "It's not necessary. We know who he is. He's the head software engineer on Mr. Grainger's newest project. He doesn't drive." She pushed a square of plastic with the word VISITOR in block letters through the slot in the window at me. "There's your temporary admission badge. Show that to Darla at Reception. Drive straight back, park in Visitors against the wall, and enter through the main gray door."

I pinned the badge to my jacket and hurried outside. As I moved toward the SUV, a dark, expensive-looking sedan suddenly came roaring out of a side lot. I caught a glimpse of a high forehead, wide eyes, and a cruelly slanted mouth as I jumped backward. The driver barely cut his wheel in time to avoid making me roadkill.

"Geez," I said. "Someone's in an awful hurry."

"Sure is." I glanced up to see the female guard almost at my elbow. She shook her head. "Guess he couldn't wait for his driver."

I stared after the vehicle, which had turned out of the driveway and was now little more than a speck in the distance. "Driver?"

The guard nodded. "He's had one ever since his wife's accident. That was Kevin Grainger."

I parked in the section marked VISITORS and hurried up the cement steps and through the plate glass doors into what I can only describe as an opulent reception area.

Thick, slate gray shag carpeting the same color as the building covered the floor, and I felt my three-inch heels sink in deep. I moved soundlessly across the lobby to the massive cherrywood desk that stood on a raised dais in the center of the room—a globe with twin rings around it, KMG's logo, was emblazoned in 3-D on its center. The perky-looking brunette seated behind the desk wore a low-cut blouse and a brass name tag that proclaimed her DARLA. I showed her my badge and gave my name; she, in turn, consulted a typed list taped up to the side of her twenty-four-inch Dell computer monitor. She marked something off on a sheet, then picked up the phone, dialed a number. After speaking for about ten seconds in a very low tone, she hung up the phone, let the corners of her expertly made-up lips curve in the slightest of smiles, and pointed at the far wall with a blue-tipped fingernail.

"Take the main elevator to the sixth floor. Make a right and walk straight ahead. Patti will meet you there."

I thanked her and did as I was instructed. No one else rode in the elevator with me, and I leaned my head against the wall, mentally replaying earlier events. Where had Kevin Grainger been off to in such a hurry? The fool had nearly killed me—whoever he was meeting must be damned important. What could be so earth-shattering he didn't care if he ran an innocent person over? Several possibilities came to mind: winning the Powerball, a huge company merger—not that Grainger needed any more money—or something to do with his wife's untimely death.

The elevator dinged and the door rolled back, and my heels sank again deep into more plush carpeting, this a deep latte color. I glanced at the crown molding on the walls as I turned right and moved forward down the long, deserted hallway.

"Miss Charles?"

The woman appeared in front of me suddenly, like a wisp of smoke, and I almost jumped out of my skin. I assessed her in one quick glance. Five-five or five-six, about a hundred twenty pounds poured into a form-fitting pencil skirt and a low-cut animal print blouse. Blond hair that appeared too golden to be out of a bottle was cut in a becoming style that framed an oval-shaped face with full lips and ice blue eyes. She had no identifying marks, tattoos, or scars—none that was visible to the naked eye anyway. I glanced at her red leather Manolos and reassessed my original take on her height, thinking how Chantal would swoon over those babies. She held out a perfectly manicured, French-tipped hand. I took it and winced a bit as her fingers closed over mine. For one who appeared so petite, she had a grip like a sumo wrestler.

"I'm Patti Cummings, Mr. Grainger's admin. Shall we?"

Her voice had a breathy quality, very Marilyn Monroe. I couldn't decide if it was real or put-on. She released my hand, and I flexed my fingers as I followed her down the long hall into a large room that boasted a mammoth oak table with at least a dozen ergonomically correct leather chairs grouped around it. She seated herself at the head of the table and motioned me to take a seat. I slid into the chair on her left.

"So you're Laura Charles's daughter." Her full lips twitched in the semblance of a smile as she opened the thick file in front of her. "On behalf of the management of KMG Incorporated, please allow me to express our condolences on your mother's death. While many of us didn't know her personally, she did a stellar job catering our events, and I know Mrs. Grainger in particular was fond of her sandwiches. Her creativity was surpassed only by her culinary skill."

"Thank you," I said. "I'm trying very hard to follow in her footsteps. As I'm sure you know, I've got some pretty big shoes to fill." I waited a beat and then added, "I'd also like to express my belated condolences on Mrs. Grainger's untimely demise. Which is, after all, the reason I'm here."

"Yes, and I can understand your concern." Patti Cummings gestured toward the stack of papers before her. "I— or I should say the committee—has been reviewing the file. Hot Bread has catered every single event KMG has thrown for the past five years. That's a significant amount of business."

"Yes it is." I nodded. "It's steady income that I'd certainly hate to lose, although I could understand the company's reluctance to offer up a firm contract."

Patti thumbed through what appeared to be a pile of receipts. "As near as we can tell, Hot Bread had no written contract with our firm. It appeared to be a matter of Mrs. Grainger's personal choice."

I nodded. "She and my mother were very friendly."

Patti cleared her throat. "Mr. Grainger was most happy to leave catering details to his wife—she excelled at that sort of thing, you know. Planning charity functions, catering, the annual picnics and Christmas parties, any sort of event—Lola took charge of it all—commandeered it, actually—and did it beautifully."

The words were no doubt meant to be praise, but there was an underlying subtext to the woman's tone that suggested something else to me: Resentment? Anger? I idly wondered why. Admins in this day and age were no longer considered "gofers"—surely she shouldn't have minded Lola's taking over what appeared to me to be a menial task.

After all, it would leave her with lots of free time for other activities.

I leaned forward and put what I hoped was a pleasant smile on my face. "Naturally, I understand your trepidation. After all, Hot Bread under my ownership is a different entity—although not that much different, I hope. I pride myself on keeping the shop pretty much the same as when my mother ran it—with a few improvements along the way, of course. I don't know if you're aware, but Cruz doesn't have many specialty sandwich shops. I pride myself on standing out in a town where fast food and chain stands are a dime a dozen."

Patti smoothed a stray hair out of her eye and nodded. "Quite true. Hot Bread is no ordinary delicatessen."

I bristled inwardly as she lingered over the word *delicatessen*. I forced myself to say casually, "You've been to the shop?"

Was I imagining it, or had her face suddenly paled beneath her rose blush? "Oh, no—sorry to say, I haven't. But—" She reached inside the file folder, held up the last incarnation of our catering menu. "I've looked this over enough to know how unique your store is." She laid the menu down on the table, her fingers toying with the paper's edge. "I know for a fact the meatloaf sandwich—the *Sly Stallone*—is a special favorite of Mr. Grainger's."

"That's nice to hear. It's praise like his that sets us apart from the competition."

"I must be honest with you, Ms. Charles. I'm not sure if Mr. Grainger has made a decision yet as to exactly who will be catering our next event." She glanced at the paper before her. "That would be our Memorial Day barbecue."

"Maybe I can give you some help with that." I opened my tote bag and pulled out the pink copies I'd found in my mother's things. "Apparently my mother and Lola had an informal agreement concerning the Memorial Day barbecue and the company picnic." I held out the slips to her. "As you can see, Mrs. Grainger gave Hot Bread the catering contract to these two events. Now I can understand the trepidation—you want assurance you'll be receiving the same quality of food. I can also understand your wanting to price out other caterers, but I'd be willing to bet they won't hold a candle to us."

The full lips twitched. "You sound very confident."

"I am. I'd be more than happy to send up samples of some of our new offerings for Mr. Grainger—and anyone else—to taste test."

Patti Cummings stared blankly at the receipts. "Yes, well," she said at last. "The quality of your food was never in question. As with anything else in this economy, it all boils down to the right price."

"Understandable," I agreed. "I also have to take into consideration the rising prices of supplies, but I'm sure if you comparison shop, you'll find my prices to be more than reasonable." I paused, then added, "Not to mention the fact Mrs. Grainger did commit to us in good faith."

"Yes, but there are unusual circumstances. When your mother and Mrs. Grainger made those commitments, I'm quite certain neither of them had any idea—" She broke off abruptly and looked away.

"It's okay," I assured her. "You can say it. Neither of them had any idea they'd be dead."

"Yes." The word came out almost strangled, as if she'd been holding her breath. "Mrs. Grainger never discussed the catering with anyone here, so we had no idea commitments this far ahead had been made. It puts us in rather an awkward position."

I frowned. "Awkward? How so?"

"While I can definitely say the Memorial Day event is still up in the air, we did sign a contract with Kennedy Park to have their facility cater the picnic event just yesterday."

Genuine disappointment arrowed through me, and my shoulders slumped ever so slightly as I leaned back against the soft leather cushions. "I see."

"It was a package deal," she went on in a rush. "If we used their catering facility, we got a twenty percent discount per head—that adds up, and in these uncertain times where every penny counts—"

I didn't feel up to another lecture on the state of our economy, and held up my hand. "No need to go into it. I am a businesswoman, Ms. Cummings. I understand fully."

"I'm sure, however, Mr. Grainger will want to be fair," she said quickly. "I'm sure we'll honor the contract for the Memorial Day event. Then, depending on how that goes, we can see what other events, if any, we can throw your way. Please understand this is nothing personal. But with Mrs. Grainger out of the picture, whoever takes over event planning will no doubt have definite ideas on how they want to handle it—which may or may not include your shop." She tossed me a bright, but phony, smile. "But not to worry. We intend to afford you the same opportunity as any other catering facility. However, I'm sure the fact the late Mrs. Grainger liked your wares enough to offer exclusivity will go a long way—provided, of course, the wares are better than or equal to what was served in the past."

I nodded stiffly. "Of course. I don't imagine there's any chance I could speak to Mr. Grainger directly?"

Her eyes widened and her tone was colder than a block of ice. "I'm afraid Mr. Grainger wouldn't get personally involved with something of this nature. However, until a new catering manager is named, he's put me in charge. As such, you have my assurance Hot Bread will cater our Memorial Day event."

I let out a whoosh of air. "Well—that's something anyway. Thanks." She started to rise, but I reached out, grazed her wrist with my fingertips. "Tell me—how is Mr. Grainger doing, really? I know his wife's accident must have been quite a shock."

"Yes it was, to everyone. He's much more adjusted now. In the first weeks afterward he was a wreck."

"I'm sure. But he had his friends and co-workers to help him through that trying time. I'm sure you were a great comfort to him."

Her eyes narrowed and her chin jutted forward. "Of course, I did—I still do—what I can."

I'll bet you do. "Of course," I murmured sympathetically. "I'm sure it hasn't been easy for him, although the police ruling Mrs. Grainger's death an accident so quickly must have been a relief."

Her lips compressed into a thin line. "The detective in charge saw no need to waste time and money on an open-and-shut accident."

"Of course, of course. I was surprised, though, how few news stories there were on the incident—considering Mr. Grainger's stature in the community, and all. I'm sure the public was interested in the details."

She wiggled around a bit in her seat. "There weren't that many details to share."

"I guess not. I understand everyone on the yacht was asleep by the time it happened—" I pursed my lips in a little O of surprise. "Golly—you were there, too, weren't you?"

Her blue eyes flashed, and then her face arranged itself in an expression of benign composure. "Yes. A small group of us were away for the weekend."

"Celebrating their fifteenth wedding anniversary."

"That and—" She hesitated, then said, "We were working on a business deal as well. Actually, we're still working on it. Our original meeting had to be postponed because of—well, because of what happened."

"Oh, wow." I scooted to the edge of my chair. "Bummer."

"Yes, well, things happen. It's another reason we didn't want too much attention. The police and press were very cooperative regarding our need for discretion."

"How kind of them," I murmured. "I must say, though, the manner of Mrs. Grainger's death came as quite a surprise to me."

She looked up sharply. "I don't know what you mean."

"Mrs. Grainger often expressed her fear of the ocean to my mother. It just seemed odd to me that she would have taken a dinghy out on what she feared the most, and so late at night."

She'd been tapping the folder in front of her—at my words, the fingers stopped mid-motion, held poised above the folder. Her smile faded for just an instant, and her eyes darkened. "You seem unusually interested in Mrs. Grainger's accident, Ms. Charles," she snapped. "It's not my policy to indulge in gossip, and particularly not gossip that concerns the head of this company."

I bristled a bit at her defensive tone, but decided a healthy measure of crow would take me further. "I am sorry," I said. "I guess old habits die hard."

The eyes narrowed. "Old habits?"

"Yes—I used to be a crime reporter in Chicago, and—"

I heard a quick intake of breath and slid a glance at Patti. Beneath her carefully applied Moonglow Pink blusher, her skin had gone chalk white.

Something I'd said had definitely seemed to upset her. Now all I had to do was figure out just what that something was.

FOURTEEN

I had to hand it to her—Patti recovered quickly. One second she looked as if she were going to barf her breakfast all over the expensive shag carpeting, and the next the brilliant smile was back in place, eyes crinkling as she offered me a nervous laugh.

"Sorry. I didn't realize you had Chicago roots. I—ah—I lived there for a few years. Couldn't wait to relocate out here. Those winters are brutal!"

I nodded in agreement. "That they are."

The smile got a bit wider. "I much prefer balmy sunshine and eighty degrees to twelve-plus inches of snow on a daily basis." Her nail beat a swift tattoo against the folder. "You were a crime reporter, you said? That's an unusual profession for a woman, isn't it?"

"Not really." Obviously Patti had never heard of Anne Rule or Aphrodite Jones. "Well, I won't kid you. It was no walk in the park." I made the sign of the cross. "It's amazing what one can get used to, if you put your mind to it. I fought for that column because I wanted to show my editor a woman could do just as well on that particular topic as a man, and I succeeded."

"I bet. What made you decide to leave Chicago—to give up reporting?"

"My mother passed away, as you know, and I thought coming home and taking over the family business would be what she'd have wanted me to do. Still, there are days when I miss the stress, the danger. There was a part of me that hated to say good-bye." I fixed Patti with a stare. "Probably the same part of me that just has to keep pecking at unsolved mysteries. I'm sorry if my questions upset you."

"Oh, you didn't upset me," she said, but her assurance came a tad too quickly for real sincerity. "Sadly, Mrs. Grainger had many personal demons, but she worked hard to overcome them. As for her being in the dinghy—well, that's supposition. None of us really know what happened that night. I'm afraid that will always be a mystery." She paused and then added, "An unsolved mystery."

"Perhaps, since the one person who can supply the answers is dead."

Patti slid the menu all the way back into the folder and then turned it on its side. She pushed the papers into the folder, picked it up, tapped it against the table. "Well, thank you for stopping by. I'm so glad we had the opportunity to meet."

"Me, too." As she started to rise, I settled back farther in my chair. "You know, it might be a good idea for me to sign a formal contract to finalize our catering agreement." I gave a short laugh. "Mrs. Grainger and my mother might have liked the hearty handshake method, but both you and I know it's not the most practical way to do business."

She hesitated, then nodded. "Of course. I'll have one drawn up immediately and messengered to the store for your signature."

"If it won't take long, I don't mind waiting."

She glanced at her watch, tapping the toe of one foot impatiently. "I'll see what I can do."

"I appreciate it." I waited until she'd gathered up all her papers and started for the door, and then I added, "Perhaps it was the alcohol."

She turned, her hand on the doorknob, and stared at me. "I'm sorry?"

"The alcohol. According to the reports, everyone was 'feeling good.' People can do very strange things under the influence of alcohol, so if Mrs. Grainger had been drinking heavily . . ."

Was I imagining it, or had little beads of perspiration started to break out across her forehead? "I wouldn't know," she said coolly. "I really wasn't paying any particular attention to how much anyone else was drinking."

"I'm sorry. It's those reporter genes again. Like I said, I just can't help but wonder . . ." I scratched at my temple absently. "She could have gotten the bruises from hitting her body against either the boat or the dinghy when she fell in, but I've got to admit—unless I were dead drunk or unconscious, if I suddenly found myself splashing around in water that I'd always regarded as my worst enemy, I'd have screamed my brains out."

Patti's eyes narrowed and her lips settled into a taut line. "Did you really come here to inquire about Hot Bread's catering contracts, Ms. Charles? Or is there something else other than business motivating this visit?" She took a step back into the room and folded her arms across her chest. "I can't answer you as to why Mrs. Grainger didn't cry out. For all I know, she might have. I was asleep. As for bruises on her body—I wasn't aware of any. Then again, I only saw her body in the casket at her memorial. Now, if you'll excuse me, I think we're done here." Her finger tapped against the file folder. "This might take a while, so there's no need for you to wait. I'll see the contracts are sent to you. I wouldn't want you to waste any more time here than necessary."

I followed her out of the conference room. As we started to turn toward the foyer, a dark-haired girl with tortoise-rimmed glasses hurried up to Patti. "Ms. Cummings, Mr. Baker needs you in Conference Room C right away. They're doing a call to China and he needs your notes on the Glass project."

"Thank you, Kristi, I forgot about that." She handed the folder over to the girl. "Have Ilena draw up the standard catering contract for our Memorial Day event for Ms. Charles's signature, and have someone messenger it over to Hot Bread this afternoon." She glanced over at me with a thin smile. "I'm sorry. Duty calls." She started to leave, then abruptly turned back. "Nice meeting you," she said in a tone that implied she'd have rather walked barefoot over hot coals.

"Interesting meeting you," I murmured. I watched her as she hurried off in the opposite direction. Her springy step indicated she was more than a little relieved to be rid of me.

Kristi tapped my arm and smiled. "I know Ms. Cummings said to messenger the contract, but it's a standard one and shouldn't take longer than a half hour to prepare. You're welcome to wait, if you wish."

I shook my head. "Messenger is fine. I'll expect them

later this afternoon. Besides, I have the feeling Ms. Cummings would prefer it if I didn't wait. I think I upset her, asking some questions about the day Mrs. Grainger died."

"Ah." Kristi's eyes widened behind the massive frames. "Yeah, I can understand that. Mrs. Grainger's death is sort of a taboo subject around here. If you ask me, Mr. Grainger is still in mourning. But"—she leaned forward and lowered her voice—"it wouldn't surprise any of us if, when he's ready to pick up the pieces of his life, Ms. Cummings is right there. I mean, she's always all over him. Like glue."

Well, now. This was more like it. "Really? So you'd say Ms. Cummings has more than just a business interest in Mr. Grainger?"

"I'd say, and so would everyone in this building, right down to the janitor." Her giggle sounded more like a nervous gasp. "I really shouldn't gossip. Ms. Cummings has always treated me with respect. But sometimes she can be a bit overbearing to the secretaries—it's like she's already assumed the role of lady of the manor." She pressed her face closer to mine and said in a stage whisper, "Mr. Grainger's got eyes. He's a man, after all. He ogled Patti plenty before the accident, but he'd never have cheated on Mrs. Grainger when she was alive. Not only did he love her, but it was her money that helped him start up this company. He'd never have risked losing either of the two things he loved most in the world."

"Do you think Mrs. Grainger knew how Patti felt about her husband?"

"Well, I don't see how she didn't know. Everyone else did. But trust me, Mr. Grainger had no interest in Patti—not back then. Now is a different story." She let out an expressive sigh. "They're always together. It's like they're joined at the hip, or something."

"I see," I said thoughtfully. "Tell me, Kristi—did you ever hear any rumors about Mrs. Grainger having an affair? With one of the men here?"

Kristi shook her head. "God, where did you hear something like that? Oh, never mind, I can guess." She waved her hand in a circle, and the corners of her mouth turned down in a derisive smile. "I couldn't swear to it—I mean there were some social functions where they did look to be pretty tight—but Mrs. Grainger was too classy for Marshall, and deep down he knew it. If Mrs. Grainger had any interest in him at all, it was only a ploy to make her husband sweat a bit. I'd bet my whole year's salary she'd never actually have *done* anything with him."

"It seems as if Mr. Connor was taking some chance, then. You'd think he'd have been afraid of rumors like that getting back to Mr. Grainger."

"Marshall doesn't always think with the right part of his anatomy," chuckled Kristi. "But he's real good at what he does—Mr. Grainger would probably overlook anything short of murder to keep him."

I refrained from saying that could well be the case, and nodded. Kristi seemed to be a talkative gal in a very talkative mood, so I decided it was worth posing another question. "How about Mr. Tabor? I heard there was a lot of resentment when he was appointed to his position."

"Um, yeah. There were others much more qualified, but Buck went to college with Mr. Grainger, and he's pretty good at selling himself." She closed one eye in a wink. "You know what I mean."

I nodded. The college angle was a good one. Had Buck learned something about Kevin there that he held over his head? "Well—this has been very interesting, Kristi."

She shifted a bit uncomfortably. "Look, please don't

repeat anything I said. I'm probably way out of line, and I'd really hate to give you the wrong idea, especially if you're going to be doing business with our firm." Her tongue darted out, licked at her bottom lip. "And if Patti knew I was going on like this . . . Well, it'd be the unemployment line for me for sure."

"No worries." I made a motion of zipping up my lips. "Mum's the word. Besides, I rarely listen to gossip. I like to form my own opinions."

Kristi gave a relieved sigh and I fell into step beside her, then let out a little cry and snapped my fingers in the air. "Damn—I must have left my purse in the conference room." As she started to turn with me, I waved my arm. "Oh, no. You go on. I can find my way to the elevators."

Kristi hesitated, then shifted the folder in her arms. "If you're sure." She moved off, and I retraced my steps. I found my purse just where I'd shoved it—under my chair. I tucked it under my arm and paused for a moment, taking stock of the situation. It was pretty apparent Patti Cummings was a master at keeping her cool, but I knew I'd managed to rattle her cage a bit in more ways than one. Good.

Now that I was on a roll, I wanted to find someone else's to rattle.

I moved into the hallway and looked around, wondering where Marshall Connor and Buck Tabor's offices might be. I paused in front of a closed door with no name on it, and jumped slightly as it started to open and I could hear the soft murmur of voices. I glanced frantically about and saw another closed door, the name ALICIA SAMUELS emblazoned across the dark wood in gold letters. I crossed to it, said a silent prayer, and grasped the knob. It turned easily, and one quick glance assured me the office was empty. I let my shoulders relax a bit, then opened the door a crack and peered out.

Two men stood in the hall. One was short, squat, and had a shock of gray hair too thick and perfectly coiffed to be natural. The other appeared a bit younger, tall and muscular, with jet-black hair swept back from a high forehead and snapping black eyes. Both wore expensive-looking suits. The shorter of the two spoke so softly I had to strain to catch his words.

"He said some reporter was asking questions. Can you believe it? After all this time? He really got pissed, Marsh."

"Yeah, Buck, I could tell by the way he peeled out of the executive lot. Almost ran some girl over, the fool," the other snorted.

Marsh? Buck? My heart beat faster at the realization that here might be the other two members of that fated weekend cruise. I forced myself to focus as the shorter of the two, whom I assumed was Buck Tabor, pressed a finger to his lips. "Who knows what set all this off? I thought the questions were long over with." He pulled a handkerchief out of his pocket and swiped it across his forehead. "Well, it's probably some hotshot out to make a name for himself. He figures he'll solve a cold case. Our luck he'd pick this one."

"It's not cold, it's closed," the man whom I took to be Marshall Connor retorted. "What does Kevin think he's going to accomplish?"

"You know Kevin." Tabor sighed. "He goes crazy whenever Lola's involved."

"Well, no one can prove a damn thing as long as we all stick to the story. We were all asleep. That way they can't prove squat." He closed one eye in an exaggerated wink.

"Well, I don't know about you, but I was really asleep," Tabor chuckled. "Can't prove anything by me."

"Or me," Connor agreed. "And we all know they'll never prove anything by Patti. She'd die before she'd rat on the big man."

"Yeah—I can't understand that. Patti could have any man she wanted, but she wants someone who I doubt will ever see her as more than an efficient right arm."

"You're just pissed because she hasn't given you the time of day since Lola's death." Connor's laugh was deep and rumbling. "Sour grapes, eh, Buck?"

Their voices faded as they turned and walked down the corridor. I closed the door and leaned against it, rubbing my palms along the side of my skirt. They were slick with sweat.

So they'd all lied—every one of them, including no doubt, Captain Lott. From the sound of things, it was a group effort to protect Kevin Grainger. But from what? Murder—or something else? Chances were excellent I was the reporter they'd referred to—and if so, there was only one way they could have known that. So much for Lott keeping our chat confidential. Well, if nothing else, now I could be certain where his loyalties lie—and to be honest, who could blame the guy, after all Grainger had done for him?

My knees wobbled. Rather than take a chance on collapsing, I moved swiftly over to the cherrywood desk and eased myself into the soft leather chair behind it. I leaned forward and rested my elbows on the desk, taking several deep, calming breaths.

I'd obviously been away from crime reporting way too long. I'd taken bigger risks than this in the past without even breaking a sweat. I leaned back in the chair, let my eyes rove over the office. The top of the desk had a thin layer of dust on it, as did the computer monitor. Obviously

Alicia Samuels, whoever she might be, had not used this office for some time. I flexed my legs, and was just about to stand up when my attention was drawn to a small pad to the left of the computer monitor, and the number scrawled across it.

368-555-9879

There was a date scrawled beneath the number: 8/14. I frowned.

August fourteenth was the date Lola died.

I opened my purse and pulled out my cell. I punched in the number and waited. After a few seconds I was rewarded with a woman's mechanical voice:

"Hello, this is Lola Grainger. I'm not available to take your call right now. Please leave a message and I'll get back to you."

FIFTEEN

I took the elevator down to the main floor, handed in my guest badge at the reception desk, and hurried out to the visitor parking lot, my thoughts in a whirl. It seemed every time I thought a little progress was made—WHAM! Something happened to throw me ten steps backward.

In this case, it was Alicia Samuels. Who was she and why would she have Lola Grainger's number in her office? What was their connection, if any? I'd never heard of her before, or seen her name bandied about in any of the news accounts. I wondered if Nick Atkins had known about her, and my thoughts drifted again to those missing pages. I suddenly felt the need to talk to Ollie. He was a professional investigator, after all. Maybe he could give me a fresh perspective. I shoved my SUV into reverse, put my foot to the gas, and heard the unmistakable crunch of metal.

Shit. It wasn't a hard collision—Lord knows I hadn't been going *that* fast. But fast enough, apparently. The sound had been loud enough to get my adrenaline going and the blood pounding in my ears. I slammed the SUV into park and got out, prepared to assess the damage. I walked around to the back bumper and saw the other car— a dark Acura, with a dent in the passenger side the size of a basketball. Swell. I forced myself to glance quickly at the driver's side, and I frowned. It was empty.

"Well, well. I wanted to run into you again, but this is going a bit far."

I whirled, and met the stormy gaze of none other than Detective Daniel Corleone.

Double shit.

"D-Detective Corleone," I stammered. "Fancy meeting you here."

One corner of his lip quirked. "Indeed. So where's the fire?"

I looked dumbly from Corleone to the dented Acura back to Corleone. I pointed to the vehicle. "Your car?"

He nodded. "Yes. My personal vehicle. I only bought it last month. It's got less than three thousand miles on it— and now it's got its very first dent."

Triple shit.

Words spilled out of my mouth in a babbling torrent. "Detective, I am *so* sorry! It was my fault! Totally!"

"No argument there," he agreed, and held out his hand. As I looked at it questioningly, he wiggled his fingers. "Insurance card? You do have insurance, I hope?"

"Oh. Yes, of course."

I turned and walked over to the passenger side of my vehicle, opened the door, and started rummaging in the glove compartment. As my fingers closed over the laminated packet that held my insurance and registration information, I could feel heat start to color my cheeks.

Of all the detectives in all the Acuras in Cruz, why in hell did I have to run into his?

I walked back to the car. Corleone was leaning casually against the rear bumper, arms folded. I handed him my insurance card. "Here. Just write down the information. The whole thing is my fault. If they won't pay, then I will." I mentally assessed what I had in my savings account. The damage couldn't be more than nine hundred dollars . . . could it?

"Of course they'll pay. And of course it was your fault."

He copied down my insurance information into a little black book he removed from his jacket pocket, then handed the card back to me. "So?" he said. "Care to explain?"

I looked at him. "Explain? There's really nothing to explain. I wasn't paying attention, I'm afraid. I was thinking about . . . something else."

He slipped his notebook back into his pocket and folded his arms across his impossibly broad chest. "Just what are you doing here?"

I didn't answer at first—I admit it, I was momentarily distracted by the way his ash-blond hair fell in slight waves over his tanned forehead, and by those sleepy, sexy eyes with their dark—and impossibly long for a guy—lashes. He leaned a bit closer, filling my nostrils with his musky, clean scent. My vision suddenly seemed a bit fuzzy around the edges, and I took a deep, calming breath—and then I felt his fingers dig into my forearm.

"Are you all right, Nora? I asked what are you doing here, at the KMG offices? Playing detective?"

Startled, I jerked my arm out of his grasp. I sucked in another breath and my vision cleared. His face loomed before me, his lips drawn into a thin line, his eyes no longer sleepy and sexy, but with a visible glint of annoyance.

"I—no. Playing detective? No. I—why would you think that?" I stammered. In spite of his hostile stare, he was still damn sexy and he smelled delicious, and dammit, it was hard for me to think cohesively around him.

Quadruple shit.

"It could be because I've always found there to be a fine line between investigative reporters and detectives, or perhaps I'm still thinking of our conversation of the other day," he said. "You remember? The one where you came to my office under the pretext of doing a story and tried to see if I was amenable to reopening the Lola Grainger case."

His words snapped me out of the funk I'd fallen into, and my eyes blazed as I stared back at him. "Now hold on a minute. You agreed with me! Are you changing your mind?" I paused, and then added, "And there was no pretext. I *am* thinking of doing a story on the Lola Grainger case."

"Funny. I spoke to your editor at *Noir*. Louis, right? He seemed to be very much in the dark about your story. Apparently he hasn't given his approval."

I nibbled at my lower lip. "Well, of course he hasn't. I haven't gotten all my facts and written it yet. But he knew I was considering doing it." I tossed my head. "Besides, that's not why I'm here."

The eyebrow inched up another notch. "No?"

"No. I'm here, actually, on store business. Lola Grainger and my mother used to have 'gentlemen's agreements' that Hot Bread would cater all of KMG's social events. Now that both of them are deceased, I felt the need to make more concrete arrangements."

"I see," he said slowly. "So the reason for your visit today had nothing to do with Lola's death?"

"No—it had to do with the fact I needed to firm up

whether or not KMG still wants Hot Bread to do their catering."

He was silent for a few moments, then shrugged. "Okay. Sorry. How'd it go?"

"They're taking it under advisement. Right now I still have a lock on their Memorial Day event, but I lost the Fourth of July picnic. After that—it's up to the new catering manager, whoever that may be."

"Ah, so your inattention can be attributed to worry over future catering income from KMG?"

"For the most part."

The frown deepened. "What does that mean?"

"It means I was wondering how I could possibly make up the money I'm losing over that Fourth of July contract."

"Sounds to me as if there's something else going on in that pretty head of yours. Mind sharing?"

Pretty head? Had he just called me pretty? I gave myself a mental slap upside the head and crossed my own arms over my chest. This was no time to dwell on whether or not he was flirting with me. My editor in Chicago had always told me, "When confronted with an immovable obstacle, the best defense is a frontal attack." I stared straight into Detective Corleone's baby blues and said, "Let me ask *you* a question, Detective. What exactly are you doing here? Your visit couldn't possibly have anything to do with the Lola Grainger case, now could it?"

I saw a muscle work in his lower jaw. "As a matter of fact, it does. I thought I'd do some follow-up work. As I've already mentioned to you, you made some interesting points that I feel deserve more clarification. I phoned Mr. Grainger earlier."

"Great. So—did he clarify?"

"He did not. He hung up on me, so I felt a personal visit was in order."

I chuckled. "Well, you should have made an appointment. He's not here. He left about two hours ago."

His eyes popped. "He left?"

"Yep—as a matter of fact, he almost ran me over on his way out."

"No kidding. Well, well—you have had a busy day, haven't you?" He reached out, brushed a stray lock of hair off my cheek. "I don't suppose you have any idea where he might have gone."

Shelly Lott came to mind, but I hesitated sharing that. If Lott had squealed to Grainger, he might also do the same to the detective, and then I'd really be in deep doo-doo. I wanted to keep my investigating a secret from the good detective—for the moment, at least. Once I had something really concrete, then it would be a very different story. "Not offhand. But the others who were on board the yacht that night are all in their offices. You might want to question them."

"I intend to." His eyes searched my face for a minute before he added, "I know I said I'd call you tomorrow but since we've met up now . . ." He cleared his throat. "I still want to discuss this case with you."

I offered him a thin smile. "Discuss? Or try and pry information out of me."

He grinned. "Both, actually. I thought perhaps we might do it—over dinner."

"Dinner?" I croaked. Was he really asking me out on a date?

"I know cooking is your occupation, but you still have to eat, right?" He gave me a dazzlingly wide smile. "Do you like Chinese? I thought we might get a booth at Wung Foo's. It always seems pretty quiet there."

"That's because ninety percent of his business is take-out," I said, and we laughed. "Sure, that sounds good. What time?"

"Does seven work for you?" He paused, and then added, "Tonight?"

That caught me off guard. I'd anticipated tomorrow. "Tonight?" I repeated.

"I realize it's short notice, but as it happens, I have tonight off. So I thought—"

I held up my hand. "You don't need to explain. Tonight's fine. Seven's fine. I—I'll meet you there."

"Excellent. I'm sure it will be a very useful evening." He walked around to the driver's side of his car and opened the door. "I'll take your space, if you don't mind. The lot seems quite full today." His eyes twinkled and he smiled. I noticed the dimples that accentuated either side of his well-shaped lips. "Just be careful backing up. I'm rather fond of my front fender."

Gee, he was hilarious. But I supposed when someone looked like he did, a sense of humor probably wasn't all that important.

SIXTEEN

Nick was sitting in the window when I got back to Hot Bread, looking none the worse for wear. I wiggled my fingers in greeting as I opened the front door, and got an indifferent stare for my trouble. Chantal was behind the counter, cleaning up after the last of the lunch crowd. She glanced up as I entered and raised a hand to her forehead in dramatic fashion.

"Ah, *chérie*, you are back. Thank goodness."

I set my purse down and walked over to the counter. I lifted the lid on the glass case, removed a brownie, and bit into it. "What's wrong? Bad day? Don't tell me Ramona Hickey was complaining again."

"Ach, not the customers. Our boy over there." She pointed an accusing finger in Nick's direction. "He seems to have overdosed on naughty pills today."

I glanced over at Nick, who still sat serenely in the window, tail curled under him. "He looks calm to me."

"Now he is. You should have seen him earlier. *Mon Dieu!* He shook off every collar I attempted to put on him, the rascal."

I smothered a chuckle. "Maybe having Nick as your pet jewelry model isn't such a good idea. Maybe you should look for a more docile animal—a pit bull perhaps?"

"Very funny." Chantal stuck out her tongue, then creased her brow. "I am very tempted, but—Nick is just so handsome! And he photographed so well in the poses Remy took. I swear, I don't know what got into him today. It was almost as if he were possessed." She lowered her voice to a whisper at the last word.

I glanced at Nick over my shoulder. "What do you say to that, Nick?" I asked. "Are you possessed by an evil spirit?"

He hopped down from the window and sashayed over to where I sat. He reared back on his haunches and wiggled one paw in the air, while the other grazed his neck.

"*Ma-ROW!*"

I chuckled. "I think he just doesn't like to have anything confining on him. I told you, he's a free spirit. Anyway, he seems fine to me."

"Yeah, he is now. Earlier though he was acting like a little devil. He knocked over that pouch of Scrabble tiles you had on the back counter and was pushing them all over the floor."

I shot Nick a sharp glance. He stared innocently back at me.

"The Scrabble tiles again, huh? Maybe he just wanted to play," I offered. "Ollie said that Nick Atkins was teaching him the game."

"The cat plays Scrabble." Chantal put both hands on her slender hips. "Now *that* I would pay to see."

"Ollie said he was just as smart as a dog, and I don't doubt it for a second."

Nick blinked twice. "*Er-ow*," he squeaked, then turned and dove underneath the back table. He emerged a moment later, black nose to the floor, edging out three small wooden tiles.

"Oh, ho, what's this!" I bent over and picked up the squares. They were the same ones I'd found him playing with before: a B, an I, and an F. I set the tiles on the table and tapped my finger against the tablecloth. "That is odd."

Chantal walked over, glanced at the tiles. "FIB," she said. "Nick can spell?"

"No, I arranged them like that, but—it's the second time I've caught him playing with these particular letters, and it strikes me as particularly odd, today especially since my visit to KMG has convinced me more than one of my little group of suspects is lying through their teeth."

Chantal let out a chuckle. "Well, perhaps we have underestimated Nicky. In addition to being a game player, perhaps he is also psychic."

Nick hopped up on the table, reared his paw back, and scattered the tiles back to the floor.

"Nick!" I cried, bending over to retrieve them. "Bad kitty."

"I told you," Chantal said, tapping her foot. "Whether you choose to believe me or not, he's possessed by something—or someone."

I picked up the tiles, walked over to the back counter, and slipped them inside the worn case, which I tucked promptly in the drawer. I looked down. Nick hovered at my ankles, regarding me with a watchful stare.

"You can play with them again when you learn how to behave," I remonstrated, wagging my finger at him.

"*Grr-up*," he chirped. Then he flopped down on one side and gave his manhood a good lick.

So much for discipline.

After Chantal departed, I dug out Ollie's number and placed a call. He answered on the second ring. "Well, well. Seems as if you're making a habit of this, Nora. Not that I'm complaining." He laughed.

"I hope you don't mind, but sometimes talking things out with someone else gives me a fresh perspective." *Talking it out with someone who can answer me certainly doesn't hurt either*, I added silently, giving Nick a side glance.

"Not at all. I'm used to it. Nick used to do the same thing, so talk away."

I hit the highlights of my trip to KMG, my conversation with Patti, my almost run-in with Kevin, the conversation I'd overheard between Buck and Tabor, and finally, my findings in Alicia Samuels's office. The only thing I left out was my run-in with Detective Daniel. I'd omitted filling in Chantal as well. I didn't need to hear her romantic predictions right now—especially when there was nothing romantic at all about our upcoming dinner.

"Nick never mentioned an Alicia Samuels, and I never heard of her," Ollie said when I'd finished. "It is puzzling, but you also have to take into consideration her door was unlocked, right? That means lots of other people could have just walked in and used her office, the same as you today."

"True," I agreed. "Getting back to Patti Simmons—she seemed more than a little shaken when I told her I used to report on crime back in Chicago. I know I wasn't mistaken about her reaction. I'm just not certain which part elicited it."

"Maybe she just couldn't picture you hanging around people who wear five-thousand-dollar suits and carry guns. Your specialty was the mob, right?"

"Yep. Or maybe she's got something to hide. At least I did learn one good thing—Lola's phone is somewhere and still active, or else I wouldn't have gotten that message when I dialed the number." I glanced at the clock on the wall. "Well, thanks for letting me brainstorm with you, Ollie. I've got to start getting ready now. I'm meeting Detective Corleone. I need to find out just what he knows about all this, and I have to do it without tipping my hand on just how involved I am. Any suggestions?"

"Order club soda. Alcohol loosens lips, and you might find yourself revealing a bit too much." I could hear the twinge of irony in his tone. "I speak from experience."

I exchanged a few more pleasantries with Ollie and then hung up. I made sure the downstairs door to the sandwich shop was locked and the CLOSED sign in place, and then headed upstairs to get ready to meet Daniel. Nick followed, arranging himself on my comforter while I sat down on the edge of the bed to pull on fresh stockings.

My mind kept flicking back to that last sentence in Nick Atkins's journal. What could Lola have known about her husband big enough to possibly kill over? That he was cheating on her with Patti? Maybe, if he'd been the aggressor, but from all accounts, Patti was. So then what else could it be?

I sighed. My head hurt from trying to figure all this out.

A squishing sound demanded my attention. I glanced over and saw Nick back on the floor, pushing something around on the hardwood floor with his paw. I cried aloud when I saw what it was.

More Scrabble tiles.

"How on earth did these get up here?" I demanded, giving the cat a stern look. He must have gotten into the pouch and hoarded a small supply to play with. "You have nice catnip toys, Nick. Mice, and some balls. If you lose these tiles, we won't be able to play the game."

He gave me a classic cat look—eyes narrowed, nose up in the air. *"Yargle."*

I looked at the tiles I held in my hand. A G, an O, a T, and a V. "Gotv," I said. I laid the tiles on the bed, moved them around. Togv wasn't a word. I rearranged them again.

GOVT. An abbreviation for government.

"Hm," I said, eyes narrowing. "Maybe this secret of Kevin's has something to do with those big government contracts his company has? That might make sense—maybe Lola found out he was cheating Uncle Sam. But would he kill her over that?" I looked at Nick. "I wonder what Daniel would make of all this."

I stepped into my skirt, pulled my T-shirt over my head, and did a slow turn in front of my full-length mirror. Now that I thought about it, it certainly was a coincidence, my running into Daniel at KMG. Our meeting seemed convenient—perhaps a bit too much so.

Something furry brushed my leg. Nick sat there, his head bobbing up and down.

"Convenient," I murmured. "Like—like he'd been following me. But why would he do that?"

I could think of only one reason—he wanted to know how much I knew about Lola Grainger. But if he wasn't considering reopening the case, why was he so interested?

"Of course," I said to Nick, "he could be interested in me, you know. And he really doesn't have the authority to reopen the case on his own. He's just a fill-in."

Which begged another question—just exactly where

was he from? He'd never mentioned that. What did I know about Detective Daniel Corleone, other than he was blessed with devastatingly good looks?

Hey, if I played my cards right, maybe tonight I'd find out lots of answers. But would they be the ones I wanted to hear?

My iPhone chose that moment to vibrate wildly around on my dresser. I snatched it up, thinking perhaps the good detective had to cancel at the last minute, but the number was one I didn't recognize as local. Frowning, I answered, "Hello."

"Nora Charles?" A man's voice, raspy, a shadow above a whisper floated over the wire. "I've got to talk to you, Ms. Charles. Now."

The voice was oddly familiar but I couldn't quite place it. "I'm sorry. Who is this?"

An impatient sigh, and then, "Lott—Captain Lott. We spoke yesterday. I've got to see you, and right now."

"Is something wrong, Captain?"

He gave a mirthless chuckle. "There's lots wrong, but I think the time has come to make it right." He hesitated and then said, "I lied to you, Ms. Charles. That last night on the boat—things didn't go down quite like I described it."

I gripped the phone more tightly. "What do you mean?"

"What do you think I mean? I lied."

"Oh? How so, Captain?"

"Well, there was a lot of drinkin' goin' on, but Mrs. Grainger, she retired a lot earlier than the others." He paused. "'Round about midnight, I thought I heard her out on deck. And there were scuffling sounds. Like a fight."

"A fight? Did you see who Mrs. Grainger was fighting with?"

"No. It was pretty dark. I only saw a shadow. I went back

to the galley, but not long after that, Mrs. Grainger went missing. And . . ."

"Yes?" I prompted as he fell silent.

"When I came on board today, I found some drawers open that I know I'd shut and some cabin doors open. Someone was on board here."

I thought of Daniel and said, "Maybe it was the police."

"I don't think so. I think someone was on board lookin' for something. That night, I heard Mrs. Grainger tell someone she'd found it. Maybe they're after whatever 'it' is. Mrs. Grainger had a lot of hidey-holes for stuff—sometimes she could be a real pack rat."

"Where are you now, Captain Lott?"

"On the *Lady L*. Pier nine, slip seven."

"Okay. I have an appointment with Detective Corleone at seven thirty, but I'm sure if I call him—"

"No, no police." Panic and something else tinged his voice—fear? "Listen, there's no time, trust me. You've got to come here now—right now."

The line went dead. I swore with frustration and clicked off the phone. I didn't want to cancel my date—excuse me—appointment—with Daniel, but I felt the urgency of hearing what Lott had to say. Plus I was curious as to what Lola might have hidden. "I guess I have no choice," I muttered. "This could break the case wide open."

I reached for the phone, and as my fingers grazed the case, it rang again. This time the Cruz PD number showed up, and I answered. "Hello."

"I'm really sorry," Daniel said, sounding apologetic, "but I'm going to have to cancel tonight, Nora. The detective who was supposed to be on duty tonight had to take off—his wife's having a baby. So I'm afraid we'll have to put off our conversation yet again."

I pushed my hand through my hair and inwardly breathed a sigh of relief. "Don't worry about it. It's fine, really."

"I promise I'll make it up to you. I *will* call you tomorrow."

I hung up and eyed Nick. "Problem solved. He has to work."

Nick ambled over to my purse, and now had my car keys between his teeth. He padded over to me and dropped them into my lap. I gave his head a quick pat, tucked the keys into the pocket of my jacket, and went down the stairs. As I exited the side door, I felt something furry brush my leg. I glanced down.

Nick squatted beside me, his golden eyes wide.

"Oh, no." I unlocked the door and pushed it open. "Sorry, pal, you're staying here. The marina's no place for you."

Nick turned and, tail held high, marched straight to my SUV. He squatted down beside the passenger door and stared at me as if to say, "Get a move on, human. We've got things to do."

I sighed. "Okay," I said. I unlocked the car, then walked around to the passenger side and swung the door open. "You can go with me. But you're staying in the car—no arguments."

Nick drew back his lips to show his sharp teeth and hissed.

"I said no arguing, dammit."

Another hiss, louder. He jumped onto the passenger seat in one fluid motion, paw scraping against the soft leather.

I got in, slipped the SUV into reverse, and started to

back out of the driveway, conscious of his golden gaze boring into me. I stole a sidelong glance. His eyes were slits, his lip curled on one side. If ever a cat could look pissed, Nick was the epitome of it right now.

"Determined, aren't you? Okay, okay, you win. I'll think about it," I mumbled. "If you're good, then maybe I'll let you accompany me onto the boat."

No hiss, but a slight *grr* emanated from between his lips. I could almost envision two horns sprouting up in place of his ears, and that black plume of a tail morphing into a pitchfork. Chantal was right—today Nick had definitely become one devil cat.

"Fine. You can come with me. But you stick close, y'hear?"

"*Er-up.*" That little stinker blinked twice, turned around in a circle, then lay down on the seat and promptly closed his eyes, the corners of his lips tipped up in an almost human expression of triumph.

Oh, sure. He knew I'd give in. How could I not? If I were to be entirely truthful with myself, I was glad to have someone else along on this quest—even if my companion was of the four-footed variety.

SEVENTEEN

Dusk was settling in as I parked my SUV near the marina. Nick, curled up in a ball on the backseat, jerked to attention as I shut the motor off. I got out and walked around to the passenger side and opened the door. He stretched his forepaws, then hopped out, landing in a furry ball at my feet. I cast a rueful glance at my dinged rear fender as I locked the car and then started toward the pier, Nick trotting right along beside me. Midway down I halted and pulled a slip of paper from my sweater pocket.

"Pier nine, pier nine." I gave a quick glance around. "How do I find pier nine? There are no numbers on these things. Must one be psychic, like Chantal?"

Nick regarded me for a moment, his head cocked to one side. Then he ambled over to one of the slips and squatted over to one side.

"What, tired already? Come on—help me find pier nine."

When he made no move to get up, I moved closer. As I approached him, he sprang up, and I saw what his body had covered—the numbers were posted off to the side of the slips, not in the middle. I'd been looking in the wrong spot—how helpful of Nick to show me the error of my ways.

"Well, thanks," I said to him.

"*Er-ul*," he trilled, whiskers tipping up just a tad.

"Yes, I can tell you're pleased with yourself. Maybe Chantal's not that far off the mark. Maybe you are psychic," I said. "Or psycho."

His whiskers twitched, and he fell into step beside me as I continued on down the line. We passed pier thirteen—twelve to the right, and then suddenly nine loomed in front of me. My eyes widened at the sight of the sleek boat that was the size of a small airplane. Sure enough, the name *Lady L* was emblazoned in scarlet script along its side. A slight breeze sprang up, and I wrapped my thin cardigan more tightly around my shoulders. Even though it was early April, the temperature was barely sixty degrees—colder than usual for this time of year in Southern California. We approached the boat, and I saw the gangplank was down—an invitation to board. I shivered involuntarily. It was quiet—almost too quiet.

Nick must have sensed it, too, because he pawed at my legs.

We stepped onto the deck and Nick turned around in a circle, head lifted. I felt a chill steal through my entire body, and I squared my shoulders. "Well, if this were a *Thin Man* movie," I said to Nick, "the first thing we'd find here would be Lott's body, staring sightlessly into space." I took a quick glance around. "We're okay so far. No body."

Yet, I added silently.

The boat was pitch-dark; apparently Lott had been afraid to put on a light. Good thing I'd come prepared. I dug into my other pocket for my mini-flashlight, courtesy of the good people at QVC, and switched it on. A bright circle of light cut into the blackness. "Captain Lott," I called, my voice just above a stage whisper. "Captain Lott, it's Nora Charles. I'm here and I'm alone, as you requested. Where are you?"

The yacht was silent—deadly silent.

At my feet, Nick let out a little bleat. "Yeah, Nick. I know. I don't have a good feeling about this, either," I muttered. I moved forward, my eyes darting to and fro, looking for some movement, a shadow, anything—some assurance that another living person was aboard the vessel.

"Captain Lott," I called again, a bit more loudly this time. "Are you here? It's Nora Charles. I'm here, and alone, as you requested."

Suddenly I stopped still. Had I imagined it, or had I just heard the faintest sound—a creak, like an unoiled door closing ever so softly? I turned in that direction, then jumped at the sensation of needles digging into my calf and looked down to see Nick, his claw clamped firmly around my leg, as if imploring me to go no farther.

I hesitated, then raised my voice again. "Captain Lott? Are you here?"

My gut told me I'd get no answer, and it was correct. Nothing greeted us but utter and complete silence, so thick you could cut it with a knife.

I shook my leg free of Nick's clawing grasp and moved slowly forward. I felt along the wall and my fingers found a light switch. I flicked it on and immediately the cabin was lit in a soft glow. Off to my right was what appeared to be the main cabin. It was decorated in soft blue, the furniture fine leather, the rug a thick, plush pile. It looked comfortable—homey, as if a woman's fine hand had decorated. The breeze off the water wafted through the cabin, eerily quiet except for Nick's ragged breathing and the sound of the waves lapping against the yacht's side.

I shut off my flashlight, stuffed it back in my pocket, and proceeded slowly down the long corridor. There were doors on each side of the walkway—I assumed these led to the individual staterooms. I walked to the first one, turned the knob. The door swung inward at my touch.

The bedroom was elegantly appointed, a king-size bed commandeered a good portion of the room, its navy quilted comforter drawn back to reveal satin sheets in a soft teal blue. The furniture seemed to be of good quality—oak, if I wasn't mistaken. There was one end table and a long dresser with an ornate mirror positioned against the far wall. The other boasted a large armoire on which rested a flat-screen television and a Bose sound system.

I wondered if all the rooms were so lush. Most likely they would be. Apparently nothing was too good for Grainger's guests.

Nick's claws dug into my ankle again, and I let out a little yelp of pain. "Will you stop that?" I pushed at his rotund fanny with the toe of my shoe. "Come on—we've lots more to explore. He's got to be around somewhere."

No one was more surprised at my sudden bravado than me. Any fear I felt was overshadowed by my niggling sense of curiosity. Where in hell was Lott? He'd sounded desperate enough on the phone. Had something happened? Had someone else come to the yacht, maybe scared him away?

Lord, I hoped that was the reason he wasn't answering and not . . . something else.

I opened the door to the next room, and my breath caught in my throat. She was lying faceup, spread-eagled across the slick satin sheets, arms flung out in a gesture of helplessness, one perfect bullet hole in the middle of her forehead, and another gone through her chest, judging from the big red stain in the center of her blouse. My feet took me forward, like a somnambulist caught in a dream, overcome by the shock of my discovery. My aforementioned luck had run out.

In death, Patti Simmons's eyes didn't appear as blue as the deep blue sea. Instead they were mere slits, glassy like hardened marbles. Her lips were twisted in a grimace: Shock? Surprise? My gaze went to her forehead and that perfect, round bloodied hole. Long-buried memories forced their way into the forefront of my brain. I'd seen killings like this before, way back when I'd first started writing crime stories in Chicago. They hadn't been pretty then, either.

"Execution," I murmured. "It looks like a murder, execution style." I continued to stare, my eyes riveted in fascination to the bullet hole. "What in hell is she doing here anyway?" I paused as a sudden thought came to me.

Had Patti been the person who'd gotten under Lott's skin—whom he seemed to be afraid of? Had Lott shot her? Was that the reason he'd vanished?

Or was yet another person responsible?

Nick's ears suddenly perked straight up. He cocked his head to one side, as if listening to something, and then began to frantically paw the air in front of him. His claws dipped down, clamped firmly in the hem of my skirt, and he gave a little tug.

His meaning was obvious—he wanted me to leave, which was, no doubt, the prudent thing to do.

But I wasn't quite ready to do that. Call it leftover investigative reporter syndrome, but there was more to be learned from studying the scene here; I'd bet every sandwich in my shop on it. I shook myself free of him, no easy feat—this cat was strong with a capital S. I finally managed to disengage his claw and I looked down at him. His eyes were wide, and if I didn't know better, I could swear they held a hint of panic. I felt compelled to bend down and give his head a reassuring pat. He meowed plaintively and I could feel a tremor rock his furry body as he pressed himself against my ankles.

"Okay, Nick. We'll go. Just give me a minute, buddy, okay?"

I moved closer to the bed and stared down at Patti. Nick hopped up on the dresser next to the bed, tail bristling, swishing impatiently to and fro. I pointed. "Look at her hand. Doesn't it seem like she's pointing to something?"

"*Er-ow!*" Nick answered. He twisted his head toward the doorway.

"Yes, yes, we'll go. I just need a minute more."

I followed the line of her finger. There was a small chest in one corner of the room. I moved over to inspect it. It was medium-size, made of elegant carved wood. There were brass handles on either side. I grasped the handles and pulled. The chest was lighter than I'd expected. As I turned, something caught my eye. I set the chest back down and moved to the spot where it had previously stood.

"Look at this floorboard," I said to Nick. "The edge is slightly raised."

I bent over, gave it a tug. The floorboard jerked upward, and I caught a flash of yellow inside a small hole in the floor. I bent down and pulled out an eight-by-ten manila envelope.

"Well, well. Maybe we finally got lucky." I turned the envelope over in my hand. Could this be what Lott said Lola had hidden? What he thought an intruder had been searching for?

I sucked in my breath and resisted the impulse to tear it open right then and there. Best to get off the boat and back home first. I'd see what was inside, and then decide whether or not to call Daniel. Maybe not the wisest course of action, considering, but—it was the one I'd decided to take.

Suddenly Nick let out a "*meow*" and dived right at me. His teeth bared, he clamped them right into the envelope. Startled, I loosened my grip and he jerked it out of my hand in one movement. He vanished underneath the bed, claws clicking against the polished hardwood floor.

"Nick," I muttered. "What the hell—"

"*Meow*," came from the depths underneath the bed. "*Ffft.*"

"Nick, dammit. What's wrong? What do you sense?"

I leaned over and raised the sheet. Nick cowered in the corner, the envelope clamped securely underneath his paws.

"Nick," I said sternly. "Get out here right now. Give me that envelope."

He drew back his lips and hissed.

"Hey! What did I tell you about attitude, mister?"

My hand snaked underneath the bed toward the envelope. Nick pushed it farther underneath himself, hissed again, and took a swipe at me with one paw. I pulled my hand back just in time to avoid getting a nasty scratch.

"What is wrong with you?" I cried. Good God, maybe he really was possessed. I could think of no other reason why this formerly docile cat would suddenly turn into a mini-tiger. I stared at him, half-expecting to see horns sprout up on his forehead at any second.

"I'm going to get that envelope, Nick. Scratch me and you'll pay for it, I warn you. No steak, no chicken, none of Hot Bread's lunch leftovers for a week. Just canned Purina, how do you like that, you spoiled little brat?" I lifted the edge of the sheet and had just started to inch my arm toward Nick again when the door to the stateroom was kicked open. I snapped my arm back and turned around, my jaw dropping at what I saw.

Two police officers stood framed in the doorway, guns drawn—and pointed right at me.

"Hands up, lady," one of them said.

Startled, I raised both arms slowly. "Officers, you're making a mistake. This isn't what it looks like . . . I can explain."

The taller of the two shot me a look that clearly indicated he wasn't buying what I was trying to sell. "You can tell your story at headquarters," he barked. "Right now you're under arrest. You have the right to remain silent . . ."

EIGHTEEN

"Well, I certainly didn't expect to see you tonight, Nora—and certainly not in my interrogation room."

After I'd been taken down to Police Headquarters (over loud protests, I might add), I'd been put into this small room with only a table and two chairs. I asked if I was being formally charged, but my question fell on deaf ears. I was tempted to make a scene, demand I be allowed to make my one phone call—the only problem is, I had no idea who I would call. I didn't want to bother Chantal or Remy, I hadn't gotten around to hiring a lawyer yet, Louis was out of town—and I certainly couldn't call Ollie. For one thing, I hadn't known him that long. For another, I didn't want to listen to the "told you this case was dynamite" lecture that I had no doubt I'd be subjected to. Plus, I was worried about Nick.

What had happened to him after I'd been hauled here? The last I'd seen of him, he was hiding beneath the bed—had the police searched the entire room? If they were anything like the Chicago force, they'd have left no stone unturned—and if Daniel Corleone was in charge, no doubt every nook and cranny had been thoroughly examined. I started to replay those last few moments before everything had been turned upside down over in my mind, but I confess all cohesive thought went out the window the minute Detective Corleone entered the room. He carried a thick sheaf of papers in a plain brown file folder and wore no jacket, just a light pink shirt, no tie, and his collar was loosened. I could see a glint of a gold chain around his neck as he eased himself onto the wooden chair across from me.

"Yeah." I leaned forward, resting both my elbows on the hardwood table. "Fancy meeting you here. I didn't expect to see you tonight, either, since you canceled our da— our appointment."

If he'd noticed my slip, he paid it no heed, just opened the folder and started to riffle through the papers within. "Your appearance on the *Lady L* does complicate matters," he said at last. "Would you mind telling me what you were doing there?"

My eyes searched his face, but his expression remained impassive. "I was following up on a lead."

"A lead?" His fingers hesitated over the stack of papers. "What sort of lead?"

I shifted, trying to find a comfortable position on the hard wood chair. The furniture wasn't built for comfort. "I—ah—I don't really know if I can say. The conversation was confidential between me and one of my sources."

"Ah, yes. Your sources. So you have been playing detective?"

"I don't know if I'd call it playing exactly."

He leaned back in the chair, and a sigh of exasperation escaped his lips. "I don't think you realize the trouble you are actually in. Two officers caught you standing over the dead body."

"Oh, for the love of God," I burst out, "you know damn well I didn't kill Patti Simmons. What was my motive, for heaven's sake? Not to mention the fact no weapon was found on or near my person."

His lips twitched slightly, as if he were choking back a laugh. I personally didn't see what was so damned funny about my situation. He had nothing to hold me here on, and he damn well knew it.

"That may be true," he said at last. "But I'd still like to know what you were doing on the *Lady L*. You didn't mention any plans to go down to the docks when I called earlier."

I grimaced. "Well, my original plans were canceled, as you well know. Besides, I didn't have those plans when we spoke."

"You could have called back."

"Why? If I had, would you have blown off work and gone with me?"

"I might have."

I sighed and shifted again in the chair. "I bet you get a lot of confessions in here, just so people can get out of this damned chair," I muttered.

"Not as many as you might think." He crossed his arms over his chest, regarded me with a benign expression. "I'm waiting."

"And if I refuse to talk—wait, don't tell me. You've got ways to pull the information out of me, right?"

He leaned across the table, his nose scant inches from mine. "I have a few."

Ooh, did that conjure up images. I could hear my heart pound in my chest as some of those ways flitted through my brain. Champagne, soft lights, music, the two of us dancing cheek to cheek . . .

"How does spending the night locked in a jail cell appeal to you?"

My bubble burst and the image of us doing the cha-cha faded, replaced by one of me trying to get comfortable on a metal cot. So much for that. I sucked in a breath. "You wouldn't! On what charge?"

"Trespassing, for one. Breaking and entering for another."

"I didn't break into anything," My temper flared. "The yacht was wide open, and besides, I was invited aboard." I paused and bit my lower lip.

I'd have liked to wipe the satisfied smirk off his face as he opened the file folder again and leaned both his elbows on top of it. "Ah, now that's more like it," he said. "Who invited you aboard, Nora?"

I clamped my lips together and glared at him.

"Well, I know it wasn't Kevin Grainger," he said. "So there's only one other person it could possibly be. What did Shelly Lott want? Why did he want to see you tonight, and why on board the *Lady L*?"

I resisted the impulse to sneer. "I don't know what he wanted. He wasn't on board."

"That's where you're wrong."

My breath constricted in my throat, and my hand fluttered over my chest. "Oh my God—he was there? You found him?"

"We did."

I swallowed. "Is he—was he—did you find him dead, too?"

"No. We found him in the galley, unconscious. He's at Cruz General with a monster headache. They're keeping him overnight for observation." He paused. "He admitted calling you, and then he thought he heard noises—scuffling noises, like someone prowling around. Something conked him on the back of the head and that's the last he remembers."

"Did you find the weapon?"

"We're still searching the yacht. Maybe the prowler took it with him."

He reached across the table and captured one of my hands in his. The feel of his flesh against mine sent my senses skyrocketing, particularly when he started to rub his forefinger against the back of my hand.

"I'm not the enemy, Nora," he said softly. "Believe it or not, you were brought in for your own protection."

I arched one brow and jerked my hand away. "In handcuffs?"

"Well, I wanted to be certain you didn't do something foolish—like try to run off and find the person who killed Patti Simmons."

"We wouldn't be that stupid," I began and then stopped. I regretted my little slip the minute the words came out of my mouth. Daniel's eyes lit up like a Christmas tree.

"*We?* So you did bring someone with you?"

I swallowed. I certainly wasn't about to squeal on Nick—I had a feeling telling Daniel I'd brought a cat along with me for company would only make me appear daffier than he already thought me to be, and I did not want him to think of my name as synonymous with the term *crazy cat woman*. "Of course not," I said. "It was just a slip of the tongue. I guess I said it because I had been thinking of bringing you with me."

His look of surprise was genuine. "You were? Really?"

"I told Lott I was supposed to meet you, and I'd bring you along, but he was adamant I come alone. He admitted he'd lied to me the other day about what happened on the yacht the night Lola died. He wanted to talk to me." I paused. "And he told me he thought someone had been poking around on the yacht. He thought they might have been looking for something Lola might have hidden."

"I see." Daniel's eyes were dark. "And did he say what that might be?"

I shook my head. "He just wanted me to come right down, alone. When I arrived, the yacht was dark. I put the lights on, started looking around."

Daniel's lips slashed into a thin line of annoyance. "Rather a foolish move, don't you think? The killer could have still been on board."

"It's possible. I'm positive I heard a floorboard or a door creak, a few minutes before I found Patti Simmons's body."

His eyes searched my face. "And that's all you found, correct? Nothing else?"

I shot him a look of mock innocence. "Of course, Detective. Why do you ask? Don't you believe me?"

"In a word—no."

"Well, tough."

He looked at me for a long moment. Suddenly he reached into his pocket and pulled out his cell phone. He glanced at the screen, shook his head, then murmured, "Excuse me," and picked up the file folder and went back out the door. I took the opportunity to rise out of the chair and do a few stretches. If they kept me in this room much longer on that chair, I was definitely going to have to visit a chiropractor. Thankfully he returned about ten minutes later, with two file folders tucked under his arm this time. He set them down and motioned for me to take my seat.

"My men have finished searching the yacht," he said. "They didn't find anyone on board."

My head snapped up. "No one? No one at all?"

"That's what I just said. No one, or anything hidden—including the murder weapon or whatever was used to knock Lott out."

"The killer must have taken it with him." I couldn't resist a shudder. We'd had a pretty close call, Nick and I, and I couldn't help but wonder how the heck he'd gotten out of there unseen, and what he'd done with the envelope he'd snatched from me.

I felt a sudden urge to get home, make sure my feline compadre was all right. "How much longer are you going to hold me here?"

"Why? Is there somewhere you have to be?"

"You and I both know you can't hold me without evidence, and you have none against me," I returned. "Or is this the part where you're going to ask me if I want a lawyer?"

Daniel paused and sighed.

"You're not under arrest, Nora. You're not a suspect. But I'd appreciate your cooperation. Is that all right with you?"

I was tempted to ask what might happen if it weren't, but instead smiled sweetly. "Of course. I'm always happy to cooperate with the police in any way I can."

"Good. Now, do you recall Lott saying anything about Patti Simmons when you had your first conversation?"

"He didn't say much about her at all, just that she'd spilled some wine on the chair cushions and it upset Mrs. Grainger. But I can't vouch for the veracity of that account, because when he called me tonight, he told me he'd lied before."

"Did he say what he'd lied about?"

I shook my head. "Do you think he called Patti also? Is that why she was on board?"

"I really couldn't say at this time."

My eyes narrowed. I was getting that odd vibe from him again, the vibe that told me he knew more than he was letting on—a lot more. "You know something," I said.

"I'm supposed to know things," he replied. "I'm the police."

Nice wiseass answer. "Perhaps this would be a good time to have that discussion we've been putting off—about Lola Grainger's death not being an accident."

His eyes widened. "I don't recall saying that. I believe I said I agreed with you that certain aspects of the investigation could have been handled better."

I half rose out of my chair, palms splayed across the desktop. "Listen, Detective. I may have quit reporting full-time, but my instincts are still with me. And they're telling me you know a lot more about the Lola Grainger case than you want me to know."

He looked at me in much the same way one would look at a maiden aunt afflicted with Alzheimer's, lips twisted in an expression of pity. "Are they, now."

"Yes, they are. Adrienne Sloane thought her sister was murdered, and quite frankly, I'm inclined to agree with her." I paused. "Honestly, for someone so interested in seeing justice done, I can't understand why you're so unwilling to try and track Adrienne down. After all, she might not have gotten on that plane to Bermuda. Maybe she's holed up somewhere. She might have some important information to share."

He picked up the folder, tapped the edge of it against the desk. "I greatly doubt that."

"Why? You haven't even tried—"

"It's kind of hard to get information out of a dead woman."

My jaw dropped and I stared, stunned at Daniel's casual confirmation of what Ollie had told me Nick Atkins had thought he'd seen. "Adrienne is dead—that's terrible," I stammered. "Are you sure?"

His blond head inclined in a curt nod. "Quite sure, yes."

"Oh. Well, do you know how she died? Where was her body found?"

He looked me straight in the eye. "I do. Her body was found in the infirmary of the Metropolitan Correctional Center in Chicago."

My breath caught, threatened to choke me. "P-prison? She died in prison? But—that's impossible! How could her body have gotten there?"

"It was there because she was a resident."

I shook my head. "I'm sorry. I'm confused."

He removed a sheet of paper from the folder and passed it across to me. "Read for yourself. Adrienne Sloane died in prison, the apparent victim of an asthma attack. She choked on her own vomit." He paused. "And her sister, Lola Sloane Grainger, claimed her body—two years ago."

NINETEEN

It was close to eleven o'clock when the police cruiser dropped me off at Hot Bread. Daniel had insisted on a police escort for me, over my protests that I could take a cab. For my own protection, he'd said. Personally, I had the notion he thought that, left to my own devices, I'd head right back to the marina, and he'd have been right. I was dying of curiosity—and worry. I needed to know what happened to Nick.

I let myself in through the store entrance, switched on the lights, and went straight into the kitchen. My rumbling stomach reminded me I hadn't had anything to eat since lunchtime. I pulled eggs, a slab of bacon, some boiled ham, and a stick of cheddar cheese out of the fridge and set them on the counter. I put some slices of bacon on a plate and slipped it into the microwave, then set a frying pan on the stove on low flame. I sliced some ham and cheddar, then cracked eggs in a small bowl, added a dash of milk, and pulled my whisk out of the drawer. A few minutes later I poured the mixture into the frying pan, added some bits of the bacon slices and chopped-up ham and cheddar. Ten minutes later I was seated at the table nearest the rear entrance, a fluffy omelet and glass of milk in front of me. My fork was halfway to my lips when I paused.

Was I mistaken, or was that a scratching sound at the rear door?

I gave the omelet a longing look, set down the fork, crossed over to the door, and opened it. Nick squatted there, golden eyes wide. His fur was matted and he had some leaves and twigs sticking out of his back. His white ruff was slightly soiled, but otherwise, he looked none the worse for wear. As I stared at him, startled, he pushed past me and walked right inside, straight over to where I'd been sitting. He hopped up on my chair, squatted right in front of my plate, and proceeded to eat my omelet.

I stared at him, and then closed the door and hurried over to where he was busily chowing down on my dinner. I snatched him up and enveloped him in a big hug.

"Nick! You're all right." I held him back a bit and frowned. "How did you get all these leaves in your fur? What happened? Where have you been? And what happened to that envelope?"

"*Er-up!*" He blinked at me and then his tongue darted out to graze my cheek.

"Aw, I'm glad to see you, too. But how in hell—"

"*Meower*," he bleated and squirmed out of my arms, gave me a baleful look, then squatted back in front of the plate. He continued eating.

"Okay, I get it. First things first."

I was damn curious as to what had transpired—maybe even as curious as a cat. I had no idea, though, how I was ever going to find out what exactly had gone down—probably because the one person who could tell me couldn't talk. He glanced up from the plate and flicked his tail, and I got a good whiff of him.

"Hoo boy," I cried, waving my hand in the air. "You smell like you've been digging ditches."

I paused as a sudden thought occurred to me and I gave Nick a stern look. "Is that what you did with the envelope? Did you bury it somewhere?"

He glanced over his shoulder at me and I swear he grinned.

"Like a dog—that's an understatement." I shook my head. "Well, fine, be that way. Tomorrow you and I will take a ride back to the 'scene of the crime,' so to speak. Maybe we'll pay Ollie a visit, too. I've got a lot I need to talk over with him."

My stomach growled again. I gave it a swift pat, crossed back to the fridge, pulled out some more eggs and cheddar. I saw Nick's head jerk up as I closed the refrigerator door.

"Oh, no." I wagged my finger at him. "You've had an entire omelet. *My* entire omelet, to be exact. Now it's my turn."

He tossed me a plaintive look. "*Ew-werr*," he said, and then began to purr softly. I set the eggs and cheese on the counter and went over, gave his ears a quick scratch.

"I really wish you could talk, Nick. Tell me where you've been, how you got so dirty—and what you did with that envelope. But not to worry—I'll figure something out." I wrinkled my nose. "Would you like me to clean you up a bit? Give you a quick bath?"

His head snapped up and then he hopped off the table and, tail held high, stalked over to the far corner, where he flopped on one side and proceeded to lick himself.

"Okay, fine." I laughed as I started beating up some more eggs. "Do it yourself."

"*Meower,*" he answered. Then he coughed up one honey of a hairball.

Yuck.

I'd just finished my omelet and sat down (again) when I heard a soft knock at the back door. I frowned over at Nick, who'd stretched out in front of the back counter and was now fast asleep. I crossed over to the door, opened it a crack, then gave a little cry when I saw who stood outside and swung the door open.

"Ollie! What on earth!"

"Hello, Nora. I hope you're not upset by me dropping by. I know it's very late."

"Are you kidding?" I grinned. "I'm glad to see you. I was planning to call you tomorrow. Come on in. What are you doing here?"

Ollie took off the light jacket he wore and draped it across one arm. "Like I said, I hope you don't mind. I have a few friends on the Cruz force, and I happened to be talking to one when you—ah—happened to drop in."

I felt my cheeks start to flame. "Oh."

"Of course, he didn't tell me all the details, but it seems to me you were pretty brave." His tongue clucked against the roof of his mouth. "You know, you could have called me. I'd have accompanied you."

"Thanks, but I didn't want to bother you."

There was no mistaking the twinkle in his eyes as he answered, "Are you sure? Or could it be you just didn't want me to reiterate my earlier warning to you—you know the one about TNT."

I grinned. "A little bit of both, I guess."

"Fair enough." His eyes darted around the room, lit up as they rested on Nick, who'd arisen, wakened no doubt by the sounds of voices, and was stretching his front paws out. "Ah, and there's little Sherlock—sorry, little Nick now. It'll take me a bit to get used to his new name. He looks splendid, Nora."

"Yeah, pretty splendid indeed considering he had to walk at least twenty miles tonight. It's at least that far from here to the marina, wouldn't you say?"

Ollie's eyes widened. "You took him with you?"

I shrugged. "I know. I should have left him here, but to tell you the truth, I wanted company. And he was pretty insistent on accompanying me."

"Yes, he always did hate to be alone."

I moved over to my coffeepot. "How about I make some coffee and fill you in on what happened? There are some new aspects to this case I sure could use a fresh perspective on."

He held up his hand. "Say no more. I said I'd help you any way I can, and I meant it."

Nick sidled up to Ollie, plopped down right in front of him, and began to purr loudly.

"Ah, he remembers me, I think. How are you, cat formerly known as Sherlock?" He laughed. His gaze swept Nick up and down and he shot me a puzzled look. "Is that a leaf in his fur?"

"Yep. Guess I missed this one." I reached down, plucked it out, and tossed it into the trash. "Say, how would you feel about taking a little ride with us?"

"A ride?" His eyes narrowed. "Now? Where?"

"No, not right now. We'll have some coffee first." I folded my arms across my chest. "As to where—honestly, I'm not sure. It depends."

"Depends on what?"

"On where Nick might have buried the evidence."

Ollie's jaw dropped. "Evidence? Of what?"

"Not sure about that, either," I admitted. I reached for the coffeepot. "Have a seat. It's a long story."

A half pot of coffee later, Ollie was pretty much up to speed.

"It sounds to me as if the killer was specifically after Patti," he observed.

I paused, mug halfway to my lips. "Why do you say that?"

"Because Lott was only knocked out and not killed. Of course, your arrival could have saved the man. We'll probably never know."

I held up my hand. "I'd agree with you, Ollie, if I hadn't seen her body with my own eyes. Patti was killed with two clean shots—head and heart. Do I have to tell you what that means?"

He frowned. "But why would a professional hit man be after her?"

"Maybe he wasn't. Maybe he was after the envelope I found, and she was in the wrong place at the wrong time." I leaned forward and cupped my chin in my hand. "What if Adrienne wasn't off the mark with her suggestion to Nick? Maybe the evidence has something to do with Kevin, and Patti was trying to get it back for him." I sighed. "I asked a friend of mine to check into a possible connection between Grainger and West Coast mobs, but—what if he's not a born-and-bred Californian?"

Ollie considered this, then slowly nodded. "Good point. I can't ever remember reading much about Kevin Grainger's early years, now that you mention it. Most articles that touch on his past begin with college."

"Then there's a chance he's a transplant." I pulled a pad over to me. "I'll make a note to call Hank, have him check out some East Coast crime families, see if anything turns up." I scribbled on the paper, and then met Ollie's gaze again. "The most significant thing I learned tonight, though, is that Nick Atkins was right in what he told you. Adrienne Sloane is dead."

Ollie's eyes widened. "Really? Her body was found?" His tongue darted out, licked at his bottom lip. "Did they—did they also find . . ."

I shook my head. "No, your partner is still MIA. As for Adrienne, well, she didn't die on the docks."

"She didn't?"

I stretched my legs out in front of me. "She died in prison. Complications from an asthma attack, as I understand it—two years ago."

Ollie's eyes popped wide. "*Two years?*" He rubbed absently at his temple. "But that can't be. Nick spoke with her the day he disappeared, and then he got that text—and she was most certainly not in prison."

I reached into my tote and pulled out the sheet of paper Corleone had given me. I placed it in front of Ollie. "See for yourself. It's dated two years ago, and while it's pretty brief, all the salient facts are there. Including the fact she was survived by her only living relative, her sister, Lola Sloane Grainger."

Ollie skimmed the article, then handed it back to me. "This doesn't make any sense at all. If Adrienne Sloane is dead, then who hired Nick? Her ghost?"

"I don't know, but it couldn't have been the real Adrienne Sloane." I took the paper back and eyed him. "It is odd, though. There was a note in Nick's journal—it said he checked her out, and she passed."

Ollie pursed his lips. "Nick may not have done as thorough a job as he should have. Oh, I recall she showed him tons of ID, but as for any background checks—he only did the bare minimum. He was so intrigued by the case, and the potential notoriety . . . Besides, who'd ever expect Lola Sloane to have a jailbird sister?"

"True—let alone one who's already dead."

"What prison did she die in? This article doesn't say."

"Metropolitan Correctional Center in Chicago. Oh!" I stopped speaking as a sudden thought occurred to me. "You said Nick checked out mob families and crime in Chicago. Do you think it could have had anything to do with Adrienne? That perhaps he suspected something wasn't quite right?"

"Nick never said what he was looking for," Ollie said thoughtfully. "If he had suspicions, he never shared them with me."

I thought of the missing journal pages. "Might he have written them down somewhere?"

"He could have."

We sat silently for several minutes, sipping our coffee. At length, Ollie turned back to me. "It just doesn't make sense, Nora. Why would someone masquerade as Lola's dead sister and hire Nick to prove Lola was murdered?"

I tapped my chin. "Why indeed? Unless we're looking at this all wrong. Perhaps there is no masquerade. Maybe the Adrienne Sloane who was in prison isn't dead. Maybe she faked her death. Maybe the woman who came to Nick *is* Adrienne Sloane."

He cocked his head to one side. "O-kay. Why would she fake her own death?"

I shoved the heel of my hand through my hair. "Damned if I know. Maybe it's connected to her prison stay. Maybe she made enemies who swore to kill her."

Ollie scratched at his left ear. "That seems rather melodramatic to me. What could she have done that would be so life-threatening? We need to know more about what she was in prison for. You were in Chicago during this time frame—you never heard of her at all?"

"No, but that doesn't necessarily mean anything." I pushed back from the table and stood up. "I'll look into this more thoroughly but right now, it's time for our field trip." I raised my voice. "Nick!"

The cat rose from his position in front of the stove and trotted over to us. Ollie leaned down to rub his ears, and frowned.

"I never noticed that white streak behind his ear before," he murmured. "Nick had one, too—behind the same ear, I think."

Nick glanced up at us, and his whiskers twitched. "*Er-ow!*"

Ollie laughed. "I'm telling you, he understands every word we say. He's a real smart cat—smarter than some humans."

"And we're about to find out just how smart he is," I said. I picked up my car keys and dangled them in front of Nick, who blinked back at me. Twice.

"Come on, Nick. Flex those kitty paws of yours. It's time for you to dig up some evidence."

TWENTY

Norton Park, located adjacent to the pier, wasn't exactly a small, kiddie-type park. I imagined it was probably quite busy in the daytime, and quite beautiful, too. Fortunately it wasn't one of those that were kept closed at night—anyone could walk, or drive, through its spacious grounds, as Ollie, Nick, and I were doing now. Nick rode shotgun in the front, and Ollie sat in the back, his long legs swung off to the side.

I drove my SUV along its panhandle and wound around its curving roads, past beds of beautiful, multicolored flowers, past the children's park with an honest-to-goodness antique carousel, past the small petting zoo. I turned down a lane heavy with trees, and felt like Snow White when she'd been trapped in the forest after the Huntsman had spared her life and told her to get the hell out of Dodge. It was spooky being here at night, especially with the moon playing peekaboo from behind the dark clouds, appearing at intervals to bathe us in its silvery glow.

"I'm not certain I'm clear on what we're supposed to be looking for," ventured Ollie.

"Neither am I," I replied. "That's Nick's department. I'm hoping he'll let me know when to stop."

"Are you sure this is the right placc?"

"It's situated beside the marina, and it's the only place I can think of where Nick would have gotten so dirty. Let's hope I'm right."

At last we reached the wooded section of the park that was closest to the pier. Nick pressed his nose against the windowpane. As I rounded a fork in the road, he suddenly let out a loud wail.

"Uh-oh, I think I may have passed it." I put the SUV into reverse and slowly backed up. When I got to the fork, Nick tapped his paw against the window and wailed again.

"Okay, okay." I turned onto the wide trail that stretched through the thicket of trees and drove at a snail's pace. "Nick—is anything familiar?" I asked after I'd gone about half a mile.

He sat up on his hind legs and tapped his paws against the glass, his chubby body shaking. I pulled over to the side. "Okay, okay. Don't get excited."

In the backseat Ollie snickered, then looked a bit chagrined when I shot him a look. I couldn't actually blame him too much, though—after all, it was like something out of a fantasy novel. I spoke to Nick like he was a person and could answer me, although to be perfectly honest? I wouldn't have been a bit surprised if he had.

Nick took off at a brisk canter through the heavily wooded area, so fast, in fact, that Ollie and I had a bit of a struggle keeping up. Nick ducked under the low-slung branch of a large elm and almost vanished; a second later we caught sight of him, cantering down the winding path to a small open circle. I could smell the salt air, and knew the pier wasn't too far away. When we reached the clearing, we caught sight of Nick, pacing around a mound of freshly packed earth.

"How on earth did he ever manage to do this?" I muttered. I kicked at the ground with the toe of my sneaker, and Ollie did the same. A few minutes later I saw the edge of an envelope peep out of the brown earth.

"Bingo!" I cried, and bent to retrieve the thick manila envelope out of the hole. As I thrust my hand in, my fingers also came in contact with something hard. "There's something else in this hole." I pulled out the envelope and the other object—a cell phone, covered in leaves and grime. I brushed the leaves off, and saw a tooth mark embedded in its supple leather case.

I waved the phone under Nick's nose. "Did you find this, too? Good Lord, Nick—however did you get both of these off the boat? Did you drag them? Those choppers of yours must be superstrong, just like those forepaws. You're not from this planet, are you? You're from Krypton, right?"

Behind me Ollie chuckled. "If he answers you, do let me know, Nora. I'll be glad to give up the investigation business to act as his agent. It would be no problem to get him into Vegas, maybe even on Letterman's Stupid Pet Tricks."

"If he actually answered me, I assure you—it would be no trick. If there ever was a candidate for the world's first ever talking cat—it's him. But no chance of that ever happening. He has his own method of communicating."

Nick gave me a look as if to say, *Get with the program.*

I ran my hand along the case, and the ridge of my nail fit perfectly into the tooth mark Nick's canines had left. "Nice case," I observed. "Good leather." I slipped the phone into the back pocket of my dark indigo washed jeans, tucked the envelope under one arm, and then started kicking the dirt back into place with my sneaker. Ollie helped, and twenty minutes later we were all back in my SUV. I brushed an errant curl out of my eyes, leaving a streak of mud across one cheek as I turned the envelope over in my hands. I tapped my finger on the tape that sealed it.

"Whatever is in here must be important enough to kill for," I said. I lifted the envelope and shook it. "There's something heavy in here." I let out a low whistle. "Man, if I wasn't impressed with Nick's resourcefulness before, I am now."

Ollie inclined his head toward the wood. "Let's take it back to your house and look at it. This place creeps me out."

We exited the park, but instead of turning right and heading back toward Hot Bread, I made a left.

"Shortcut?" asked Ollie.

I shook my head.

"I just want to take one more look at the yacht. I know, I know—it's crazy, and I'm sure Daniel has men watching it, but—dammit, I just can't figure out how the darn cat did all this."

Ollie laughed. "Haven't you ever learned that in life there are just certain things you have to accept without question? I believe they call it faith."

I drove down the pier, slowing down considerably as we approached slip number nine. We all peered out the window. The yacht looked much as it had when I'd left it, dark and deserted, everything the same save for the yellow crime scene tape stretched across the front entrance. A sudden thought hit me and I glanced over my shoulder at

Ollie. "Maybe this envelope wasn't even Lola's. What if it was Patti's?"

Ollie's eyes narrowed. "Then what was it doing hidden in Lola's stateroom?"

I considered this for a moment. "Maybe Lola found out that whatever's in here had something to do with this secret her husband is supposed to have. I'll bet anything Patti found out Lola took it. They fought over it, and that's how Lola went overboard." I sat back, quite impressed with my deductive reasoning, hoping Ollie was as well.

"So if we go along with your theory and accept that Patti is the one who killed Lola, the only people who would possibly want to see her dead would be (A) the grieving husband, provided he didn't want Patti in his life as the next Mrs. Grainger, or (B) her sister, Adrienne Sloane, who wanted revenge for her sister's murder, but whose very existence is now questionable."

"Oh, I think she definitely exists," I said. "We just aren't sure at the moment if she's dead or alive."

"This case has more twists and turns than the Runaway Train at Disneyland." Ollie sighed. "Nick—human Nick— used to love that ride."

"So do I," I admitted. "Frankly it surprises me Nick Atkins would enjoy something like that. From the little I know." I bit my tongue and stopped speaking.

Ollie laughed. "You can say it. From the little you know, Nick Atkins is a jerk, a real piece of work, not the type of guy who'd enjoy an afternoon at Disneyland. You can say it. I have, and so have many, many others."

I shot him a sheepish grin. "I admit, at first he sounded like a real jerk. But then . . ." I tugged at a curl. "I don't know. I think—maybe I might have ended up liking him."

In the seat next to me Nick made a rumbling sound.

"Most women did." Ollie sighed. "He had a charisma that was difficult to pass up."

"I can't speak to his charisma," I said. "But I certainly can speak to his taste in pets. After all, he adopted little Nick here, the world's smartest cat—right?"

Ollie smiled. "Remember when I told you the cat found you, Nora? Well, it was pretty much the same with Nick. Little Nick found him, not the other way around. Nick was hesitant about having a pet at first, too, but it wasn't long before he was hooked."

I raised one eyebrow. "Really? That sounds like it has all the makings of a very intriguing story."

"Oh, it does." Ollie nodded mysteriously. "Remind me to tell it to you . . . someday."

I glanced over at Nick and cocked one eyebrow. "So— you picked out both me and Atkins to be your master, huh? What's that all about?"

Nick blinked his golden eyes twice. Then he coughed up another huge hairball.

B ack home, I searched in my cabinet and came up with the hairball medicine Chantal had thoughtfully purchased. I put some on a tiny plastic spoon and held it out toward Nick. He hesitated, sniffed at it, then lapped it off the spoon.

"Sorry, pal. I know it probably doesn't taste as good as cherry cough syrup, but this is the best they make for cats. Next time you decide to dig a giant hole, maybe you'll let me help you clean up afterward, instead of doing it all yourself."

He looked at me, squeezed both eyes shut, and stuck his nose up in the air. So much for friendly advice.

I picked up the envelope and carried it to the kitchen table, where Ollie had fresh mugs of coffee waiting. I pulled the cell phone out of my pocket and laid it next to the envelope. Then I took my letter opener, picked up the envelope, and made a clean slit across the tape. I lifted the flap, turned the envelope on its side.

Three photographs fell out, and a square of tissue.

Ollie shot me a puzzled look. "This is it? This is what you think Patti Simmons got herself killed over? This is what tipped Lola off to the big secret about her husband?" He snorted. "Looks like junk to me."

I picked up the first photograph, a black-and-white studio shot of a young man with wide eyes, a pug nose, and light hair. His face was split in a wide, carefree smile. There was something about his eyes that struck a chord in me—maybe it was the oddly haunted expression in them, for one so young—he looked barely seventeen. I turned the photo over.

"Karl Goring," I read. "Who the hell is Karl Goring?"

Ollie, meanwhile, was unwrapping the square of tissue. "There's something hard inside here," he announced. "Lots of tape, too. Whoever wrapped this up did an excellent job."

While Ollie busied himself with the tissue, I turned my attention to the next photograph. It was apparently taken at a dinner honoring the KMG staff, some months before. Seated in a circle around the table were Kevin, Lola, Buck Tabor and his wife, Marshall Connor and a date, and Patti Simmons, obviously alone, seated on Kevin's left. Patti wore a very low-cut dress, with a large brooch square in the middle of her cleavage. The only other piece of jewelry she wore was a ring on the middle finger of her right hand. Her face was turned slightly toward her boss, and there was no denying the light in her eyes as she looked at him, or the look of rapturous happiness on her face.

"God, Patti was in love with Kevin." I shook the photograph in the air. "I mean, it's so obvious in this photo. And look at Lola's face—she sees it, too. How could you miss it!"

Ollie took a quick glance. "Nothing looks out of the ordinary to me."

"That figures. You're a man. Men can't see it. But it's very obvious to a woman. Maybe this is the secret—proof Patti was in love with Kevin."

The last photo had tumbled out facedown. I turned it over. It was a smaller group shot, three men and two women at a table. The men all looked dapper, in three-piece suits. One was smoking a cigar. I turned my attention to the women and pointed to the one on the left.

"She's a redhead in this photo, but I could swear that's Patti Simmons," I said. "That's some dress she's got on. If it were cut any lower, this would be in *Playboy*."

"I don't believe it."

Ollie's eyes were round and wide, practically bugging out of his head. I gripped his arm. "What's wrong?"

"I—I'm not sure," he stammered. "But that picture . . . not Patti. The other woman."

I leaned in for a closer look. The woman seated next to Patti gave the impression of being slender, with long, red-brown hair curling to her shoulders. Her makeup was skillfully applied and showed off high cheekbones, full lips, sparkling eyes. "She's pretty. Why, Ollie, what's wrong about it?"

His voice trembled. "I could be wrong, but I don't think so. I saw her once, when she visited Nick, and I'd seen other pictures. I know that woman." His finger shot out, tapped at the face.

"*She's* the one who hired Nick. *That's* Adrienne Sloane."

TWENTY-ONE

"Adrienne Sloane," I cried and peered more closely at the photo. "Are you sure?"

"Well, let's put it this way. It's the woman who claimed to be Adrienne Sloane. Her real identity is yet to be determined. It's her, I know it as sure as I know my name is Oliver Jebediah Sampson." He stopped speaking abruptly, clapped one hand across his mouth. "Oh, dear!"

Ah, the damage had already been done. I grinned at him. "Jebediah? Really?"

He sniffed. "Yes, really. It was my mother's father's name."

"Oliver Jebediah Sampson. Say—O. J. Sampson. Sounds almost like—"

His hand shot out. "You don't have to say it. I've heard all the jokes a million times since that trial in 1995. Why do you think I never tell people my middle name?" He massaged his forehead lightly with his fingers. "I never told Nick, either. God—he'd never have let me live it down."

I stifled a grin, then turned the photo over and pointed to numbers written in ink on the reverse. "See the date? October, four years ago. It can't be Adrienne. Adrienne would have been in prison then."

Ollie blinked. "Maybe, maybe not. After all, we don't know what she was jailed for, or when. All we know is she supposedly died there two years ago."

"I guess." I traced each of the women's faces with the edge of my nail. "So, let's say this is a photo of Adrienne and Patti—where do they know each other from?"

Ollie leaned in for a closer look. "Well, judging from the attire—one would almost think they were in the world's oldest profession."

I worried my bottom lip as I stared at the photo. "There's something wrong with that theory, though. Kevin's company does work for the government. His HR Department has to do extensive background checks on everyone. If Patti had a prison record, would she have been hired as his confidential admin? I doubt it."

"Background information can be faked. After all, Adrienne Sloane—or whoever she was—apparently was able to do it. Of course, that begs the question, why did she go to all that trouble?"

I got up, crossed over to one of the drawers, and returned holding my Ginsu knife. I picked up the tiny square and made one quick, clean incision. The tissue separated, revealing the object buried square in its middle.

I picked up the ring and turned it over in my hand. It had a thick, gold cigar band, inlaid with a large square cut stone. The cameo in the stone's center was a knight's helmet in profile, and it stood out, deep gold against stark black, giving it an almost 3-D effect. I turned the ring over in my hand, then set it back on the tissue.

"It's definitely an expensive piece. That black stone looks like pure onyx, and the carving is most likely gold, I'm guessing eighteen karat. But I agree, this just doesn't seem like the type of jewelry Patti would own." I studied it, my brow furrowed. I had the distinct feeling I'd seen it—or something similar—somewhere before, but the memory was elusive, like a wisp of smoke.

"Maybe she bought it as a gift," suggested Ollie. "In any event, I wonder why it's in with those pictures."

I rewrapped the ring in the tissue. "I'm sure it means something—but as to what, I wouldn't even attempt to hazard a guess. Onyx is a very energetic stone—the ancient Egyptians used it for protection. Maybe this was her good luck talisman."

I set the rewrapped ring down on top of the photo and reached for the cell phone. I slipped it out of the case and held it up. It was an older model, I'd guess a good four years at least. "Well, Lola didn't go for the newest in phones apparently. This model is several years old. Can't get Internet access or take pictures with this model," Ollie observed.

"My mother always said Lola was a simple, no-non-sense type of woman who didn't care much for frills or bells and whistles. She probably just wanted a simple phone—you know, one you could just turn on and make a call from. She must have felt she didn't require all the other adornments."

I pressed the green button and the phone lit up. "I'm not familiar with this model. I want to find the call history."

I touched the key in the upper-left-hand corner. A screen appeared that said, *Messaging*. Number 5 was voice mail, and the number in brackets after that title indicated there were three voice messages waiting retrieval.

I bit at my lower lip. "We'll need a password for this, right?"

"Maybe there's a way around it. Hit 5."

"Here goes nothing," I said, and pressed the required button. A tinny mechanical voice instructed me to "Please enter your password, then press pound."

"Aargh." I ran both hands through my mass of hair. "Still need a password. Any ideas?"

"Most people use something simple, like a birthday, or a name, or initials."

I had no idea in hell what Lola's birthday was, so I keyed in her name. The mechanical voice said, "Sorry, your password is incorrect. Please try again."

This time I keyed in Kevin's name. Same response. I tried just Lola's initials. Same response.

"We're probably going to get locked out soon," I growled. "Something's gotta work."

"Her anniversary," suggested Ollie. "That's the day after she died—August fifteenth, right? Try that?"

I keyed in the date. Same negative mechanical response. This really sucked.

"Try that date and their combined initials: LKG," Ollie said at last. "If that doesn't work I don't know what to tell you. I'm fresh out of ideas. Nick was the hacker in our partnership."

I keyed that in, and Bingo! The screen changed again. Now it displayed three numbers, which were all the same: 555-621-9875.

"So how do I play 'em?" I asked. "Just highlight the number and hit Enter?"

"Let's try it."

I highlighted the first one, hit Enter. Then I pressed the speaker button so we both could hear. A few seconds later, a woman's tinny voice filled the room.

"Lola? Call me back. I've got some other information for you."

That was it. The caller clicked off. I glanced over at Ollie, whose features had twisted into a deep scowl.

"I could be wrong. I only heard her voice once or twice, when I took a message, you understand . . ."

I stared at him. "Don't tell me you think that voice was Adrienne's?" I picked up the phone, twirled it around. "This baby has a direct line to the afterlife?"

Ollie shifted in the chair. "I could be mistaken."

"Or you might not. If Adrienne Sloane isn't dead—but that can't be." I frowned. "Lola ID'd the body."

"There is another possibility. Two, actually. Lola was in on whatever deception Adrienne was undertaking, or she didn't know the body wasn't her sister's. After all, they were estranged for years. If the body was the same general build . . ."

"If that's so, why any deception at all?" I asked. I grabbed the phone, highlighted the number, then pressed Call. The phone rang once, twice, three times. I was about to disconnect on the sixth ring when the answering machine clicked on.

"Hello, you've reached the desk of Alicia Samuels. I'm not available to take your call at the moment. Please leave a detailed message and I will get back to you as soon as possible."

"This Alicia Samuels again," Ollie said when I'd hung up. "There's got to be some sort of link among these three women—but what?"

A sudden thought occurred to me. I jumped up, went

over, and got my laptop. I booted it up, and then called up the KMG website. I went to the tab marked NEWS AND MEDIA and then clicked on KMG IN THE NEWS. A screen filled with pictures appeared. I scrolled down until one caption caught my eye: *KMG's Marketing Dept accepts Citizen Award.* I clicked on the photo to enlarge it. She was standing in the very last row, her face averted, but enough of it was visible for me to make a positive ID.

Alicia Samuels and Adrienne Sloane were, apparently, one and the same woman.

TWENTY-TWO

"**Y**ou look horrible. Didn't you get any sleep last night?"

I frowned across the counter at Chantal. It was just past nine o'clock, and the worst of the breakfast rush was over. Chantal had bustled in at eight thirty and helped me with my last few customers—a gesture I greatly appreciated, since I was truly running on empty. I'd spent most of what was left of the night tossing and turning, trying to make sense of everything I'd learned and not having much success at all.

I swiped the back of my hand across my forehead and offered my friend a thin smile. "A little. It was a rough night."

"That good, eh?" She shot me a wiseass grin. "Might I ask if the good detective had anything to do with it?"

"He did, in a sense. I spent a good part of the night down at headquarters."

Chantal's eyebrows rose. "Headquarters. Rather an odd choice for a first date, no?"

"It wasn't a date. That's generally where they take you when they find you standing over a dead body."

"Dead body?" she squeaked. "You've got to be kidding."

"Sadly, no."

I hit the highlights, detailing my quest for justice on Lola's behalf, my interviews with Corleone, Lott, and Patti, Lott's mysterious phone call and finding Patti's dead body. I omitted, of course, my midnight sojourn with Ollie, and the fact that Nick had been the one to hide the cell phone and envelope with its packet of photographs and ring. I also mentioned the possibility that Alicia Samuels and Adrienne Sloane could be one and the same, despite the fact that Adrienne Sloane was supposed to have died two years earlier. The story sounded even more fantastic as I went through it step-by-step, and when I'd finished, I couldn't begrudge the look of utter incredulity on Chantal's face.

"Well—it certainly is a puzzler," she said at last. Abruptly she thrust out her hand. "Do you have the photos and ring handy?"

I nodded and motioned for her to follow me into the back room. She took a seat at the table, and I brought out the envelope from its hiding place. I handed it to her, and she took it, turned it over in her hand. She opened the envelope and spilled the contents onto the table. Her eyes lit up as she saw the ring. She picked it up, turning it over in her hand.

"Good workmanship," she said. She ran her nail along the edge of the helmet. "This is beautifully done. Did you know that in the thirteenth century they called the helmet a bascinet?"

"Not to be confused with what you put a baby in, right?"

Chantal laughed. "Right." She held the ring up to the light. "I'll bet I could duplicate this—maybe even make a pin out of the cameo. I would love to make a copy. Would you mind if I borrowed it?"

I reached out and plucked it from her outstretched hand. "Sorry. I'd better not loan it out. Technically, it's evidence. Evidence of just what, I'm not sure yet, but—it was taken from the crime scene. If Detective Corleone knew I had this, he'd probably lock me up and throw away the key."

"Then I'll just take a few minutes now to draw it, if you don't mind." She was already reaching into her tote bag for the sketchpad and pencils she kept in there. "I can visualize how grand this would look—I could do multicolored plumes, and maybe a matching necklace of aurora borealis . . ."

I couldn't imagine who might want a pin of a knight's helmet, but I knew that Chantal often went to Renaissance fairs, where there might indeed be interest in such a piece. "Knock yourself out."

I busied myself cleaning up and making things ready for the impending lunch crowd as Chantal worked. After about twenty minutes, she had a few sketches she seemed satisfied with.

"What else was in the envelope?" she asked.

I showed her the photographs. She studied them, her face impassive. I could tell from the way she handled them, and the way she ran her finger across each and every one, that she was trying to pick up some sort of psychic impression. Normally I pooh-pooh her efforts because I've never really believed in that sort of thing, but at this point I was willing to take any help I could get.

Finally she looked at me. "There is a connection," she said. "I can sense it."

"Between Patti and Alicia—or Adrienne, whoever she is?"

Chantal nodded. She picked up the photograph of Karl Goring. "And between them and this boy. The feeling is very strong." She flipped the photograph over. "When someone wishes something to stay hidden, there are ways. I see a cloudy white aura around all of them. That can indicate denial or a cover-up. Maybe you should start there?"

"Cover-up might actually make sense." I glanced at the clock. "I placed a call to my Chicago contact early this morning. I'm hoping he might be able to supply some of these answers."

She reached out, grabbed my hand. "Just be careful, *chérie*. I can see flashes of black around you—a sure indication of involvement in issues relating to hatred or death. There is also something else." Her fingers slashed a capital D in the air in front of my face. "Danger, *chérie*. It is all around you. Oh, my!" Her hand shot out and her fingers twined around mine and squeezed. Hard. "This is the dangerous mission my friend warned you about. You must use extreme caution."

I smiled thinly. I'd always taken Chantal's predictions at face value, but this somehow gave me the willies. "I'll be on my guard, believe me."

Her eyes were dark with concern. "Promise?"

"Cross my heart and hope to—you know what I mean."

She nibbled at her lower lip. "I guess I should not worry. After all, you are in good hands."

I gave Nick a quick sidelong glance. "You mean paws?" I chuckled.

She gave me a swat on the arm. "Not Nicky, silly. Your King of Swords, the yummy detective you refuse to admit you like. Never fear. He will come to your rescue."

I bit out a chuckle. I had dismissed her prediction about Daniel. "My King of Swords would probably like to put one through me if he knew just how involved I am in this." I pushed the heel of my hand through my hair and sat down next to her. "We almost had a date the other night."

Chantal's eyes gleamed. "Really! Oh, I knew it the minute I saw him. You are perfect for each other."

"Yeah, well, don't get too happy. We never had the date. And now my finding the dead body has put a definite damper on our relationship."

She gave my hand another squeeze. "Don't worry—it will all work out. The cards never lie."

"It's too bad the cards can't tell me who killed Lola and Patti." I sighed. "Or if Adrienne is dead or alive."

"You will figure it out." Chantal nodded. "Just like your favorite detective Nick Charles—which reminds me, where is our Nick? I have some new collars for him to try."

I felt something furry and warm brush against my ankles. I lifted the edge of the tablecloth and bent over. Nick hunkered near the wall, paws tucked under him, eyes blinking. His posture practically screamed, *Hide me! Please!*

Chantal leaned down. Nick lumbered up and tried to move away, but Chantal reached underneath the table, grabbed him by his ruff, and pulled him out. The ease with which she hefted him onto her lap amazed me. Nick squatted there, his girth taking up the entire space.

"Nicky," she crooned. "You bad boy, hiding from me. And here I thought we were doing so well!"

Nick blinked, and said nothing. But the look he slid me spoke volumes.

"Well, I forgive you," Chantal went on. "After all, you probably have better things to do than model for me, right?

Like catch some mice maybe? Or some flies? Find a sweet little calico to spend time with?" She pulled her tote bag over and reached inside. "Still, I have a present for you. I think you will like this one—ah, here it is."

Chantal held up a dark navy blue collar. Emblazoned across it the name NICK stood out in light blue stones. She looked at me anxiously. "I know you said clear stones, but they did not show up well on the navy material. Besides, blue is for boys, no?"

My gaze was fixated on the tiny object positioned just above the K in NICK. "Is that a gun?" I asked.

Chantal nodded. "I get the strangest impressions when I touch him—I see trench coats and guns, like he is a little detective himself, you know? So I put this on the collar for him. It is like his own personal symbol. Nicky can be your detective partner, Nora."

She leaned over and slipped the collar around Nick's neck. I had to admit, it looked pretty sharp. For his part, Nick raised his paw and started to scratch at the offending material.

"Ooh, I guess I made it too small." Chantal reached over and removed the collar. "I'll make it a little bigger. I thought I measured correctly—Nicky, have you gained weight?" She gave him a stern look.

Nick jumped off my lap and headed straight for his food bowl.

Enough said.

I t was one o'clock, and the bulk of the lunch rush was over for the day. I pulled off my apron and headed straight for my computer. Nick was curled up in a ball, snoring loudly by the stove. Oddly, I found the sound comforting. I searched Google Images for Lola Grainger and her sister Adrienne, then hit Enter.

Three images appeared. I clicked on the first one. It was a picture taken many years before, when the girls were barely ten. Pretty young things, but no way to tell from that if Alicia Samuels was indeed Adrienne Sloane.

I moved on to the next one. This was an APA newswire photo, and it showed Lola Grainger walking beside a closed casket. I increased the size so I could read the minuscule printing below the photo.

Socialite Lola Grainger leaves the Metropolitan Correctional Center with the body of her deceased sister.

No name was given. If Nick Atkins had run across this while checking out Adrienne, it wouldn't have proven anything. After all, there could have been yet another sister.

Well, nothing to be learned from that photo. I clicked on the last one. This one looked to be a candid shot of a much younger Lola; I'd put her age at around twenty or twenty-one. She was walking with another girl, whose face was partially in shadow. The caption below it read, *Lola Grainger and sister before the tragedy*—the tragedy, no doubt, being the sisters' separation and Adrienne's incarceration. There was no photography credit given. I frowned as I studied it. The girl had the same long red-brown hair as Alicia Samuels, and her face was the same shape, but it was impossible to make a definite identification from that photo, either. It could be Alicia—or not.

I sighed. I was still no further along in proving whether or not Alicia Samuels and Adrienne Sloane were one and the same person. Maybe I should take a different approach.

I went back to the main page and typed in "Karl Goring." Three sites came up. The first was a Dr. Karl Goring accepting an award. The guy lived in Minnesota and was sixty-three. Not likely. The second Karl Goring was a twenty-something vet out of Arizona. I clicked on the last site.

It was an obituary for a Karl Goring, seventeen years old, who'd died in a car crash twenty-five years earlier. No photo. He'd lived on the outskirts of Chicago.

The bell over the shop door tinkled, heralding the arrival of a customer. I minimized the screen, then grabbed my apron and hurried out front. "Hello, can I help you? We have clam chowder today and—" The rest of my little speech died right there, on my lips.

Daniel Corleone stood there, and he didn't look happy. Not at all.

"Hello, Nora," he said.

"Detective Corleone—what a nice surprise. Did you come for lunch? As I started to say, today we have clam chowder, and—"

He held up his hand. "No, thanks. I've already eaten. I came to see you."

"Really? Well, I'm flattered."

He moved over to the counter and eased one hip against it. I had to admit, the man looked good. Today he had on a gray jacket, a dress shirt, and a blue-striped tie. The suit and shirt looked to be expensive, and that tie had to be silk. I wondered how he could afford such nice clothes on a detective's salary. I wasn't sure how much the Cruz force paid, but I was pretty positive Brooks Brothers suits would be a luxury. He looked me straight in the eye. "A little birdie tells me that you're still digging into the Lola Grainger case—I thought you were going to cease working on that story."

My eyes narrowed. "We were supposed to have a discussion, if you'll recall. And I never said I'd cease working on the story—just that I wouldn't turn it in to be published until you and I talked. And I haven't, so . . . where's the problem?"

His expression darkened. "I don't think you appreciate the seriousness of this situation, Nora. This is not something that you should be involved in."

"Why not? Is there something you're afraid I'll find out?"

"Are you really just writing an article? Or is there something more to all this?"

I thrust my lower lip out. "Don't be ridiculous. What more could there be?"

He leaned all the way across the counter so that his nose was almost level with mine. "I don't think you realize just how much trouble this investigation of yours can land you in."

"Well, then why don't you enlighten me?"

He blew out a breath. "I would if I could."

I slammed my hand down on the counter. "And what does that mean?"

He was momentarily quiet, his gaze lowered, which I didn't take to be a good sign. He seemed to be filtering out just how much information he should impart.

"What's the matter?" I persisted. "Cat got your tongue?"

He pushed his hand through his hair, making little ends stick up. "You took me by surprise, Nora. When you first came to the office, I confess, I didn't realize what you were up to—or rather, I did, but not the magnitude of it."

"I'm sorry—what do you mean, what I was up to?"

"You claim to be writing a story, yet your boss at that magazine knows nothing about it. You claim that your mother and Lola were friends, and as a former crime reporter, you have a certain sense of justice that's been outraged—that I can understand. But then you go poking around, interviewing suspects, trying to dig up confidential information—now that makes me think you have another motive in mind for wanting to pry into Lola Grainger's death. And the only thing I can think of is you're trying to help someone—but I can't figure out just who that someone could be." He tapped my counter with his forefinger. "Unless it's that PI—the one you said Adrienne Sloane hired. I haven't been able to get a line on just who that was, unless you'd care to share that information?"

I was honestly shocked by that admission—it seemed he'd done a damn good job getting the lowdown on everything else I'd done so far. I placed both my hands on my hips and glared at him. "Sorry, I can't help you. The only suspects I interviewed were Lott and Patti—and neither of them turned out very well," I said. "As for digging up confidential information—you've got me there. You were the one who presented me with the printout on Adrienne Sloane's death—are you now saying that it's confidential information? Or are you referring to my calling my source in Chicago and asking him to find out a few things? And if that's what you're referring to—then I'd damn well like to know how you found out. I've always been under the impression wiretapping is illegal."

"It is—under usual circumstances."

I raised one eyebrow. "And these are unusual?"

He blew out a breath. "Look, I'm going to have to ask you to trust law enforcement here, Nora. There are certain things I can't tell you."

I folded my arms across my chest. "That's not very fair, now is it? You want to know all my information, my sources, but you won't tell me jack?"

"All I can say is you're treading on sensitive ground and

I suggest—strongly suggest—you back off. Before something happens."

"Is that a threat?"

"Heck no. It's a warning. I can appreciate your zeal, and what you've accomplished so far. But please, for your own good, and your own safety—promise me you'll drop it."

"Drop what?"

He raised his eyebrows. "You know what. Now I'm asking you nicely, as someone who likes you—how did you find out about Karl Goring?"

I started. "Karl Goring? I'm sorry, but—"

"I know you've inquired about him," he said. "That's why I'm asking you nicely."

I hesitated, then crossed over to the knife drawer. I slipped out the photo of Adrienne and Patti and the knife, and then walked over and handed the envelope with the other two photos to him. He took it, opened it, stared at the contents, then wordlessly slipped the envelope into the inner pocket of his expensive jacket.

"I'd ask where you got that, but I've got a feeling I already know. Don't confirm it!" He held his hand up as I opened my mouth to speak. "It's better if I don't know. If I do, I might have to arrest you for withholding evidence in a murder investigation, and neither of us would like that very much." He patted his breast pocket. "Too much tedious paperwork."

I cut him an eye roll—a big one. "You're kidding, right?"

He sighed. "I wish I were. So—is that all of it?"

I put my hands behind my back, crossed all my fingers. "Yes. That's all of it."

He studied me a moment. "Now why don't I believe you?"

"You have some nerve," I burst out. "You come into my shop and accuse me of meddling, of confiscating evidence—"

"Which you did." His gaze narrowed. "How did you get hold of this anyway?"

I merely shrugged. I could hardly say Nick had retrieved the evidence, although I wondered just how he'd react if I did. Judging from his demeanor thus far, he'd probably have me committed.

He raised both hands in a gesture of surrender. "Okay. Okay." Then he reached across, lightly grazed my cheek with the back of his hand. "Try not to hate me too much, Nora. It's just that these photos shouldn't be floating around."

I pounced on his statement like a cat on a mouse. "Why? Do they have something to do with Patti's murder? Surely you're not suggesting she was killed over a few photos?"

"I'm not at liberty to reveal any information concerning these photos, or the investigation into Patti's death. You'll just have to trust me when I tell you it's not safe."

"Why?" I was having a hard time concentrating due to the fact his skin felt so warm against mine. "Why isn't it safe? Can't you at least tell me that?"

He withdrew his hand and shook his head. "I'm afraid not. Believe me when I say I'm looking out for you. After all, how can we ever go on that date if you're behind bars—or worse?"

Worse? I licked at my lips, forcing myself not to obsess on the fact he'd referred to our missed dinner as a date. I picked up a dish towel from a nearby rack and twirled it in my hand. "Maybe if I knew just what was at stake here, I'd be more inclined to forgive you. And cooperate."

He paused, and for a minute I thought he might actually break down and spill his guts, but then his expression hardened, and he shook his head.

"Sorry. It's really better for you if you don't know. Look, I can't arrest you—yet. But if that's what it takes to keep you safe, I will. I'll be watching you, so keep your nose clean, okay, Nora?"

He turned and walked to the door. As he turned the knob, I called out, "So what's in it for me? What's my incentive to drop all this? Besides a dinner date with you, that is."

He gave me a swift glance over his shoulder. "Staying alive," he said, and walked out the door.

TWENTY-THREE

"**B**oy, that guy's got nerve!"

I waited until the door had closed behind Daniel before I threw the dishrag I'd been holding to the floor and stamped on it. A childish action, to be sure, but it made me feel much better. Nick crawled out from under the table the moment the door closed. He leaped over the towel and hopped up on the counter, his golden eyes flashing sparks. I reached out and gave him a swift pat on the head.

"Sorry, Nick. He just makes me so mad!"

I stamped my foot again, harder this time. Nick sat motionless, staring at me. His whiskers twitched, and then he arched his back in a taut stretch, opened his mouth in a large yawn, and jumped back onto the floor with a grunt.

I walked over to the drawer and removed the few photos I'd held back from Daniel. "He really seemed pissed about these photos, didn't he?" I tapped the envelope against my chin. "I'd sure like to know how he found out I was asking about Karl Goring. How does he get all this information anyway? He always seems to be a heck of a lot more informed than our usual Cruz police force, I can tell you that."

I remembered back in Chicago, most of the detectives used NCIC—the National Crime Information Center—as a source of information. It was pretty reliable, but even that had errors at times. I thought back to the information he'd gotten on Adrienne Sloane—information that seemed pretty hard to pinpoint. I knew prison records were made public, but the information one could gather online was sketchy and detailed reports cost money—money I was relatively certain wasn't in the Cruz police budget. No, information like that usually came from the inside, but most prison guards and wardens were canny with info, unless they were on the take, or there was something in it for them, or . . .

I opened the drawer where I'd put the tiles Nick had been playing with the other day and pulled them out. They spelled FIB, all right, but if you switched two letters . . .

"FBI." I cocked a brow at Nick, who had darted his long pink tongue all over his face and was now concentrating on his right paw. "People in prisons don't like to spill stuff unless there's something in it for them, or unless they're talking to a Fed. What do you think, Nick? Do you think the FBI is somehow involved in this? That Detective Daniel has an 'in' with someone there?"

Nick raised his golden gaze to meet mine, and then let out a shrill howl.

I frowned as I recalled Nick's choice of Scrabble letters.

One set spelled either FIB or FBI. The other was GOVT, an abbreviation for *government*. The FBI was a branch of the government.

The first time I'd caught Nick with the FBI letters had been right after I'd met Daniel. Had Nick sensed something about the detective? After all, what did I really know about him? I only had his word he was substituting for O'Halleran—I'd never checked with anyone else down at headquarters. Even the night before, I'd been sequestered until he came to the interrogation room. Could it even be possible?

I gave the cat a sharp glance, but right now Nick wasn't interested in me; it was grooming time. He licked his left paw and made a pass across his whiskers, his cheekbones, twice over his eyes, once over the back of his head before sticking his left leg straight up in the air and cleaning his manhood.

"Crap, Nick. What were you trying to tell me? That Corleone doesn't have to have an informant at the FBI, because he *is* the FBI?"

Nick paused in his ablutions. "*Ew-owr.*" He bleated, and then returned to his grooming.

Well, it would explain a lot. How he had the clout to get information not available for public consumption—that, for all intents and purposes, has been buried—to anyone except FBI or CIA. Chantal said the auras on those pictures were indicative of a cover-up—what if she was right? What if Adrienne Sloane's death was part of some cover-up—something that included Patti Simmons and Karl Goring?

I flopped into a chair, pushed my hand through my hair. "Whatever it is has to be big for the FBI to be involved, and we're talking *really* big. Huge. Gigundo. What would be huge enough to warrant a massive cover-up and the FBI's involvement?"

I got up, crossed over to my laptop, opened it, and started typing. Nick, done for the moment with his grooming, hopped up on the chair next to me. A couple of seconds later, the FBI website appeared on my screen. I read the "Breaking News," my teeth jamming into my bottom lip when I spotted an item about a newly sentenced mob boss.

"Mobsters. I'm back to the damn mob after all. Sheesh— I can't get away from 'em."

Nick sat back on his haunches, began grooming his other side.

I continued to stare at the FBI's website. "Best reason I can think of for a cover-up is someone turning state's evidence. Ratting on the big boys." I could feel the beginnings of a monster headache start to form, and I absently rubbed at my temple. "It's possible. I've seen it before. She— Adrienne—might have been incarcerated on some charge, and the Feds approached her with a deal—her freedom for info on her boss. Depending on who and how powerful the mobster was, it could be a viable reason for faking her death. She might have needed to establish a whole new identity."

I got up, walked over to the counter where I'd dropped the envelope, and brought it back to the table. I pulled out the one of Patti and Adrienne/Alicia and held it up.

"The sisters were estranged for years. Adrienne could have gotten in with bad company, maybe even one of the mob heads. He sells her out to protect his own skin, but the Feds approach her with a deal in prison, offer her a shot at an entirely new life if she rolls over. She's jaded now—got no loyalty or love left in her—so she takes the deal and for all intents and purposes Adrienne is dead. The Feds get her testimony, put the mobster away, and Adrienne starts life all over as Alicia Samuels—either ironically or by design, in the company her brother-in-law owns."

I pulled a pad in front of me. Feds always recommended that people in WPP use their same first name, or else choose first and last names that start with their initials—makes the transition easier. I wrote down:

Adrienne Sloane
Alicia Samuels
A and S. Bingo.

Nick hopped up on the table, walked over, peered over my shoulder, and a shrill howl emitted from his throat.

"You're right, Nick. There's still a lot unexplained. For one, how does Patti figure in all this? How far back did she and Adrienne go, and how tight were they? And let's not forget Karl Goring, or how he might tie into all this. Chantal said they were all connected, so maybe—maybe Patti was in the mob, too? As for Goring—well, I've got no clue there. What I need is some link, something that will tie the three of them together."

Nick laid his paw on my shoulder, butted his head against my chin.

Well, it was clear what I needed to do. I needed another look-see into Alicia Samuels's office. After all, she'd gotten careless and left Lola Grainger's cell number on her desk—maybe there was something else that would shed some light left behind. And quite frankly, I wouldn't have minded a one-on-one with Kevin Grainger, either. I probably should go to Daniel, but after that little lecture I doubt he'd be pleased at my interference. However, if I could get proof Adrienne was alive, and a lead on who killed Patti . . .

"KMG, here I come," I murmured. I reached for my cell and punched in a number, while Nick watched, eyes slitted. "Only this time, I won't need an appointment. Hey, Chantal! Does your brother still have his old bicycle?"

TWENTY-FOUR

Chantal delivered the bicycle just as I was ushering my last lunch patron out the door. She wheeled it into the back room and bestowed a dubious glance my way.

"Here it is, *chérie*. Remy oiled the wheels—he has not used it in years. He said you could keep it, if you want."

"I don't think that will be necessary, but thanks."

She continued to give me her version of the "evil eye" after I locked the door, took off my apron, and loaded all the lunch crowd dishes into the dishwasher. She folded her arms across her chest and leaned against the kitchen doorjamb.

"So—you are tired of driving your SUV around? You feel riding a bike will be better exercise?"

"Sorta kinda."

"Or," she said shrewdly, "you are planning on channeling Jessica Fletcher, and thus needed a similar mode of transportation?"

I pulled my hair into a ponytail and shoved it under an *NCIS* cap that I'd gotten on eBay. Gotta love that Mark Harmon. "Sorta kinda."

I could tell my friend was struggling hard to keep her temper. "This has something to do with this investigation you are involved in, right, *chérie*? The dangerous mission? Do not say 'sorta kinda' please or I will be forced to slap you."

I pulled an old SF Giants jacket over my T-shirt and dark denim jeans. "Could be."

Chantal rolled her eyes and let out an impatient sigh. "For heaven's sake, Nora, please tell me you are not doing anything foolish—like confronting a suspected killer."

I zipped up the jacket and went over, patted my friend's hand. "You know me better than that. I never did stuff like that when I was paid to do it. Well, maybe only occasionally."

"Sure." She snorted. "I know how you can get when you are faced with a puzzle. You have a tendency to take chances."

"Me? A risk taker? Good old dependable me?" I shot her a look of mock disdain. "You must have me confused with someone else."

"I was happy when you decided to take over your mama's store, and do you know why?"

I beamed at her. "Because I moved back to Cruz, and we could see each other regularly again?"

"That, and the fact that you would no longer be out prowling the streets of Chicago, helping to put the bad guys away. You had some pretty close calls you never told anyone about."

"That I did, but how did you—"

She tapped her temple. "I am not psychic for nothing. I know you laugh at it, but it is nothing to laugh at. My predictions—my visions—have a ninety-seven percent success rate."

"I do believe in intuition," I told her. "What I don't believe in is anyone's ability to predict the future—the exact future. I'm more than willing to believe that you get intuitive glimpses into certain events. Heck, I might have experienced some of that myself. Plus . . ." My face split into a big grin. "I may be the owner of the world's first psychic cat."

Her breath exploded in a long, drawn-out sigh. "Well, it is good you are open-minded in that respect, at least. Please trust what I say to you. That cloud is still around you—if anything, it is thicker. My psy—my intuition—is telling me that you are walking headlong into danger. That you are putting your very life in jeopardy."

I took both my friend's hands in mine. "I'll be careful, and I'm not about to do anything foolish, Chantal. But if something unforeseen should happen—you'd take care of Nick for me, right?"

Nick's head popped out from underneath the table. "*Oooowwwwrrrr*," he howled.

Chantal smiled. "See, Nicky will accept no substitutes. He wants you to get *your* tail back here in one piece."

I picked him up and buried my nose in his ruff. "Nothing's going to happen," I whispered. "I'll be back in one piece before you know it. I wouldn't leave you to spend the rest of your nine lives as a cat jewelry model."

I set him down, and Nick turned around twice. "*E-yow!*" he cried.

I was a bit out of practice, so it took me a good forty-five minutes, but I cycled all the way from Hot Bread to the other end of town and the KMG building, a feat I could have accomplished in fifteen minutes with the SUV—but then I might have had a hard time getting through the gate. I'd remembered the engineer on my previous visit sailing through the entrance without having to flash a badge—I was hoping for the same sort of luck now. I'd worry about how I'd actually get into the building once I'd passed the first hurdle.

It seemed luck was on my side as I made the turn onto KMG property. There was a large delivery truck at the guard shack, and it seemed the guard on duty was occupied checking out the driver's paperwork. Of course, that didn't mean they couldn't look up and see me, or catch me on their video cameras. Squaring my shoulders, I pulled my cap down low over my eyes and pulled my Giants jacket collar up around my neck.

Then I sailed straight through the entrance onto the back parking lot.

One hurdle down—several more to go.

I pedaled all the way to the back of the lot and found a small bicycle rack. Apparently the engineer wasn't the only one who rode his bike—there were four others chained there. I propped mine in the last slot, and then stood, debating my next move. It was to get inside obviously, but without a badge, that posed a definite problem. I imagined I could have avoided all this subterfuge had I just called for an appointment, but to be honest, with Patti gone, I had no idea who my new contact should be, nor any desire to get shuffled around for a half hour while people attempted to find out. I've always found the personal approach infinitely more satisfying—it usually produces immediate, if not effective, results.

The rear door opened and I saw two suited figures emerge. I sucked in my breath as the first one turned and I caught a good view of him full face—Daniel. Swell. His companion was tall—I guessed around six feet, with a good build and reddish hair that seemed in need of a decent haircut. The suit he wore hung on his frame, as if it were two sizes too big. I couldn't tell much else, because the sunglasses he wore concealed much of his face. They walked over to the far wall, and I recognized Daniel's Acura, dent and all. The two got into it and then drove off. I heaved a sigh of relief. At least I wouldn't have to worry about running into him here.

A small Nissan drove up, slid into the space Daniel had just vacated. Two girls exited the car, laughing and talking. I pulled the rubber band out of my hair and fluffed it out, then stuffed the cap into my jacket pocket. Grabbing my purse out of the bicycle basket, I hurried over to join them. They regarded me curiously as I stepped forward.

"Hello, I was wondering if you could help me?" I pointed to the bicycle. "I tried to sign in at the guard shack, but the guard was pretty busy with the deliveryman. I was kind of surprised she waved me in."

The taller of the two girls looked me up and down. She had on a blue and white dress that showed off her trim figure, and her honey-colored hair was cut in a becoming style. A slight frown creased her skillfully made-up face— I judged her to be in her late twenties. "They do that sometimes with the bicycle riders. You have no idea how we've complained about it. I mean, think about it—they could just let anybody in—no offense."

"Yeah," agreed the shorter girl. She was plumper, but had a prettier face. Her violet-colored suit wasn't as expensively cut as the other girl's, but if those stilettos she wore weren't Manolos, I'd eat leftover tuna for a week. She brushed a hand through her raven curls, and I noted her nails were French tips, and professionally done. KMG must pay their admins well. "It would be so easy for a terrorist to just ride in here and leave a suitcase with a bomb lying around—you know."

I nodded, and offered what I hoped was a sympathetic smile. I held my arms out. "I couldn't agree more. See—no suitcases." When that was met with blank stares, I decided that either they had no sense of humor, or my stand-up routine needed work. "I came here hoping to see Mr. Grainger, or possibly whoever's been appointed the new catering manager." I reached into my cross-body bag and dug out a business card for each of them. "I'm Nora Charles. I own Hot Bread, and I'd been negotiating some catering contracts with Ms. Simmons."

They took the cards and looked at them, and their attitudes suddenly did a one-eighty degree turn. "Oh, Hot Bread," the blonde gushed. "Specialty sandwich shop, right? I love that place! You own it?"

I nodded.

"Wow—I'm crazy over those sandwiches. Those names are so catchy! I was in the other day—I had the *Ricky Martin*." She smacked her lips. "It was great."

"Me, too," said the brunette. "I like the tuna melt. And the Ryan Reynolds Reuben. And practically everything on the menu. Can't you tell?" She ran her hands over her plump hips before she stuffed the card into her jacket pocket. "What events are you catering for us?"

"The Memorial Day event definitely. There were others under negotiation. Ms. Simmons was going to send me a final contract, but . . ." I shrugged and injected a note of sympathy into my voice as it trailed off.

The two exchanged a quick look, and then the blonde nodded. "Yeah, we saw the story in the paper this morning.

It's pretty gross. I mean, Patti wasn't the nicest person in the world, but no one should die like that. It's crazy."

"Well, I thought I'd better come down and see what's happening with my contracts in person. It's hard sometimes to get through with a phone call."

"You're right. Especially around here." The blonde wiggled her fingers. "I'm Irene, by the way, and this is Jody. Marshall Connor is handling the catering for now, I think. You can check in with Darla, and then we'll take you up to his office, if you want."

I fell into step beside them as they flashed their badges and the door swung open automatically. "Marshall Connor?" I said as we walked into the reception area. "Funny, catering is the type of job you'd think a woman would have—like Alicia Samuels perhaps."

Both of them turned to stare at me. "Alicia Samuels? Why would you think she'd get that job?" Irene asked.

I shrugged. "No particular reason. I've just heard that she's painstaking with detail and very thorough—although I'd guess one would have to be, dealing with the media, right?"

"She was." Jody shrugged. "It's hard to say just what she's doing now. She doesn't work here anymore. She quit the week after Mrs. Grainger died."

I tried to sound neutral and not let my tone convey any of the excitement I felt at that announcement. "She quit? Really?"

"Yeah, it surprised us, too. She was good at what she did, and everyone seemed to like her, especially Mr. Grainger. Patti wasn't too fond of her, though." Irene gave a wise nod.

"Yeah." Jody giggled. "And vice versa. Alicia used to avoid Patti like the plague. If she saw her coming, she'd duck into someone's office, or bury her nose in a file. She tried to have as little to do with her as possible."

"Amazing what jealousy will do. Patti was so afraid Alicia'd make a move on Grainger, it was pathetic." Irene sighed. "Not that Mr. Grainger had eyes for any other woman—at least not when his wife was alive. Patti didn't waste any time sinking her hooks into him once she was gone, though."

"Well, I think he only let her because he was still in shock," put in Jody. "Mark my words, he'd have come to his senses sooner or later—if Patti hadn't died first." She flushed and made a quick sign of the cross. "May she rest in peace."

We were in front of the reception desk now. Irene motioned to me that they'd wait over by the bank of elevators, and I waited my turn behind a FedEx man who seemed infinitely more interested in the cleavage displayed by Darla's low-cut blouse than in anything she was saying to him. After he panted and drooled for ten minutes, he finally went on his way, and I stepped forward and stated my name. Darla gave me a blank look at first, but when I handed her my card, her eyes lit up like a Christmas tree.

"Oh, yes, Ms. Charles. I am so sorry. Ms. Simmons never did mail out your contract. I'm sure Mr. Connor would be happy to discuss terms with you, though. Everyone here just loves Hot Bread." She smiled and picked up the phone. "Let me just tell him you're coming up."

She turned away and spoke briefly into the phone. After a few minutes she replaced the handset and smiled. "Mr. Connor's out, but his admin says she remembers seeing that contract. Mr. Connor did re-sign it, so if you want to go up to the eighth floor and ask for Betsy, she'll be happy to give you your copy. Just turn right when you get off the elevator and walk all the way down." She paused. "You can ask about making another appointment with Mr. Connor. I'm sorry, but everyone's just been so stressed since—ah—the incident."

"Understandable. Thanks."

Irene and Jody must have got tired of waiting for me, because when I reached the bank of elevators, neither girl was in sight. I rode up to the eighth floor by myself and, when the doors opened, made a left instead of the prescribed right. I passed the conference room where I'd sat with Patti only two short days ago and then I found myself back in front of Alicia Samuels's office. I turned the knob, and the door yielded an inch and then stopped, stuck. I tried the knob again, putting more of my weight behind it this time. The door shook and then groaned inward, its creaking hinges suggesting an oiling might be in order. I closed it carefully and moved swiftly over to the desk, sat down in the leather chair. The sticky pad with Lola's cell number on it was still in the same spot as when I'd seen it.

Okay, Nora. Now what?

I leaned back in the chair and looked the desk over. I opened the middle drawer and peered inside. It was empty save for two Bic pens, some rubber bands, a small magnifying glass, and two pennies. I closed the drawer and opened the drawer on the right. This time I scored a box of breath mints and a box of staples. The drawer on the left was totally empty. I pulled out both bottom drawers. Aside from some thin files with press releases, they were empty as well. There were certainly no clues here. Alicia/Adrienne had covered her tracks well.

Or had she?

I'd moved offices about eight times in the six years I'd

worked on the *Chicago Tribune*, and each time I'd left something behind without realizing it. It wasn't intentional—it's just one of the hazards of moving. You're usually so irritated that you have to move in the first place and usually so rushed by the time the big day finally rolls around that there's always *something* that gets cast by the wayside.

In Alicia/Adrienne's case, I was certain it might be something she'd hidden, something she might have even forgotten about. I'd done that—hidden something so very well that I often forgot I had it, or when it came time to look for it, damned if I could remember the "safe place" I'd stored it in.

I got up, walked over to the massive cherrywood bookcase. The shelves overflowed with books on marketing, media, and other related subjects. I ran my finger along the spines, idly noting the titles: *The Social Media Marketing Book*, *Marketing Made Easy*, *Marketing and the Media*, *Book of Crests*, *Marketing in the New Media* . . .

Whoa!

I backed up and looked over those titles again. *Book of Crests* stood out like a sore thumb. I pulled it out of its slot and took it over to the desk. I settled myself into the soft leather and opened the thick volume. A quick perusal revealed it to be a sort of encyclopedia of coats of arms of various family names. I noticed a small Post-it sticking out and turned to that page.

On it was a photograph of the Gianelli family crest. It depicted the usual coat of arms, and right at the top was a large knight's helmet (or as Chantal would say, a bascinet) with long, flowing plumes.

A memory stirred at the back of my mind, elusive, just out of reach. I pushed the chair back and rose. As my fingers closed over the book, I felt my back hip pocket vibrate. Startled, I dropped the book. The heavy volume crashed to the floor. I winced at the sound and dug in my pocket, pulling out my cell. I snapped it open.

"Nora Charles."

"Hey, babe. Hank told me to give you a call. He thought I could dig up some info you asked him to check on quicker. You know, because of my contacts."

Petey Peppercorn was a PI from Chicago, one of the best. He'd been another of my confidential sources for years when I worked the crime beat, and we'd become fast friends. His tone was light, but there was a steely undercurrent to it that told me he had something important to tell me. "I hope this isn't a bad time?"

I sank back into the chair. "It could be worse. What do you have? Something on Karl Goring?"

"Yeah, and I had a devil of a time getting it. I see why old Hankie passed the buck to me. That trail is buried deeper than Captain Kidd's gold. The only reason I got anything at all is my guy at the FBI owes me big-time." He blew out a breath. "Listen up—I'm only gonna say this once. When Goring was young, he got in with the mob. At first it started out small, and then it grew into something pretty big. Anyway, long story short, the kid realized he was in over his head and turned on the mob leader. You know what that usually means."

"Witness Protection?"

"Yep. My source couldn't tell me any more than that, but he did tell me the name of the mob guy Karl's testimony put away."

"Who?"

"Giancarlo Gianelli."

And now I remembered why that crest seemed so familiar. I'd done a story on Giancarlo Gianelli when the former mob kingpin had died after a long stretch in prison. He'd had a large and loyal family, who always wore symbols of the Gianelli name—usually something in the shape of a knight's head, the symbol on their family crest. I remembered something else, too.

"Giancarlo has siblings, right?"

"Yeah—one's Mickey. He got busted two years ago. Money laundering. He's got thirty-five to life in Chicago State." Petey's chuckle was dry. "One of his ex-dolls blew the whistle on him—a deathbed confession from prison, I heard."

"Really. Deathbed." My mouth was so dry, I could barely form the words. "You don't remember her name, by any chance?"

"Ada, maybe? Adele—no wait. Adrienne. That was it. That help you any?"

I tightened the grip on my phone. "You have no idea."

"Listen, I don't know what you're mixed up in, and I don't wanna know. I thought you got out of the crime reporting business—thought you went back to run your mama's deli."

"I did—I am. What can I say? Old habits die hard."

"Yeah, well, if you're foolin' around with the Gianellis, there's something you should know. Aldo—that's the last remaining brother—the Feds are watchin' him too. Got to do with offshore accounts and terrorist ties, but so far they can't prove anything. Since they're under observation by the Feds, they gotta keep their noses clean, but my guy on the inside told me that Aldo's been mouthing off a bit lately, hinting he's about to settle an old score. I'm not quite sure what that means, but it can't be good. You know the Gianellis—they're into revenge." He paused. "So whatever you're into, Nora, be careful. I'd hate to hear they pulled your body out of the ocean wearin' a pair of cement shoes, if you get my drift. Hank and I—we'd miss ya."

I tried a laugh, but it came out sounding like a hyena on crack. Loud and shrill. "You know me, Petey. I'm always careful."

"Yeah, right. Well, you need anything else, just holler. We never had this conversation, by the way."

"What conversation?"

He chuckled. "That's my girl."

The line went dead. I slipped my phone back into my pocket and bent to retrieve the book. As I picked it up, I saw the edge of a photograph peeping out from underneath the dust jacket. I set the book back on the desk, removed the jacket. The photo had been taped to the inside, but the fall must have shaken it loose. I picked it up and looked at it.

There were two men in the photo. One was heavy, his fat belly protruding over the waistband of his expensively cut suit. He had slicked-back black hair, beady eyes, and a smile that showed expensively capped teeth. The second man was medium height, slight build, with a sharp nose, protruding chin, and small, slitted eyes. There was a cruel slant to his mouth that indicated he could probably be a pretty tough customer. Looking at him sent a chill racing up my spine. There was something about him that struck a chord, yet I was positive I'd never seen him before. God, I'd certainly have remembered him!

The fat man was handing the shorter man a small object. I squinted, trying to get a better look. I blinked, unable to trust what I'd seen. I pulled open the middle drawer, grabbed the magnifying glass, and pored over the picture.

Nope. I hadn't been mistaken. It was a ring, and it looked almost exactly like the one I'd found in Lola's envelope, except the inlay was different—I couldn't quite make it out. Damn grainy photos! I flipped it over—there were initials printed there: MG and CW—and a date, some five years earlier. MG—Mickey Gianelli? I had no idea who CW might be. I stuffed the photo into my cross-body bag and replaced the *Book of Crests* on the shelf. Then I shut off the light and started for the door. As I approached it, I froze. The outline of a person was visible through the door's thick frosted pane. As I stared, the knob slowly turned, hesitated, and then the door burst open. I found myself looking straight at none other than Kevin Grainger. He seemed as startled to see me as I was him.

He found his voice first. "Who are you, and what are you doing in this office?" he demanded.

All I could do was stare. Kevin Grainger cut a far more impressive figure in person. He was tall and well built, the gray suit he wore draping nicely on his frame. He had a firm chin, well-shaped lips, and his eyes, a rich cornflower blue, blazed with a mixture of fury and puzzlement as he assessed me.

I opened my mouth, but I was so startled that no words came out, just a plaintive squeak. He folded his arms across his chest and continued to glare. "Well? I'm waiting. Who are you?"

I found my voice. "Mr. Grainger, I presume?" At his curt nod, I continued, "I am so sorry. I'm—my name is Nora Charles. I own a specialty sandwich shop in town—Hot

Bread. I came here today to pick up a catering contract, and I'm afraid my sense of direction is a bit off." I offered him a small smile. "As you can see, I got a bit turned around. I just stopped in here to—to get my bearings."

The fury seemed to subside and he ran his hand absently through his thick mass of iron gray hair. "I see. Well, I'm sorry to bark at you, Ms. Charles, but—well, I didn't expect anyone to be in here. The occupant is out on leave."

I nodded. "Alicia Samuels. Yes, I know."

One brow rose. "Oh?"

"I've done some research on KMG," I said quickly. "When I spoke with Ms. Simmons, she indicated you were in the process of naming a catering manager. From all I've read, Ms. Samuels seems a good fit—someone I'd enjoy working with."

"Yes, well, to be quite frank, Ms. Charles, I'm not at all sure if she will be returning."

"That's too bad. She seemed perfect for the position. Her leaving is nothing serious, I hope?"

His frown deepened. "I'm sorry. I don't discuss employees' personal matters with outsiders."

"Of course. I'm sorry. It's just that I would like to discuss the possibility of Hot Bread taking on more of your event catering, and since Ms. Simmons was my only contact here, I'm not quite sure whom I should approach."

"Marshall Connor has the position for the moment. Not permanently, you understand, but he's a very organized individual and he'll be a good interim replacement. You can make an appointment to speak about it with him." His hand waved in the air, an impatient gesture. "KMG has sustained a number of losses of key personnel recently. If you read the papers, I'm sure I don't have to tell you that."

I said a silent prayer of thanks that Grainger apparently did not know I was the one who'd found Patti's body. I wondered briefly just how much—or how little—Daniel might have told him. Aloud I said, "No, sir, you don't. Might I offer my condolences on both your personal and professional losses."

He hesitated, then gave a curt nod. "Thank you."

"My mother was quite fond of Mrs. Grainger," I went on. "They'd formed quite a bond. She had a respect for my mother's talent, and I know for a fact my mother appreciated the business Mrs. Grainger threw her way."

"My late wife had a definite talent with details such as that." Kevin Grainger's tone took on a wistful note. "When it came to that particular function, I was more than happy to turn the reins over to her. She had a knack for knowing just how to put an event together."

"Ms. Simmons seemed to have the same quality," I ventured. "Or at least, that's the impression I got when we spoke earlier in the week."

One brow lifted. "You think so? Well, so far you're the only one to offer any positive feedback on her. We received many complaints on her brusque manner—at least, that's what Marshall reported back to me." He shook his head. "I'm sorry. I don't mean to speak ill of the deceased, particularly someone who was such an asset to the company. Patti's manner was excellent for getting reports and presentations in on time, but dealing with the public wasn't her forte. She wouldn't have been left in charge, had she lived. Quite honestly, I'm not certain who'll take it over. Marshall has an eye for detail, but he feels such a function is beneath his stature, and he's probably right. The catering position should most likely fall to a woman, but for the moment, I've got no one qualified."

"It sounds like a very interesting job."

His lips twitched. "Would you like to apply?"

I laughed. "Sorry. I gave up a nine-to-five grind in Chicago to come back and be my own boss. Been there, done that."

"Ah, yes. Chicago." He let out a long sigh, and as I stared at him, a niggling sense of familiarity crept through me. There was just something about the way he looked that struck a chord, an elusive memory, but for the moment I couldn't quite grasp it.

"Have you ever been there?" I asked. "It's a great city."

"Once or twice," he murmured. Then he added, so softly I had to strain to catch the words, "Long ago."

"Perhaps you've sailed the *Lady L* there? That would be quite a journey from here, but rather a nice one, I imagine," I ventured.

His head jerked up. "I confess, since my wife's death, I can count on one hand the times I've been back on the *Lady L*. I plan to sell it, once all this is over," he said shortly. "Too many memories—I'm certain you understand."

"Of course." I nodded sympathetically. "Between your wife's accident and Patti's shooting, I imagine it would be hard for you to look at the boat in quite the same way again."

He gave me an odd stare and suddenly his hand shot out, encircled my wrist in a grip of steel. "How did you know Patti'd been shot?" he demanded. "The newspaper accounts hinted at foul play, but none of them described the manner of death. How could you possibly know, unless . . ." His fingers bit into my wrist, harder. "Good God. What did you do back in Chicago? Is it possible— you can't be—"

"You're hurting me," I cried, and he released me, took a step backward. His face darkened like a thundercloud.

"Charles. Nora Charles. I seem to recall Lola telling me the Charles woman's daughter was a writer. A reporter, to be precise. You wouldn't happen to be the one who's been snooping around, asking questions, claiming my wife was a victim of foul play?" he hissed. "Because if you are—"

The unspoken threat hung in the air like a cloud of smoke as the door suddenly eased open again, and Kristi stood on the threshold. She looked at both of us, cleared her throat nervously.

"Mr. Grainger, sorry to interrupt. Mr. Tate needs you in Conference Room A. I saw you come in here, and—"

He whirled on the girl. "Can't you see we were having a discussion?" he blurted out.

"No matter, I was just leaving," I said quickly, moving toward the door before Grainger could utter another word. I smiled brightly at Kristi. "Well, I need to find Mr. Marshall's office. It's been a real pleasure meeting you, Mr. Grainger."

I moved past them and out into the hall before either of them could speak, thinking that now might be an excellent time to make my exit. I decided not to take a chance waiting for the elevator—just in case—and hurried over to the stairwell. I wondered briefly just why Kevin Grainger had gone into Alicia's office in the first place, and instinctively tightened my grip on my cross-body bag and the photos I'd shoved inside. A thought had occurred to me when he'd mentioned Chicago, and I had an idea just why he seemed familiar to me, but I wasn't one hundred percent certain.

I needed to check some things out, and the best place for what I had in mind was the Cruz Public Library. I stole a quick glance at my watch. Of course, tonight was the library's early night.

Five thirty on the dot was like a grand exodus on Thursdays, but with any luck, I'd be able to get down there before closing time.

But I'd have to pedal like hell.

TWENTY-FIVE

I made it down to the Cruz Public Library with twenty minutes to spare. I propped the bicycle against the side of the massive gray granite building and quickly climbed the short flight of stone steps to the iron-bound door. The comforting smell of hundreds of thousands of musty pages greeted me as I stepped through the glass door—maybe it's the writer in me, but I've always found that smell to be inspiring—and at times, oddly comforting.

Jemina Slater, who'd held the post of head librarian for as far back as I could remember, glanced up from her issue of *Woman's Day* and frowned at me as I shoved through the door. She pushed her wire-rimmed glasses down on her beak-shaped nose and pointed at the wall clock, which read five ten.

"Sorry," I mouthed. "But it's important."

She held up ten fingers, paused, then ten fingers again. I chuckled. Jemina was a creature of habit who didn't enjoy having any routine of hers interrupted. She'd practically had a stroke when I discontinued the *Jay Leno*—baloney and mayo on rye—from Hot Bread's menu. Tonight was her usual food shopping night, followed by a light supper of tuna casserole for her and her Yorkie, Thurston, capped by an evening of *Gray's Anatomy* and *Scandal*. If I set her schedule off by as much as a second, I'd never hear the end of it.

"I'll be out of here in nineteen," I said as I passed her desk.

"*Hmpf,*" she grunted, giving her iron gray beehive hairdo a quick pat. Her stern blue gaze was icy and sharp. "See that you are."

I tossed her a breezy smile, knowing that would infuriate her more. "Microfilm still in the same place?"

"Hasn't changed since you were in high school." She glanced pointedly at the clock again. "You remember how to work the machine?"

"Sure do." With an impish grin I added, "If I forget, I'll give you a shout."

The stare got icier. Her hand shot out, indicating the clock. "Stop wasting time. You're down to seventeen minutes," she hissed.

I descended the marble steps to the even mustier-smelling basement, which housed the newspaper morgue, the computer lab, and the microfilm machines. I went over to the bins that housed the microfilm itself, found the one for the *Cruz Sun*, and picked over half the contents before I found the reel with the date I wanted. I carried it over to one of the machines and turned the reader button on. I lifted the glass plate, inserted the reel of microfilm onto the left spindle, and proceeded to thread the film under the small rollers then under the plate and onto the right-sided rollers and onto the empty film spool. As I worked, I couldn't resist a chuckle. What memories this brought back!

I closed the glass plate and used the manual knob on the front of the machine to advance the film. Another button in the middle aided me in getting the picture into sharp focus. I went through about half of the reel before the story I wanted appeared on the screen:

Man Survives Car Crash

The story went on to detail how Lott had gone over the guardrail, barely made it to safety, and been rescued. Two photos accompanied the short article. One showed the smashed guardrail and a downward shot of the steep ravine. The outline of the wreckage was barely visible. Two men in white coats wheeled a still figure toward a waiting ambulance. I wondered how anyone could survive a crash like that and yet he had. It seemed nothing short of a miracle.

The other photo was of Lott himself. The caption indicated it had been taken about a week before the accident. It was a fairly close shot, and showed him beside the scrimshaw case proudly pointing to the middle shelf, to the figures I'd noticed on my initial visit—the grouping of animals, the money clip with the clipper ship. The shock of thick gray hair looked the same as the Shelly Lott I'd met, but the man in this photograph was clean-shaven, no thick growth of beard concealing the lower portion of his face. I attributed his bushy addition as an attempt to conceal skin that had been badly burned. Too bad, because Lott had an attractive dimple right in the center of his chin, à la Kirk Douglas. The caption below the photo read: *Lott with his pride and joy: Scrimshaw.*

I pored over the photo. Nope. What I was looking for wasn't there.

I checked the side of the machine and was relieved to see it did have a printer function. I quickly ran off a copy of the article, then rewound the reel and carefully took it off the spindle. I crossed back over, replaced it in its box, and then moved over to the bank of computers. I typed in the address for a site I'd often used as a research tool— PapersPast.com, and went immediately to the *Chicago Herald*, then typed in "Mickey Gianelli—photos."

Almost immediately the screen filled with images— and according to the legend at the bottom, there were thirty-seven pages more.

A sharp rap made me look up. Jemina was standing about ten feet away. She waved her wrist back and forth in the air like a flag, and pointed to her watch. "You've got six minutes," she said flatly.

I groaned. No way could I get what I wanted in six minutes. "I need a little more time," I said. "But I hate to make you late. You could leave the key—I'll make sure I lock up after me, I promise."

She folded her arms across her chest and regarded me over the rims of her glasses. "Like you did that time before the SATs?"

I flushed. "I'm a lot older and wiser now, Jemina."

"Older maybe. Wiser—jury's still out." She shook her head and turned to go back up the stairs. "I can give you an extra ten minutes—that's it. Then I lock up, and if you're not done, well—you can spend the night."

"Ten minutes. Great." I was already pulling up page three of images. "I'll only need eight—I hope."

On the twentieth page I found what I was looking for. It was a duplicate of the photo I had in my bag, only this time there was a caption accompanying it: *Mickey Gianelli with one of his right-hand men, Carlo Wyatt.*

Ah, good. Now I could put a name to the face. I printed out a copy of this photo, too, then turned back to the machine. I had one more item to check, and I crossed my fingers. With any luck, I'd find it within the next seven minutes.

I switched off the computer, stuffed the other articles back in my bag, and hurried up the stairway. As I reached the top, I glanced at my digital watch: five thirty-nine.

I held my wrist up as I sailed past Jemina's desk. "See— I'm early."

"*Hmpf*," she grunted. "That's a matter of opinion."

As I mounted my bicycle, I debated my options: (A) I could go home and discuss my findings with my silent partner, Nick, and maybe Chantal; (B) I could go to the police station and try to discuss my findings with Daniel, if he were so inclined to listen; or (C) I could go to the Poker Face, have a drink, review my own findings, and try and figure out my next move all on my own.

Lance made a great appletini; I opted for Plan C.

The Poker Face resided about five blocks away from Hot Bread, hunkered near City Hall and the high school. It had been an old fire station that the original owner had converted into a bar. When Lance and Phil had taken over, they'd made some additions: a jukebox, a stage for a band that was used mostly for karaoke on Monday nights (and bad karaoke, at that), and restrooms of questionable variety. A large, cherrywood bar took up most of the room, but there were a few tables scattered about, in case anyone wanted to sit and partake of the few selections on the sparse menu—hamburger, cheeseburger, plain garden salad, bland turkey club, and a varied selection of fries. Lance was smart enough to know that while he might be a king in the liquor and drink area, when it came to food, he had the sense to defer to those who knew what they were doing—namely *moi*.

I entered and cast a casual glance around. Lance stood behind the bar, wiping off a glass. He saw me, smiled, and waved. A man in a suit sat hunched over a tall glass at a small table in the rear near the jukebox, his back to me. Two other guys in sweatpants and ragged T-shirts sat at the bar, large frosted mugs of beer in front of them, their eyes glued to the forty-two-inch flat-screen TV above the bar. Some sort of sports event was on; I wasn't quite sure just what, since I am not a sports aficionado. It looked like some sort of game men played in their shorts—soccer came to mind.

I slid onto one of the stools and almost immediately Lance came over. He slung his towel over one shoulder and placed first a tiny square of a napkin and then a large martini glass with a decorative apple-slice garnish in front of me.

My fingers closed around the glass's stem. "How did you know?"

His laugh was easy. "That an appletini's your favorite drink? Heck, you've loved 'em ever since high school. Plus the way you slurped 'em down the first time you were in here since you came back was a great clue."

I lifted the glass to my lips, took a sip. One thing, Lance surely wasn't stingy with his vodka. "I only had two the last time."

He tossed me a wink. "Sweetheart, it's not the quantity, it's the quality."

"Well, if you make all of your drinks as powerful as this, I don't see how you can possibly turn a profit."

He leaned in a bit closer to me. "Yours are special," he whispered.

I took another sip. "You make a mean appletini."

"If you think that's good, you should try my lemon drop." He made little kissing noises with his lips. "I'm known far and wide for my lemon drop."

"I may take you up on that."

He rested both his elbows on the counter. "What's up, Nora? You don't usually come in alone and sit at the bar. Got troubles at the shop? Got man troubles?" Lance put his finger up to his ear and wiggled it back and forth. "I'm a great listener. That's why I'm such a good bartender."

I toyed with the stem of my glass and slid him a smile. "It's a few things, all rolled into one. I just needed some downtime. Time to think, sort things out."

He nodded. "I hear ya. You picked a good night, too. Slow as molasses. Although"—he pointed to the table in the rear—"those two have been here since three o'clock. One's on his fifth glass of club soda, the other on his fourth Coke. Good thing they both ordered the club sandwich, or I might have to call them a cab."

I leaned across the bar, swatted him on his arm. "Very funny."

He tapped his forefinger on the bar. "I'd do the same for you. If you're planning on tying one on, you can just hand over your car keys now."

"As a matter of fact, I didn't drive."

He frowned. "You walked?"

"Bicycled."

He wiggled his eyebrow. "Well—this is a new side of you. Are you striving to keep gas prices down by alternating your modes of transportation, or just channeling Jessica Fletcher?"

"Actually, it's complicated."

His hand shot up. "No, don't tell me. Something tells me I'm better off not knowing all the sordid details."

I raised my glass. "You're probably right."

One of the men at the other end of the bar waved his hand and held up his empty mug. Lance tossed me an apologetic look and moved away. I picked up my glass and turned so that I had a good look at the bar's interior as I sipped my drink. The man seated at the rear table turned his head, affording me a clear view of his profile, and I started as I recognized Marshall Connor. He pulled a cell phone from his pocket and started talking into it. I quickly slid off my stool and wandered over toward the jukebox. I stood, pretending to study the listing of songs, as I strained to hear what he was saying.

"Well, Kevin will be away indefinitely, so I'll be in charge of that now, not Buck. No, no, that contract can go forth as planned. What? What catering contract? Oh, yes, the one Patti drew up—what's that? She came in, but never picked it up? Well, that is odd . . . go on ahead and mail it out."

Ah, yes. I'd been in such a hurry to get to the library, I'd forgotten all about my original mission. As Marshall Connor laid his phone back on the table, I turned around and stepped right over to his table. I tapped him on the shoulder, and his head jerked up immediately, his sharp eyes raking me over head to toe.

"Yes? Is there something I can do for you?"

"I'm sorry to bother you, Mr. Connor." I held out my hand. "I'm Nora Charles—the owner of Hot Bread. I was at KMG earlier today."

He stared at me blankly, and then his expression cleared. "Oh, yes. My admin just mentioned you. You were supposed to pick up a contract."

"Yes, sir. May I?" I indicated the empty seat with a wave of my hand. He hesitated, so I slid into the seat before he could protest. "I won't be long. I just wanted to explain about the contract."

He hesitated, then nodded. "Go ahead."

"I did intend to pick it up, and I actually did speak to Mr. Grainger about making an appointment with you to talk about the possibility of our catering future events."

Connor's brows knit together. "Kevin saw you?" His tone clearly implied he found that to be incredulous—I wasn't quite sure if I should feel insulted or not.

"We, ah, kind of ran into each other. I had intentions of stopping by your office but I suddenly remembered another appointment I couldn't break. I was going to call your admin when I got home, tell her to just mail it on out." When he didn't say anything, I went on, "I'm not sure how much Ms. Simmons might have told anyone, but my mother had an exclusive agreement with the late Mrs. Grainger to cater all of KMG's functions. Naturally, I wouldn't expect any favors or preferential treatment, but as I indicated to Mr. Grainger, I would like the opportunity going forward to bid on any catering events KMG might be planning."

His lips quirked, a half smile. "I've never been to your shop, Ms. Charles, but I have sampled some of the food your mother used to prepare. If you're half the cook your mother was, and your price range is in the ballpark, I don't see any reason why we couldn't do business."

I tossed him a bright smile. "Thank you. That's certainly a load off my mind." I paused for a fraction of a second before adding, "Mr. Grainger mentioned he hadn't made a decision as yet on his new catering manager."

"That's correct."

"I imagine you'll hold the position for a while, then. I couldn't help but overhear you say he'd be away indefinitely?" At his nod, I said, "It must be a real emergency—I spoke with him at KMG less than two hours ago."

Connor's gaze narrowed. "Yes. It's something that came up rather suddenly. It has to do with our new defense contract." He glanced first right, then left, and said in a whisper, "I'm sorry, Ms. Charles. I really can't talk about it. I'm sure you understand."

"Oh, of course. I didn't mean to pry. It's just I mentioned to Mr. Grainger that I thought perhaps he'd give the job to Alicia Samuels, but he intimated she might be away for quite a while."

"That's correct."

"He didn't seem at all certain whether or not she'd be back. Some of the secretaries I spoke to seemed under the impression she wouldn't be."

He leaned back in the chair, his fingers toying with the edge of his napkin. "Office gossip is rarely correct, although it usually holds a grain of truth. Alicia is out on leave—a family emergency, I believe. It's true, she didn't specify a return date, but she didn't hand in an official resignation, either. As a result"—he spread his hands—"we're in limbo, and I've got myself another hat to wear. Does that clarify things for you?"

"Yes, thanks. Since you'll be in charge for a while, I do have some catering brochures I'd like to drop off, and—"

"No problem. You can mail them directly to my attention." He drummed his fingers on the black-and-white-checked tablecloth. "As for your contract, you should receive it tomorrow. My admin FedEx'd it out this evening."

"Great. I'll be certain to look for it."

Connor scraped his chair back, but I wasn't quite ready to end our conversation just yet. "You've been aboard the *Lady L* a few times, I understand. Not only just on that tragic weekend?"

He paused and looked at me. "Kevin often treated the men to fishing weekends. We haven't had one, though, since Lola's death."

"Understandable." I inclined my head toward his tie clip. "I couldn't help noticing. That's a lovely piece. Scrimshaw?"

Connor's fingers lightly touched the clip. "Yes. It was a birthday gift from Kevin, as a matter of fact."

"I take it you like scrimshaw, then?"

"I've collected some pieces in my time."

"Have you ever been to Captain Lott's office on the marina? He has quite a scrimshaw collection himself."

Connor nodded. "I've seen it. Very impressive."

"Some of those pieces are really unusual. I thought the animals were very unique. And that ring—I've never seen anything like it."

Connor frowned. "Ring?"

"Yes, I noticed it in his case when I was there a few days ago. A beautiful scrimshaw of a knight's helmet, quite large. It's set off to the side, but it's such an unusual piece, I think he should give it more prominence."

"Really?" His brow puckered in thought. "Odd—I don't ever recall seeing a ring in that case. It must be a new addition."

"When was the last time you were in his office?"

"Well, let's see. I dropped off some correspondence from Kevin on my way home a few weeks ago. I didn't notice a ring. If it's as unusual as you say, I'd certainly like to have a look at it." He stared off into space for several seconds, then turned back to me. "It had an etching of a knight's helmet, you say?"

"Yes. It was quite . . . unusual."

"Not so unusual, if you ask me." Connor rose, dropped a twenty on the table. "Now that I think of it, Alicia had a ring with a knight's head on it as well. Used to wear it around her neck on a chain."

"Really? Was it scrimshaw, too?"

He shook his head. "Heck no. One of those bas-relief cameos, gold against black onyx. It was set in a thick gold band, real expensive. Looked more like a men's ring."

TWENTY-SIX

Pedaling back to Hot Bread, I was reminded of a quote—oddly enough from Nick Atkins's favorite detective, Sherlock Holmes:

"When you have eliminated the impossible, whatever remains, however improbable, must be the truth."

Well, my solution was neat, even if there were some gaping holes. And I was certain it would sound very improbable, particularly to Detective Daniel (or was it Agent Daniel?) but . . . I was relatively certain it was the truth—the pieces, however ragged, certainly fit. I just needed to find some bit of evidence to confirm my suspicions.

Chantal greeted me as I walked in the back door. Everything had been quiet, and except for Nick clawing a few of her cat collar drawings to shreds, nothing of any event had occurred. Before she left, she enveloped me in a giant bear hug; I hugged back, a bit restrained. I didn't need Chantal's psychic powers picking up on my theory, or on what I planned to do about it—even though I still wasn't quite sure of the latter myself.

Nick looked serene, almost angelic, as I filled his bowl with some leftover tuna salad. As he plopped his rotund bottom in front of his dinner, I poured myself a cup of coffee and sat down at the table next to him. I sipped slowly and recounted aloud the afternoon's events, what I'd found out, my conversation with Connor, and finally my theory on what must have happened.

For one, I was convinced that Adrienne—or Alicia—had taken that job at KMG to be near her sister, even though she couldn't reveal her true identity.

I was also certain that Karl Goring and Kevin Grainger were one and the same. Something in Grainger's tone had struck a chord with me when he spoke about Chicago, and even before that, I'd gotten a sense something just didn't add up. Face-to-face with him, I suddenly realized what it was that bothered me—his eyes. Yes, you can change a person's overall appearance, change their name, even their backstory, their history—but there's just something about someone's eyes that defies total change, particularly when it comes to eye shape, or a certain look. When he relaxed, Kevin Grainger had that same haunted look in his eyes that Karl Goring had in that photograph. I double-checked dates while I was at the library—Kevin Grainger made his appearance in California right around the same time Karl Goring met his unfortunate end. Coupling that with the whole initial thing:

Karl Goring

Kevin Grainger

KG

It fit.

I took my theory a step further. Somehow—and I hadn't worked out just how, but no one knew better than me how the mob had its ways—the Gianellis got a tip that Karl and Kevin were one and the same. Naturally, they would want revenge on Karl for putting Giancarlo away—especially since he died in prison. But they couldn't risk killing an innocent guy and the trail leading back to them—particularly now that they were under FBI surveillance. Enter their mole—Patti. Patti's job must have been to definitely determine that Kevin was Karl, and notify her contact, who would ultimately finish the job. But she fell in love with Kevin and, even after obtaining the proof, couldn't bring herself to rat him out. In the meantime, Adrienne slash Alicia recognized her and figured she must be up to no good. Alicia decided to warn Lola that Patti was up to something, and Lola got her hands on the evidence, must have realized what it meant. Either Patti caught her or Lola confronted her—in either scenario, there was an argument and somehow—either accidentally or on purpose—Lola fell overboard. The bruise at the base of Lola's skull led me to believe her fall wasn't entirely accidental. And Adrienne, knowing full well her sister's death was no accident, takes a leave from her job as Alicia Samuels and hires Nick Atkins to help her prove it—which she has to do under her real name, of course, because why would Alicia Samuels give a rat's ass about how Lola Grainger died?

Which, of course, also meant she had to fake Adrienne Sloane's death, just in case it somehow got back to the mob. She must have called Nick Atkins down to the dock that night to witness her "death"—but then what happened? Both Adrienne—and Atkins—seemed to vanish into thin air.

Not that I expected Nick to listen—it just sometimes made more sense to voice my thoughts out loud. When I'd finished, however, I happened to glance down. I sucked in my breath at what I saw.

Nick's bowl was still three-quarters full. He squatted in front of it, his head facing me, and it was cocked to one side, his eyes slitted as if in concentration.

It almost looked as if he'd deliberately stopped eating to listen to what I had to say.

I looked at him over the rim of my coffee cup. "I'm flattered you'd stop gobbling down that tuna just for me," I said. "You're certainly a much better audience than Daniel would have been." This elicited a little purr of pleasure. "And I'd be the first one to say my solution makes everything all neat and tidy, and nine times out of ten—well, cases don't work that way. But honestly, this is the only way I can account for everything that's happened."

Nick sat up on his haunches and pawed at the air.

"Yes, I realize there are still tons of unanswered questions. Like for example, the rings. How do they figure in all this? Connor described that ring to a T, and he said Alicia used to wear it around her neck. I'll bet Patti took it from her—why, I have no idea. And how did the ring in that photo that belongs to Carlo Wyatt end up in Lott's scrimshaw case? Where the heck is Adrienne? Did she kill Patti, or is it someone else? Why hasn't another attempt been made on Grainger's life? And maybe the question that's most important to you—what happened to your owner when he went down to the docks to meet Adrienne?"

A shrill howl emitted from Nick's throat. If I didn't know better, I'd have said it was almost like a warning. I ran my fingers through my hair. "Don't worry, Nick. Nothing's going to happen to me like it happened to your former owner."

He stopped howling and cocked his head at me, almost as if to say, *How can you be sure, puny human?*

I got up, crossed to the stove, and refilled my coffee cup. I added some milk and sugar and carried it back to the table. I took a long sip, then rested my chin in my hands. "Of course, Patti could have also been the hit man. Hit person," I mused, "but somehow I don't think so. I think her job was just to be a mole—to make sure that Kevin was Karl. The hit man was someone else—her murderer, most likely. And just what is Mr. Daniel Corleone's role in all this? Is he a small-town detective, or an FBI special agent?" I made a face. "If he weren't so dead set against me participating in all this, I could have run these theories by him. Maybe I still should."

"*Owwwr.*" Nick clawed at the air. He bared his fangs and spat. "*Ow-ewer.*"

"Okay, you're right. He'd probably dismiss me with some smart-ass remark about interfering in police business." I smiled. "The focus right now should be finding Adrienne. WPP or not, if she did murder Patti, she's got to answer for it. Those shots were definitely not fired in self-defense. It was a professional hit—I've seen enough to know."

Who was left on my suspect list? Not a whole helluva lot, that was for sure. Connor, Tabor, Lott—or could there be yet someone else? I wondered idly what Carlo might be doing these days—was he even still in prison? I could check it out with Hank and Petey, but to be truthful, I was loath to involve them any more than they already were.

This case was indeed, to quote Ollie Sampson, dy-na-mite. Even more so than Ollie'd originally suspected.

I leaned back, closed my eyes. "There's something I'm missing," I muttered. "It's something obvious. In all the crime shows on TV, it's always something really obvious. Take *Murder, She Wrote*. It's usually a chance remark or an observation that enables her to crack the case. Where is Jessica Fletcher when you need her the most? Reruns probably."

I picked up my coffee cup, shut the store lights, and headed upstairs to my apartment. Nick followed, close at my heels. I walked into my den and eased myself into my mother's old Barcalounger recliner. I'd set it in front of my bookcase, right next to an antique brass floor lamp I'd picked up at a flea market for ten bucks and a small card table I'd found at a thrift shop for a song. I usually enjoyed sitting here, feet up, to read one of the classic books I enjoyed collecting, but tonight reading was far from my mind. No, my brain was busy, trying to untangle a real Chinese puzzle—one that seemed to be never ending.

Nick sat at my feet for a few minutes, then in one movement hurled himself up onto the third shelf of my bookcase, and with considerable ease at that. I stared at him, openmouthed.

Frankly, I'd thought him a bit porky for high jumping but apparently I was wrong. Apparently vertical flight isn't an issue for cats, no matter what their size.

I closed my eyes and rubbed at my temples. "That ring holds the key, I'll bet anything. Wyatt's ring matches the one I saw in Lott's scrimshaw case—how did it get there? The ring in the envelope had a knight's image as well, but it was a different style." My eyes suddenly snapped open. "The same, yet different. Of course."

Nick remained on my bookcase, his girth filling up most of it, paws folded neatly underneath him. I ran downstairs to the knife drawer to retrieve the envelope, which I carried back to the den. I tipped it, and the ring and photo slid onto the table. Then I grabbed my bag and dumped the two printouts from the library next to them.

"Gianelli liked to give his henchmen symbols," I muttered, pushing the objects around. "He used his family crest—the knight's helmet—in all of them, but he didn't give everyone the same symbol. Wyatt had the scrimshaw ring, Adrienne the onyx. They each symbolize something different—a level in his organization or—maybe a special skill?"

I jumped as something landed near my feet with a thud. I turned around and saw Nick had risen, and one claw dipped toward an empty slot on the shelf. I leaned over and picked up the small leather volume he'd decided to knock down.

It was my first edition copy of *The Thin Man*, by Dashiell Hammett.

I turned the book over in my hand and gave Nick a sidelong glance. "You do know this is a first edition? Rare, expensive. Okay, it's your namesake, but even though you can't read, you can still show some respect for the printed word."

He arranged his portly body in an imperious posture. His claw dipped forward forcefully to graze the tip of the cover. "*Owrrr.*"

"What are you trying to tell me? Geez, I wish I could read what's going on in that kitty brain of yours."

I looked at the book again, then back at the objects spread across my card table. My eyes widened and I leaned forward, poking at the photos with an outstretched finger. I stole a quick glance at Nick over my shoulder.

"You see it, too, don't you, you rascal. Ollie was right— you definitely have your own method of communicating."

"*Awwr.*" Nick leapt from the shelf to the arm of my Bar-calounger and sat there, head and tail held high.

"Sure." I laughed. "I guess I should have seen it sooner. I mean, it's all right here. Once you think about it, it sticks out like a sore thumb."

I was reminded also of two of "The Thirty-Six Strata-gems," a Chinese essay used to illustrate a series of strata-gems used in politics, war, as well as in civil interaction, often through unorthodox or deceptive means.

Prepare too much and you lose sight of the big picture;
what you see often you do not doubt.

Roughly translated: We often tend to take what we see at face value, oftentimes overlooking the obvious, which is right in front of our noses, so to speak.

Create something from nothing

Create an illusion of something's existence, while it does not; conversely, create an illusion that something does not exist, while it does.

Yep. All right there. Now all I had to do was prove it.

Nick puffed out his chest and yawned.

I leaned over, reached for my cell phone. "Guess I do have to give Hank one more call after all. Depending on his answer, I'll know what my next move should be."

Nick gave a wise nod. "*E-owl.*"

TWENTY-SEVEN

The weather had turned nasty, the strong winds and heavy rain predicted by the weatherman a reality by nine o'clock that night. I'd gotten the callback from Hank, his answer confirming my suspicions.

The weather cast a pall of gloom over the evening, increasing our feelings of trepidation throughout the evening. I made a light supper—burger and a salad for me, whitefish for Nick—and when we'd finished eating and cleared away the dishes, I made a quick phone call to Chantal. Although puzzled—and troubled—by my request, she agreed to do what I requested, no questions asked—although she did take the opportunity to remind me again about that big D on my forehead. I shrugged into my slicker with attached hood, and then Nick and I ran outside to the SUV. Twenty-five minutes later, we were parked in the parking lot at the marina. From our vantage point, we had a good view of both Lott's office at one end, and the slip where the *Lady L* was docked.

I shivered at the dampness in the air, despite my SUV's excellent heater. For the first time in my life, I wished I had a gun, even though I haven't the vaguest notion how to shoot one. To be quite honest, guns scare me—they always have—which might possibly be one reason—among many others—I'd never seriously gone after that PI license.

I couldn't wrap my head around the idea of actually killing someone, even in the line of duty.

Nick's tongue flicked back and forth across his fur. "Better to kill than be killed, right?" I said. "We still haven't figured out what might have happened to your human, but who knows? Maybe that question will be answered soon, too."

Nick stopped grooming, put his head on his paws, and shot me a beseeching look.

"I know—I'm fond of you, too, but if Nick Atkins turns up, I'm sure he'll want you back—and I'm sure he'll want to call you Sherlock again, too."

Nick drew back his gums and spat.

"Yeah, I want to keep you, too. Don't worry, I wouldn't give you up without a fight."

He blinked twice and laid his head on his forepaws. I reached over and started to scratch him on his white spot, behind his right ear. He purred for a few seconds, then suddenly shrugged away and cocked his head, ears flattened back against his skull.

"*Grrr.*"

I leaned close. "What is it? Do you hear something?"

His head moved to and fro, as if he were watching a very fast Ping-Pong game. "*Grrr.*" He rumbled again, eyes bright.

We huddled close and sat in perfect silence. For a few minutes the only sound was the steady beating of rain on the SUV's roof. Then, as we watched the pier, a shadowy form suddenly glided out of nowhere and moved swiftly toward the *Lady L*.

"Hm. That's the wrong direction. I figured he'd go straight for the office." My hand shot out, grasped the door handle. "Maybe it's not who I thought." I turned to Nick. "And you," I said, wagging my finger under his nose, "you stay here, mister, where it's safe. I can't be worrying about you."

He blinked twice and coiled his body, ready to spring. The rain had abated somewhat, but there was still a fine mist and a distinct chill in the air. I flipped up the hood on my slicker and slid out of the car, quickly eased my door shut, and hit the automatic door lock button on my key ring before he could get his rotund body moving to jump out of the car.

His nails raked at my window. His teeth were bared in a decidedly unlovely snarl. I couldn't help but toss him a saucy grin.

"Sorry, pal, but you're going to have to sit this one out."

He hissed and slammed at the window with his paw.

I frowned, knowing I probably shouldn't leave him in there with all the windows closed. The air couldn't circulate without the motor or the AC on. I reached in my pocket and pulled out my key ring. Doug, my mechanic, was a whiz with anything electrical, and he'd programmed my remote so that I could raise and lower my car windows— only problem was, I'd only used the feature once and wasn't quite sure how he'd told me to do it. I jabbed at a couple of buttons and gave a sigh of relief when the driver's side window abruptly lowered about a quarter of an inch—enough for air, not enough for Nick to slide a whisker through. I slid the key ring back in my pocket.

"Okay, you've got fresh air. Wish me luck."

I turned my back, and the air was rent with a mournful yowl—God, he was loud!

"No one's around to hear you," I shouted. The wind had started to blow again, harder now, and the mist was developing into a steady drizzle. "The wind and rain drown you out anyway."

The yowling stopped, replaced by a plaintive cry.

"Sorry, boy. I won't be long."

I gritted my teeth, pulled my hood around my face, and sprinted for the dock. I looked over my shoulder once, and almost choked at what I saw.

Nick, sprawled across the dashboard, giving me the kitty version of "the finger." Paw upraised, only his middle claw nail sticking straight up.

"Nice," I muttered as I turned and soldiered on through the rain. "See if I make you a steak anytime soon."

I slipped on board the *Lady L* and moved cautiously down the long corridor, my nerves tingling, every sense I possessed on high alert, thankful I'd decided to trade my highrise boots for thick-soled sneakers. I crept softly along, and when I reached the door of Lola's suite, I paused.

The door stood ajar. I pressed my nose against the crack and peered inside.

A figure wearing a long black cape was hunched over the exact spot where Nick and I had retrieved the envelope. I pushed the door inward a bit, wincing at the loud creak. The figure on the floor rose and whirled.

"Hello, Adrienne," I said.

Adrienne Sloane lowered the hood on her cloak. In the cabin's pale light, I could see her eyes were narrowed, her jaw set. I could also see a slight resemblance to Lola—not much, to be sure, because I was certain that perfect nose wasn't the one God had given her—but there was something to her eyes, maybe it was the shape or the color, I wasn't quite sure—that just screamed out "Lola" to me.

She regarded me warily, her hands clenched at her side. "You know who I am," she said softly.

I nodded and gestured toward the open aperture. "What you're looking for isn't there."

The eyes widened slightly. "You have it?"

"Some of it. Some of it I had to turn over to Detective Corleone."

A frown puckered her high forehead. "*Detective* Corleone?"

I decided to take a stab. "You probably know him as Agent Corleone? Maybe Special Agent Corleone?"

"Oh." A glimmer of recognition lit up her eyes. "You mean Daniel? Yes. He's been most helpful throughout this whole ordeal."

Had he now? I remembered the feeling I'd had, that he knew more than he let on. "He knew you were alive, didn't he?"

She nodded. "Oh yes. He works with the Department of Justice, which commandeers the Witness Protection Program. Daniel's been my liaison with the FBI ever since I decided to turn state's."

"And did he help get you into KMG, so you could be close to your sister?"

She nodded. "I didn't know about Kevin, though, until Patti started working there. I recognized her right away—I tried to avoid her like the plague. They altered my face after my 'death,' but—gee, you never know. Sometimes it's something real simple, like a mannerism, that can give you away, and Patti always was pretty sharp."

"I gather the two of you never liked each other."

Adrienne grunted. "Kind of hard to like the person who turned you in to the cops. Guess I can't blame her too much—she did it to save her own skin. Plus, she was jealous of my relationship with Mickey."

"That's why she stole the ring he gave you. The gold and onyx one. That was Mickey's ring, right?"

"Right. Each of the brothers had one. Mickey and I—we were involved for a long time. That's how I left my family the first time. Lola and our parents didn't want anything to do with me, and I can't say as I blame them. I did drugs, got involved in prostitution—not exactly a model citizen. But once I got thrown in the slammer—I can't explain it. My whole outlook changed. I knew I'd wasted most of my life, and call me crazy, but—I wanted to atone. I wanted to do something good." Her eyes took on a dulled cast. "Plus, the guy I loved tossed me aside for a younger model, and threw me to the wolves to save his skin—and hers. It does something to a girl." She laughed. "Knocked sense into me, that's for sure. Better late than never, I guess."

"So when the FBI approached you, you decided to turn state's evidence?" I prompted as her voice trailed off.

She nodded. "Yes. Daniel was my contact right from the get-go. Sweet man. Sometimes I find it hard to believe he's a Fed. He and the DOJ arranged for my 'death.' They passed off another inmate with a similar build to Lola and publicized it so the mob would know. We'd been estranged for so long she wouldn't have known me if she fell over me anyway. It broke my heart, though. Here I was, living in the same town, working for her husband's company, and I couldn't tell her who I was. I couldn't risk it."

"So you did the next best thing. You became friends."

She smiled. "Lola was real easy to get to know. We weren't best buds, but . . . it was enough. And then *she* came." Adrienne's hand clenched and unclenched at her side. "I knew right away something must be up. So did Daniel, when I told him."

"So you being here—working for Kevin's company— that was no accident, was it? The Feds arranged that?"

She offered me a thin smile. "Yeah. Daniel said they thought it would be good for me to be near family, even though they could never know who I really was. They suspected that Patti was there to prove Kevin was Karl, and then a hit man would be brought in—but they had to be real careful, because Aldo was being watched."

"So they wanted you to what? Spy on Patti?"

"Yes—but unfortunately that little plan backfired." Adrienne started to wring her hands in front of her. "She found my ring. My own fault—I have a bad habit of not locking my office. She was snooping around, and she found it. So then, of course, I had to disappear."

"Because she knew who you were."

"Right. And I knew she'd tell just as fast as she could, so I had to 'die' all over again. That's why I let it be known I didn't believe my sister's death was an accident, and why I hired that PI. I set it up so he'd find my 'dead' body underneath the pier. I called him and said I had something to tell him—it was possible the wrong Grainger had died. I knew that would get him over here fast. I was certain he'd say something—such a high-profile case, and he seemed eager to make a name for himself—who could have predicted someone would shoot him?"

I felt my heart thud in my chest. "Someone shot him? You saw it?"

"Well, to tell you the truth—I'm really not sure. It all happened so fast, you see, and I was hiding. I saw a figure—it looked like a woman, but as I said, it all happened so fast. I saw the person point something at him, and then I heard a shot—and after that, everything's a blur. I had to get out of there myself, fast. Been sequestered ever since—until tonight."

"You took some chance," I said. "What if that PI had continued his digging into your sister's death? He might have started investigating Kevin."

She licked at her lips. "He wouldn't have gotten far. The Feds and local police would have seen to that. They've been tapping Lott's phone for a while, you know. Once I heard that call tonight, well . . . I had to get here before he did."

"Are you working with the Feds?" At her nod, I jammed my hands deep into the pocket of my slicker. "So then they know he's really Carlo Wyatt?"

Her eyes popped wide, and her skin paled beneath her makeup. "Yes, but how on earth did you figure that out?"

"A friend of mine in Chicago ran a check for me, found out Carlo's been missing since right before Lott's accident. I just added up the pieces."

"Wow, you're good," she said, admiration evident in her tone. "It was stupid of him to put that ring in the scrimshaw case. He always had a high idea of himself—guess he just couldn't bear to be without it. Lola described it to me one day, and I knew. We've been watching him ever since, waiting for him to make his move."

I moved closer to her. "The night Lola died . . . do you know what happened?"

Adrienne licked at her lips. "Lola knew something was up with Kevin. Of course she didn't know he was worried about mob retaliation—he'd managed to keep that secret from her. She thought he might be having an affair with Patti. I knew Patti had those photographs—I wanted Lola to find them and confront Kevin. I felt he owed it to her to be honest with her, so she'd know what they were up against. I'm positive Patti found out, they argued, and Patti probably knocked her out and threw her overboard. I don't know for a fact, but that's how I figure it."

I nodded. "Well, I can understand your wanting to kill Patti—if she did murder your sister . . ."

Adrienne's eyes bugged. "Oh, no. I could never do that. Even if she did kill Lola, I didn't—I couldn't—murder Patti."

"Quite true," said a voice behind us. "I did."

I whirled around. Shelly Lott, or Carlo Wyatt, smiled at me over the barrel of the gun he held in his hand. I noticed he'd shaved off his beard, and had ditched the cane and phony limp. Instead of jeans and a cotton turtleneck, he was attired in a gray pinstripe suit. I guessed that was what the well-dressed hit man was wearing this season.

"Girls, girls. I usually take out my marks with my AR-7, but lately my 22 Ruger Mark I's been getting a lot of action."

I gestured toward the gun. "That's what you used to kill Patti Simmons," I said.

He nodded. "She was a flake. All over Mickey until he got sent to the slammer, then she switched to Aldo. But then—she goes and falls for Karl Goring, can you believe it?" He shook his head. "She's a doll who should have known better, but she thought she could beat the system. Thought about turning state's evidence herself, that's what

282 T. C. LoTEMPIO

she told me when I caught her lookin' for that envelope. She was gonna turn me in, too, and after all I'd done for her."

"What did you do for her?" I asked.

He laughed. "Why, I got rid of Lola Grainger. She was feisty and I could tell she was going to be trouble—it was time for her to go. It was easy, so easy. She got distracted, and I just whacked her on the back of the head and tossed her over. Kevin was there on the deck, too—but he'd passed out from all that liquor."

"So when Patti came, she thought Kevin had killed Lola," I said. "He was too drunk to remember if he did or didn't, but he assumed the worst, and Patti let him believe it."

"Right." Wyatt smirked. "Aldo didn't want to make a move on him without being absolutely certain, so I needed to get Patti's evidence." Wyatt snorted. "Yeah, Aldo's some mob boss. He's scared shitless of the Feds. Doesn't want to end up like his brothers. Like anyone could trace Kevin's killing back to him. I'm real careful."

"Yeah," Adrienne jeered. "You're so careful you left that damn ring of yours in plain sight. It was a giveaway to me."

"Well, you were dead once, and you will be again soon. You're not much of a threat." He glanced over at me. "I'm curious how you made the connection, though. I thought I came across pretty convincing as Lott to you."

"You did—until I saw a photograph of the real Lott's auto accident—which I'm sure the mob must have set up—and of you and Mickey. There was a slight resemblance between you and Lott, and I confess, I visualized you with a beard. Then, there was that crime scene photo. It wasn't really a good idea to be one of the MTs wheeling Lott away, or to let yourself be photographed—and wearing your ring, to boot. When I examined that photo closely, I saw it." I paused. "That's when I got the idea the bodies might have been switched."

"Well, ain't you just the smart little devil. Enough of all this—time to get down to business." He held out his hand to me. "That envelope wasn't in the office, like the phone call said it was. So I've got to assume you've got it on you. Hand it over, sister."

I licked at my lips. "I'm sorry. I don't have the envelope. It was just a ruse. I was going to see if you'd go to hunt for it, and then I was going to call the police with my theory, but—I saw Adrienne going onto the *Lady L* and followed her instead."

"Well, you made the wrong choice. Now, let me tell you how this is gonna go. We're gonna go back to your store— that's probably where you have it stashed, right? We're gonna go back to your store and get it, and then we're all gonna take a nice little ride out in the country." Wyatt shook his head. "I thought you might have taken the envelope, but the police got here too damn fast. I barely had time to knock myself out. I saw them take you away, though. You were handcuffed. How'd you ever get that envelope off the boat?"

I lifted my chin. "You'll never know."

He growled. "We'll see about that. Now, move."

He stepped forward, jabbed his gun into my ribs. Acting purely on instinct, I brought my arm up, knocking his elbow and jarring the gun. Then I crashed the heel of my sneaker right into his instep. Wyatt howled with pain and took a step back.

I grabbed Adrienne's elbow. "That would have been more effective with heels," I muttered. "Quick—make a run for it."

But Wyatt was faster than I'd anticipated. He bent, snatched the gun up, and leveled it at us. "Try one more move like that, and it will be your last." He advanced toward me, twisted my arm behind my back, and jammed the gun into my ribs. "Now walk."

We started down the corridor, Adrienne in front, then me, Wyatt right behind, the gun still in my ribs. As we approached the deck, I happened to glance over at the galley. There was a small overhang over the entrance. I blinked. Had I seen a shadow there?

"What are ya stoppin' for? Move!" Wyatt thundered. The next was a series of expletives as Nick, who'd been crouching on the overhang, dropped down right on Wyatt's face with a series of snorts and growls. Wyatt clawed frantically at the tubby cat, but Nick held on stubbornly, his sharp claws fisted deep into Wyatt's full head of hair.

I scrambled for the gun and retrieved it. I made sure the safety was on, though, before I trained it on Wyatt.

"It's okay, Nick," I said. "I've got him." I shifted the weapon gingerly in my hand.

Nick positioned his fat belly across Wyatt's face and gave me a look. "*Er-ewl.*"

I hesitated, then held the gun out to Adrienne. "You know how to shoot this?"

She shook her head, but it didn't matter. Suddenly the deck was ablaze with lights. A voice over a loudspeaker yelled, "FBI. Come out with your hands up."

A minute later Daniel burst into the cabin. He stared first at Adrienne, then at me, and then at Wyatt, who now lay on the floor, Nick's fat body plopped right across his face. Beneath Nick's furry butt Wyatt mumbled, "Help me. I can't breathe."

Daniel looked at me. I shrugged.

"I can explain," I said.

He looked at the scene before him and shook his head. "That's what I was afraid of."

EPILOGUE

"Well, to quote the Bard, 'All's well that ends well.'"

It was Monday afternoon. Once the last lunch customer was out the door, I slapped the CLOSED sign on the door and hurried to the kitchen, where I took out the special lunch I'd made for some very special people. I returned to the dining area. Adrienne Sloane and Daniel and another agent from the DOJ, Rick Barnes, were seated at the table in the back, along with Ollie and Chantal. Lying at Chantal's feet, head on paws, lay Nick. He looked at me reproachfully as I approached the table. I noted he was wearing his new collar and wondered just how hard a time he'd given Chantal.

"While our celebratory lunch is simmering, maybe we could tie up those few loose ends now?" I asked Daniel.

"Okay." He leaned back in the chair. "Well, you do seem to be quite the detective, Nora. You had it pretty well figured out so I'll just hit the high points. You already know Adrienne is Lola's sister, who got involved with the wrong crowd at a young age and became Mickey Gianelli's girl. She and Patti knew each other, and Patti was openly jealous of Adrienne, so when Patti got a chance to get Mickey's ear and convince him Adrienne was cheating on him, he set her up. Adrienne went to prison, where we approached her about turning state's evidence, an opportunity she grabbed at. In order to protect her, we faked her death, changed her appearance, and then sent her to Cruz to live, so she could be near her sister."

"It's odd, isn't it, that Lola, who wanted nothing to do with the mob and disowned Adrienne over it, ended up married to a guy from the same crime family?"

"Not so odd when you consider the fact that Karl Goring always had a crush on Lola. He knew her in high school, even though he was a few years ahead of her," Rick Barnes cut in. "Kevin Grainger's pursuit of her was definitely not accidental."

"Ooh." Chantal sighed. "How romantic."

I rolled my eyes as Daniel continued, "In the meantime, Karl Goring's whereabouts were leaked to the mob by an informant whose name we have yet to discover. Anyway, Patti was sent in as a mole to confirm Kevin and Karl were one and the same: Wyatt was right—Aldo is running scared, and didn't want to risk killing an innocent person. In the meantime, Patti realized that Buck might be able to find something out—there was that college connection—so she romanced him and he was like putty in her hands. Buck found that high school photo in Kevin's briefcase where he kept it and turned it over to her, but by that time she'd fallen in love and had no intention of turning Kevin over to the mob.

Likewise, the mob arranged for Lott to have his auto accident so they could get Wyatt on the inside."

"They took some chance with that," I said. "One would think Kevin would have been able to tell the difference between his yacht captain and an imposter."

"Under normal circumstances, maybe—but Kevin's life was far from normal. The guy was always preoccupied, if not with business, then with keeping one step ahead of the mob. And the mob knew what they were up against. Their imposter had to be picture-perfect in order to pull it off. They lucked out in the fact that Wyatt had a similar build, and a talent for mimicry. He imitated Lott's voice and mannerisms to perfection, and a bit of plastic surgery made 'em look like twins separated at birth—he fooled Kevin and Lola completely. By the way, the real Lott unfortunately did die in that accident, so there's one more charge of murder against them. Anyway, the plan was once Patti gave Wyatt the okay, he'd take Kevin out and make it look like an accident. Only thing was, Patti didn't want to turn Kevin in. Lola, under Adrienne's guidance, found the envelope and hid it. Wyatt killed Lola in a panic because when she said to him, 'I know what's going on,' he thought she'd discovered his true identity. Then it was a race between Wyatt and Patti trying to find the envelope. Patti did find it, and Wyatt killed her, but then you arrived on the scene so he called the police to get you off the boat. He was certainly surprised when the envelope was missing, too. He suspected you had it, but couldn't prove it—until you had Chantal make that phone call. And if Chantal hadn't had one of her 'feelings' that you were in deep trouble and called me—well, who knows what might have happened." He arched a brow at me. "You do realize things would have gone down more smoothly if you'd called me with your theory."

"You do realize I didn't call you because I didn't want my theories to get brushed aside like lint," I retorted.

"Sorry." He shot me a sheepish grin. "I had no choice. I had to keep you at arm's length, for your own protection—which turned out to be a moot point."

"Nick is really the one we should thank," I said, giving the tuxedo a big grin. "If he hadn't somehow managed to get out of the car and gone to the boat and dropped down on Wyatt—I think he'd have killed us before the FBI could have gotten there."

"Suffice it to say," interjected Rick Barnes, "that Wyatt is now enjoying thirty-five to life in prison, and his buddy Aldo isn't far behind. Thanks to Adrienne we finally managed to get the evidence we needed to nail him on those offshore accounts—plus ties to Israeli terrorists, to boot."

"It is a good thing Nora has excellent powers of deduction, *non*?" Chantal laughed. "If she hadn't been able to put all those clues together, Kevin Grainger might still be living in fear of mob retaliation."

"Unfortunately, Kevin's identity has been compromised now, so we'll have to relocate him again. Marshall Connor will be taking over as CEO of KMG shortly. Kevin will still realize income but it will have to be filtered and sent to him through government channels." Daniel gave Adrienne a quick smile. "Adrienne too, unfortunately. I'm sorry, I know you've established roots, but there's still valuable testimony you can give us—we can't take a chance on your staying here, possibly endangering you."

Rick Barnes nodded. "I assured Daniel we'd take good care of you, and take every precaution to ensure your future safety. Kevin's, too."

"Hey, I understand. Besides, my main reason for staying

here was Lola. I'm alive—that's the main thing." She smiled at me. "And I owe it all to Nora and her cat, Nick."

Ollie grinned at me. "See, Nora. I told you that cat was special—and smart. Smarter than a human."

"They make a great team." Chantal slid me a sidelong glance. "Nicky turned out to be your King of Swords after all," she said.

Daniel's brow arched. "King of Swords?"

"It is a long story." Chantal smiled at Daniel. "Perhaps there is a spot for them with the FBI?"

"One never knows. We've never had a cat as an agent before, but considering the circumstances, maybe we can make an exception—have them be special civilian consultants." Daniel glanced over at where Nick squatted at my feet. "Somehow I think your cat would like that, Nora. He seems to be somewhat of a ham."

Nick reared up on his hind legs. His head swiveled in Daniel's direction. Black lips peeled back to reveal glistening fangs.

"Down, boy." I pushed Nick back on the floor.

"So, Nora." Ollie leaned back in his chair. "Has all this made you want to go back into reporting? Or maybe even try and get your PI license?"

I smiled at him. "While I admit I find detective work stimulating, and the thought of my own PI license is tempting, for now I think I'll stick with something safer—like sandwich making."

"Well, if you ever change your mind—I may be in the market for a partner soon."

"I'll keep that in mind."

"Yes, and don't forget your part-time job at *Noir*," Chantal reminded me. "I bet Louis will listen to you now about those articles on unsolved crimes you wanted to do."

"We'll see," I laughed. "I'm meeting him later at the Poker Face to discuss a new column."

"Hm." Daniel stretched his long legs out in front of him. "Well, maybe I'll stop by and we can have a drink afterward. Get better acquainted. After all, we're going to be neighbors soon."

I looked sharply at him. "N-neighbors?"

He shot me a mischievous grin. "Didn't I mention? I've taken a job heading up our new FBI satellite office in Carmel—it's just fifteen minutes away. I've put down a deposit on a condo there."

"That's right," said Rick. "And I'll be working with him out of the new office as the DOJ liaison."

"That's great," Chantal cried. "Carmel is so close—and Nora's sister is living there, right? So we can visit often."

I shot her a glance and was tempted to remind her that my sister Lacey was hardly likely to invite us for a weekend, but Chantal had already turned to Rick Barnes. She smiled and lowered her lashes.

"So tell me, Mr. Barnes—do you believe in tarot?"

He smiled. "Not really, but you're welcome to try and change my mind. Oh, and you and Nora can call me Rick."

While Chantal simpered at Rick like a Southern belle, Daniel reached over and clasped my hand. "Since I'll now be living so close by, I might even actually be able to eat lunch here once in a while. Maybe squeeze in a dinner or two as well."

"Well," I stammered, "that—that would be—it would be nice."

"I thought so. I'd like to get to know you when someone isn't trying to take a shot at you. Ducking bullets can get distracting." The heat of his gaze seared right through me. "I've got the feeling being a detective is in your blood,

Nora. Once it's there, it's not easy to shake. And sometimes that's not necessarily a bad thing."

I felt my cheeks getting hot, so I excused myself to see about our lunch. I'd just finished checking the oven when Ollie came into the kitchen.

"I wanted to show you these."

He held out two crumpled sheets of paper. I stared at him.

"What are those?"

"I believe these are the pages you said were missing from Nick's journal on Lola's case. I dropped one of my cuff links and I found them jammed under the radiator. Apparently he wanted to hide them."

"Hide them? Why?"

Ollie unfolded them and pressed them into my hand. "Read 'em."

I scanned the pages quickly, my jaw dropping as I perused the cramped words. At last I met Ollie's gaze. "This cinches it. He figured out Adrienne's secret. Well, well," I breathed, handing the pages back, "I guess maybe he is the best PI in the state of California after all."

"I'm sure he would agree."

"You know, this could explain his disappearance. If the mob found out what he knew—"

"We don't know that for sure. Lots of balls in the air, remember. And maybe"—Ollie eyed the tubby tuxedo strolling into the kitchen—"maybe it is best, this time, if we let sleeping dogs lie. For you, for little Nick—for everyone." He slipped the papers into his breast pocket. "I'll give these a proper burial. Nick would want it that way—both of 'em."

Ollie left, and Nick sidled up to me.

"Well." I grinned down at him, "Looks as if you're stuck with me for the time being, Nick. Adrienne isn't quite sure just what happened to your former owner. After what Ollie just showed me, I've got an idea but one never knows. Maybe we'll find out someday—but don't blame me if I say I'm not too anxious to learn the truth."

Nick squatted on his haunches, cocked his head. "*Er-rup*," he trilled.

"Yeah, I'm kinda happy about it, too. And now I owe you a reward. After all, you did save my life."

Nick yowled with excitement, prancing beside me as I crossed to the refrigerator. I pulled out a bowl and tipped it forward so he could take a sniff.

"Yessir. That's real lobster in that lobster salad, pal. Thirty bucks a pound. Only the best for you. So don't ever say I don't appreciate you."

Nick pawed animatedly at the air as I spooned lobster into his bowl. I set it down on the floor and for the next few minutes all anyone could hear were little slurping sounds.

I watched him, tapping my finger against my cheek. "I sure would like to know how in heck you got out of that car. That's the real mystery here, if you ask me."

He lifted his head and swiveled around to look over one shoulder at me. He squeezed his eyes shut and the corner of his lip tipped upward. Then he buried his head in food bowl again.

"Nicky," sang out Chantal, "come out here. I want you to model one of my collars for the jewelry website. Remy taught me how to use the camera so I can capture you on video."

Nick's haunches angled up like fins, until he caught the word *video*—then his ears perked straight up. He spun around, gave his bib a quick lick, and then, with a wistful glance back at his bowl, trotted toward the door.

I looked after his rotund bottom and shook my head in amazement. "Geez," I called after him. "Daniel had it right. Nick, you are a ham."

But dammit, I wouldn't have him any other way.

FROM NORA'S RECIPE BOOK

THE THIN MAN TUNA MELT

1 (6½-ounce) can tuna, drained
½ cup finely chopped celery
⅓ cup mayonnaise, regular or low-fat
2 tablespoons diced onion
½ teaspoon garlic salt or powder
Butter or margarine

8 slices of your favorite bread
4 slices cheese, Swiss or cheddar
2 tablespoons crumbled bacon bits

4 thin-cut tomato slices

Combine the tuna, celery, mayonnaise, onion, and garlic salt, and blend. Butter a bread slice on one side, and place it in a toaster oven. Cover with one-fourth of the tuna mixture and spread out, then top with a cheese slice. Sprinkle liberally with bacon bits. Place under the broiler for 1 minute, then put a tomato slice on top. Butter one side of another bread slice, and place it on top of the cheese, buttered side up. Grill until golden brown on both sides, or the cheese is melted. Remove, cut, and serve. Serves two humans and one tubby tuxedo cat.

THE MICHAEL BUBLE BURGER

1 tablespoon oil
1 Vidalia onion, thinly sliced
1 pound ground chuck
1 teaspoon vinegar
½ teaspoon salt
¼ teaspoon black pepper
¼ teaspoon cayenne pepper
4 thick slices Black Forest ham

¼ cup mayonnaise
1 cup ketchup
4 thick hamburger buns, lightly toasted

1 cup shredded lettuce
4 thick slices fresh tomato

Preheat and lightly grease a grill. Heat the oil in a medium skillet over medium-low; add the onion and cook until golden and extremely soft, stirring occasionally, 15 to 20 minutes. Meanwhile, combine the beef, vinegar, salt, pepper, and cayenne in a large bowl; mix well with your hands. Form into 4 round patties. Place on the grill and cook until desired doneness, 3 to 4 minutes per side. Add the ham, and grill 1 extra minute. Remove and set aside.

To assemble the sandwich, spread 1 tablespoon mayonnaise and 1 tablespoon ketchup on each bun. On the bottom bun, arrange lettuce, one burger with ham topping, and 1 slice tomato. Serve warm. Makes four sandwiches.